THE CAPTAIN'S DEATH BED

By Virginia Woolf

THE VOYAGE OUT, 1915

NIGHT AND DAY, 1919

KEW GARDENS, 1919

MONDAY OR TUESDAY, 1921

JACOB'S ROOM, 1922

THE COMMON READER: FIRST SERIES, 1925

MRS. DALLOWAY, 1925

TO THE LIGHTHOUSE, 1927

ORLANDO, 1928

A ROOM OF ONE'S OWN, 1929

THE WAVES, 1931

LETTER TO A YOUNG POET, 1932

THE COMMON READER: SECOND SERIES, 1932

FLUSH, 1933

THE YEARS, 1937

THREE GUINEAS, 1938

ROGER FRY: A BIOGRAPHY, 1940

BETWEEN THE ACTS, 1941

THE DEATH OF THE MOTH AND OTHER ESSAYS, 1942

A HAUNTED HOUSE AND OTHER SHORT STORIES, 1944

THE MOMENT AND OTHER ESSAYS, 1947

THE CAPTAIN'S DEATH BED AND OTHER ESSAYS, 1950

A WRITER'S DIARY, 1954

VIRGINIA WOOLF AND LYTTON STRACHEY: LETTERS, 1956

GRANITE AND RAINBOW, 1958

CONTEMPORARY WRITERS, 1965

COLLECTED ESSAYS (4 vols.), 1967

The Captain's Death Bed

and other Essays

by

VIRGINIA WOOLF

A HARVEST BOOK

HARCOURT BRACE JOVANOVICH, INC.

NEW YORK

ISBN 0-15-615395-5

Printed in the United States of America

A B C D E F G H I J

Contents

CONTENTS

Editorial Note

FOUR volumes of Virginia Woolf's collected essays have already been published: *The Common Reader*, First & Second Series, *The Death of the Moth*, and *The Moment*. This fifth volume will probably be the last. As I wrote in the editorial note to *The Death of the Moth* she "left behind her a considerable number of essays, sketches, and short stories, some unpublished and some previously published in newspapers; there are, indeed, enough to fill three or four volumes." With a few unimportant exceptions, I have now included all these in the four volumes published since her death; those which have not been included were found by me to have been insufficiently revised. I must repeat what I have said before, that those which have been included would certainly have been revised or rewritten by her, had she lived. All of them have, in fact, been revised and rewritten by her, but the process would have been continued before she actually published them in a volume of collected essays.

In the previous volumes, I made no attempt to select essays in accordance with what I thought to be their merit or importance; I aimed at including in each volume some of all the various kinds of essay. The essays in this volume are, therefore, it seems to me, no different in merit and achievement from those previously published. They were written at various times in the 20 years before her death. Some are now published for the first time; others first appeared as pamphlets or in newspapers, e.g. *The Times, The Times Literary Supplement, The Nation, The New Statesman & Nation, The New Republic, The Yale Review.* Where ascertainable, I have noted the year in which the essay was written.

LEONARD WOOLF

THE CAPTAIN'S DEATH BED

Oliver Goldsmith[1]

MOST writers, to hear them talk, believe in the existence of a spirit, called, according to the age they live in, the Muse, Genius or Inspiration; and it is at her command that they write. Unfortunately the historian is bound to perceive that the lady is not altogether single and solitary. She conceals behind her robes a whole bevy of understrappers—great ladies, earls, statesmen, booksellers, editors, publishers and common men and women, who control and guide no less surely than the Muse. Change is of their nature, and as ill-luck will have it they grow steadily less picturesque as time draws on. Sidney's Lady Pembroke, dreaming over her folios in the groves of Wilton, was no mean symbol of the goddess of poetry; but her place has been taken not by one man or woman but by a vast miscellaneous crowd, who want—they do not know exactly what. They must be amused and flattered; they must be fed on scraps and scandals and, finally, they must be sent sound asleep. And who is to be blamed if what they want they get?

The patron is always changing, and for the most part imperceptibly. But one such change in the middle of the eighteenth century took place in the full light of day, and has been recorded for us with his usual vivacity by Oliver Goldsmith, who was himself one of its victims:—

[1] Written in February, 1934.

3

When the great Somers was at the helm [he wrote] patronage was fashionable among our nobility. . . . I have heard an old poet of that glorious age say, that a dinner with his lordship had procured him invitations for the whole week following; that an airing in his patron's chariot has supplied him with a citizen's coach on every future occasion. . . .

But this link [he continues] now seems entirely broken. Since the days of a certain prime minister of inglorious memory, the learned have been kept pretty much at a distance. A jockey or a laced player, supplies the place of the scholar, poet, or man of virtue. . . . He is called an author, and all know that an author is a thing only to be laughed at. His person, not his jest, becomes the mirth of the company. At his approach the most fat unthinking face brightens into malicious meaning. Even aldermen laugh, and revenge on him the ridicule which was lavished on their forefathers. . . .

To be laughed at by aldermen instead of riding in the chariots of statesmen was a change clearly not to the liking of a writer in whom we seem to perceive a spirit sensitive to ridicule and susceptible to the seduction of bloom-coloured velvet.

But the evils of the change went deeper. In the old days, he said, the patron was a man of taste and breeding, who could be trusted to see "that all who deserved fame were in a capacity of attaining it." Now in the mid-eighteenth century young men of brains were thrown to the mercy of the booksellers. Penny-a-lining came into fashion. Men of originality and spirit became docile drudges, voluminous hacks. They stuffed out their pages with platitudes. They "write through volumes while they do not think through a page." Solemnity and pomposity became the rule. "On my conscience I believe we have all forgot to laugh in these days." The new public fed greedily upon vast hunks of knowledge. They demanded huge encyclopædias, soulless compilations, which were "carried on by different writers, cemented into one body, and concurring in the same design by the mediation of the booksellers." All this was much to the disgust of a man who wrote clearly, shortly and outspokenly by nature; who held that "Were angels to write books, they never would write folios"; who felt himself among the angels but knew that the age of the angels was over. The chariots and the earls had winged their way back to Heaven; in their place stood a stout tradesman demanding so many lines of prose to be delivered by Saturday night without fail or the wretched hack would go without dinner on Sunday.

Goldsmith did his share of the work manfully, as a glance at the list of his works shows. But he was to find that the change from the Earl to the bookseller was not without its advantages. A new public had come into existence with new demands. Everybody was turning reader. The writer, if he had ceased to dine with the nobility, had become the friend and instructor of a vast congregation of ordinary men and women. They demanded essays as well as encyclopædias. They allowed their writers a freedom which the old aristocracy had never permitted. As Goldsmith said, the writer could now "refuse invitations to dinner"; he "could wear just such clothes as men generally wear" and "he can bravely assert the dignity of independence." Goldsmith by temper and training was peculiarly fitted to take advantage of the new state of things. He was a man of lively intelligence and outspoken good sense. He had the born writer's gift of being in touch with the thing itself and not with the outer husks of words. There was something shrewd and objective in his temper which fitted him admirably to preach little sermons and wing little satires. If he had little education and no learning, he had a large and varied stock of experience to draw on. He had knocked about the world. He had seen Leyden and Paris and Padua as a foot traveller sees famous cities. But his travels, far from plunging him into reverie or giving him a passion for the solitudes and sublimities of nature, had served to make him relish human society better and had proved how slight are the differences between man and man. He preferred to call himself a Citizen of the World rather than an Englishman. "We are now become so much Englishmen, Frenchmen, Dutchmen, Spaniards or Germans that we are no longer . . . members of that grand society which comprehends the whole of human kind." He insisted that we should pool our discoveries and learn from each other.

It is this detached attitude and width of view that give Goldsmith his peculiar flavour as an essayist. Other writers pack their pages fuller and bring us into closer touch with themselves. Goldsmith, on the other hand, keeps just on the edge of the crowd so that we can hear what the common people are saying and note their humours. That is why his essays, even the early ones, in *The Bee*, make such good reading. That is why it is just and fitting that *The Bee* and *The Citizen of the World* [1] should be re-printed again today, at a very modest price; and why Mr. Church should once more draw our attention in an excellent introduction to the unfaded merits of a book printed so long ago as 1762. The Citizen is still a most vivacious companion as he takes his walk from Charing Cross to Ludgate Hill. The streets are lit up for the Battle of

[1] *The Citizen of the World* and *The Bee*. By Oliver Goldsmith. Introduction by Richard Church.

Minden, and he pokes fun at the parochial patriotism of the English. He hears the shoemaker scolding his wife and forboding what will become of shoemakers "if Mounseers in wooden shoes come among us . . . when perhaps Madam Pompadour herself might have shoes scopped out of an old pear tree"; he hears the waiter at Ashley's punch house boasting to the company how if he were Secretary of State he would take Paris and plant the English standard on the Bastille. He peeps into St. Paul's and marvels at the curious lack of reverence shown by the English at their worship. He reflects that rags "which might be valued at half a string of copper money in China" yet needed a fleet and an army to win them. He marvels that the French and English are at war simply because people like their muffs edged with fur and must therefore kill each other and seize a country "belonging to people who were in possession from time immemorial." Shrewdly and sarcastically he casts his eye, as he saunters on, upon the odd habits and sights that the English are so used to that they no longer see them. Indeed he could scarcely have chosen a method better calculated to make the new public aware of itself or one better suited to the nature of his own genius. If Goldsmith stood still he could be as flat, though not as solemn, as any of the folio makers who were his aversion. Here, however, he must keep moving; he must pass rapidly under review all kinds of men and customs and speak his mind on them. And here his novelist's gift stood him in good stead. If he thinks he thinks in the round. An idea at once dresses itself up in flesh and blood and becomes a human being. Beau Tibbs comes to life: Vauxhall Gardens is bustling with people: the writer's garret is before us with its broken windows and the spider's web in the corner. He has a perpetual instinct to make concrete, to bring into being.

Perhaps it was the novelist's gift that made him a little impatient with essay writing. The shortness of the essay made people think it superficial. "I could have made them more metaphysical had I thought fit," he replied. But it is doubtful if he was prevented by circumstances from any depth of speculation. The real trouble was that Beau Tibbs and Vauxhall Gardens asked to be given a longer lease of life, but the end of the column was reached; down came the shears, and a new subject must be broached next week. The natural outlet, as Goldsmith found, was the novel. In those freer pages he had room to give his characters space to walk round and display themselves. Yet *The Vicar of Wakefield* keeps some of the characteristics that distinguish the more static art of the essayist. The characters are not quite free to go their own ways; they must come back at the tug of the string to illustrate the moral. This necessity is the stranger to us because good and bad are no longer so positively white and black; the art of the moralist is out of fashion in fiction. But Goldsmith not only believed in blackness and whiteness: he believed—perhaps one belief depends upon the other—that goodness will be rewarded, and vice punished. It is a doctrine, it may strike us when we read *The Vicar of Wakefield*, which imposes some restrictions on the novelist. There is no need of the mixed, of the twisted, of the profound. Lightly tinted, broadly shaded with here a foible, there a peccadillo, the characters of the Primroses are like those tropical fish who seem to have only backbones but no other organs to darken the transparency of their flesh. Our sympathies are not put upon the rack. Daughters may be seduced, houses burnt, and good men sent to prison, yet since the world is a perfectly balanced place, let it lurch as it likes, it is bound to settle into equilibrium in the long run. The most hardened of sinners—here Goldsmith stops characteristically to point out the evils of the prison system—will take to cutting tobacco stoppers if given the chance and thus enter the straight path of virtue again. Such assumptions stopped certain avenues of thought and imagination. But the limitation had its advantages; he could give all his mind to the story. All is clear, related, and uncrowded. He knew precisely what to leave out. Thus, once we begin to read we read on, not to reach the end, but to enjoy the present moment. We cannot dismember this small complete world. It hems us in, it surrounds us. We ask nothing better than to sit in the sun on the hawthorn bank and sing "Barbara Allen," or Johnny Armstrong's last good night. Shades of violence and wrong can scarcely trespass here. But the scene is saved from insipidity by Goldsmith's tart eighteenth-century humour. One advantage of having a settled code of morals is that you know exactly what to laugh at.

Yet there are passages in the Vicar which give us pause. "Fudge! fudge! fudge!" Burchell exclaims, and it seems that, in order to get the full effect of the scene, we should see it in the flesh. There is no margin of suggestion in this clear prose; it creates no populous and teeming silence which would be broken by the physical presence of the actors. Indeed, when we turn from Goldsmith's novel to Goldsmith's plays his characters seem to gain vigour and identity by standing before us in the round. They can say everything they have to say without the intervention of the novelist. This may be taken, if we choose, as proof that

they have nothing of extreme subtlety to say. Yet Goldsmith did himself a wrong when he followed the old habit
of labelling his people with names—Croker, Lofty, Rich-
lands—which seem to allow them but one quality apiece.
His observation, trained in the finer discriminations of fiction, worked much more cunningly than the names suggest. Bodies and hearts are attached to these signboard
faces; wit of the true spontaneous sort bubbles from their
lips. He stood, of course, at the very point where comedy
can flourish, as remote from the tragic violence of the
Elizabethans as from the minute maze of modern psy-
chology. The "humours" of the Elizabethan stage had
fined themselves into characters. Convention and conviction and an unquestioned standard of values seem to support the large, airy world of his invention. Nothing could
be more amusing than *She Stoops to Conquer*—one might
even go so far as to say that amusement of so pure a
quality will never come our way again. It demands too
rare a combination of conditions. Nothing is too far
fetched or fantastical to dry up the life blood in the characters themselves; we taste the double pleasure of a comic
situation in which living people are the actors. It may be
true that the amusement is not of the highest order. We
have not gained a deeper understanding of human oddity
and frailty when we have laughed to tears over the predicament of a good lady who has been driven round her
house for two hours in the darkness. To mistake a private
house for an inn is not a disaster that reveals the hidden
depths or the highest dignity of human nature. But these
are questions that fade out in the enjoyment of reading—an
enjoyment which is much more composite than the simple
word amusement can cover. When a thing is perfect of its

kind we cannot stop, under that spell, to pick our flower
to pieces. There is a unity about it which forbids us to
dismember it.

Yet even so, in the midst of this harmony and completeness we hear now and again another note. "But they are
dead, and their sorrows are over." "Life at its greatest and
best is but a froward child, that must be humoured and
coaxed a little till it falls asleep, and then all the care is
over." "No sounds were heard but of the shrilling cock,
and the deep-mouthed watch-dog at hollow distance." A
poet seems hidden on the other side of the page anxious to
concentrate its good-humoured urbanity into a phrase or
two of deeper meaning. And Goldsmith was a true poet,
even though he could not afford to entertain the muse for
long. "And thou, sweet Poetry," he exclaimed,

> My shame in crowds, my solitary pride,
> Thou source of all my bliss, and all my woe,
> That found'st me poor at first, and keep'st me so;

—that "dear charming nymph" fluttered her wings about
him even if she made no very long stay. It is poetry of
course at one remove from prose: poetry using only the
greys and browns upon her palette: poetry clicking her
heels together at the end of the line as though executing
the steps of a courtly dance: poetry with such a sediment
of good sense that it naturally crystallizes itself into epi-
gram:—

> And to party gave up what was meant for mankind;

or:—

> How small of all that human hearts endure
> That part which laws or kings can cause or cure.

The argument of his poems has already been stated in prose. Kingdoms grow to an unwieldy size; empires spread ruin round them; nothing is more to be valued than "a happy human face"; power and independence are to be dreaded. It has all been said before; but here the village is Auburn; the land is Ireland; all is made concrete and visualized, given a voice and a name. The world of Goldsmith's poetry is, of course, a flat and eyeless world; swains sport with nymphs, and the deep is finny. But pathos is the more moving in the midst of reserve, and the poet's sudden emotion tells the more when it is obviously not good manners to talk about oneself. If it is objected that Goldsmith's imagination is too narrowly and purely domestic, that he ignores all the rubs and struggles of life to dwell upon

> . . . the gentler morals, such as play.
> Through life's more cultured walks, and charm the way,

it is also undeniable that what he loves is not an artificial and foppish refinement. "Those calm desires that ask'd but little room" are the pith of life, the essence that he has pressed out from the turbulent and unsatisfying mass.

Yet Goldsmith has a peculiar reticence which forbids us to dwell with him in complete intimacy. It is partly no doubt that he has no such depths to reveal as some of our essayists—the solitudes and sublimities are not for him, rather the graces and amenities. And also we are kept at arm's length by the urbanity of his style, just as good manners confer impersonality upon the well-bred. But there may be another reason for his reserve. Lamb, Hazlitt, Montaigne talk openly about themselves because their faults are not small ones; Goldsmith was reserved because his foibles are the kind that men conceal. Nobody at least can read Goldsmith in the mass without noticing how frequently, yet how indirectly, certain themes recur—dress, ugliness, awkwardness, poverty and the fear of ridicule. It is as if the genial man were haunted by some private dread, as if he were conscious that besides the angel there lived in him a less reputable companion, resembling perhaps Poor Poll. It is only necessary to open Boswell to make sure. There, at once, we see our serene and mellifluous writer in the flesh. "His person was short, his countenance coarse and vulgar, his deportment that of a scholar awkwardly affecting the easy gentleman." With touch upon touch the unprepossessing portrait is built up. We are shown Goldsmith writhing upon the sofa in an agony of jealousy: Goldsmith thrusting himself into the talk and floundering on "without knowing how to get off": Goldsmith full of vanities and jealousies: Goldsmith dressing up his ugly pock-marked body in a smart bloom-coloured coat. The portrait is painted without sympathy save, indeed, of that inverted kind which comes from knowing from your own experience the sufferings which you describe. Boswell, too, was jealous, and seized upon his sitter's foibles with the malicious insight of a rival.

Yet, like all Boswell's portraits, it has the breath of life in it. He brings the other Goldsmith to the surface—he combines them both. He proves that the silver-tongued writer was no simple soul, gently floating through life from the honeysuckle to the hawthorn hedge. On the contrary, he was a complex man, a man full of troubles, without "settled principle"; who lived from hand to mouth and from day to day; who wrote his loveliest sentences in a garret under pressure of poverty. And yet, so oddly are human faculties combined, he had only to take his pen

and he was revenged upon Boswell, upon the fine gentleman who sneered at him, upon his own ugly body and
stumbling tongue. He had only to write and all was clear
and melodious; he had only to write and he was among
the angels, speaking with a silver tongue in a world where
all is ordered, rational, and serene.

White's Selborne [1]

"... there is somewhat in most genera at least, that at first sight discriminates them, and enables a judicious observer to pronounce upon them with some certainty." Gilbert White is talking, of course, about birds; the good ornithologist, he says, should be able to distinguish them by their air—"on the ground as well as on the wing, and in the bush as well as in the hand." But when the bird happens to be Gilbert White himself, when we try to discriminate the colour and shape of this very rare fowl, we are at a loss. Is he, like the bird so brightly coloured by hand as a frontispiece to the second volume, a hybrid— something between a hen that clucks and a nightingale that sings? It is one of those ambiguous books that seem to tell a plain story, the *Natural History of Selborne*, and yet by some apparently unconscious device of the author's has a door left open, through which we hear distant sounds, a dog barking, cart wheels creaking, and see, when "all the fading landscape sinks in night," if not Venus herself, at least a phantom owl.

His intention seems plain enough—it was to impart certain observations upon the fauna and flora of his native village to his friends Thomas Pennant and Daines Barrington. But it was not for the benefit of those gentlemen that he composed the sober yet stately description of Selborne with which the book opens. There it is before us, the

[1] Written in August, 1939.

15

village of Selborne, lying in the extreme eastern corner of the county of Hampshire, with its hanger and its sheep walks and those deep lanes "that affright the ladies and make timid horsemen shudder." The soil is part clay, part malm; the cottages are of stone or brick; the men work in the hop gardens and in the spring and summer the women weed the corn. No novelist could have opened better. Selborne is set solidly in the foreground. But something is lacking; and so before the scene fills with birds, mice, voles, crickets, and the Duke of Richmond's moose, before the page is loud with the chirpings, bleatings, lowings, and gruntings of their familiar intercourse, we have Queen Anne lying on the bank to watch the deer driven past. It was an anecdote, he casually remarks, that he had from an old keeper, Adams, whose great-grandfather, father and self were all keepers in the forest. And thus the single straggling street is allied with history, and shaded by tradition. No novelist could have given us more briefly and completely all that we need to know before the story begins.

The story of Selborne is a vegetable, an animal story. The gossip is about the habits of vipers and the love interest is supplied chiefly by frogs. Compared with Gilbert White the most realistic of novelists is a rash romantic. The crop of the cuckoo is examined; the viper is dissected; the grasshopper is sought with a pliant grass blade in its hole; the mouse is measured and found to weigh one copper halfpenny. Nothing can exceed the minuteness of these observations, or the scrupulous care with which they are conducted. The chief question in dispute—it is indeed the theme of the book—is the migration of swallows. Barrington believed that the swallow sleeps out the winter;

White, who has a nephew in Andalusia to inform him, now inclines to migration; then draws back. Every grain of evidence is sifted; none is obscured. With all his faculties bent on this great question, the image of science at her most innocent and most sincere, he loses that self-consciousness which so often separates us from our fellow-creatures and becomes like a bird seen through a field-glass busy in a distant hedge. This is the moment then, when his eyes are fixed upon the swallow, to watch Gilbert White himself.

We observe in the first place the creature's charming simplicity. He is quite indifferent to public opinion. He will transplant a colony of crickets to his lawn; imprison one in a paper cage on his table; bawl through a speaking trumpet at his bees—they remain indifferent; and arrive at Selborne with Aunt Snookes' aged tortoise seated beside him in the post chaise. And while thus engaged he emits those little chuckles of delight, those half-conscious burblings and comments which make him as "amusive" as one of his own birds. ". . . But their inequality of height," he muses, pondering the abortive match between the moose and the red deer, "must always have been a bar to any commerce of an amorous kind." "The copulation of frogs," he observes, "is notorious to everybody . . . and yet I never saw, or read, of toads being observed in the same situation." "Pitiable seems the condition of this poor embarrassed reptile," he laments over the tortoise, yet "there is a season (usually the beginning of June) when the tortoise walks on tip-toe" along the garden path in search of love.

And just as the vicarage garden seemed to Aunt Snookes' tortoise a whole world, so, as we look through the eyes of

Gilbert White, England becomes immense. The South Downs, across which he rides year after year, turn to "a vast range of mountains." The country is very empty. He is more solitary at Selborne than a peasant today in the remotest Hebrides. It is true that he has—he is proud of the fact—a nephew in Andalusia; but he has no acquaintance at present among the gentlemen of the Navy; and though London and Bath exist, of course—London indeed boasts a very fine collection of horns—rumours from those capitals come very slowly across wild moors and roads which the snow has made impassable. In this quiet air sounds are magnified. We hear the whisper of the grasshopper lark; the caw of rooks is like a pack of hounds "in hollow, echoing woods"; and on a still summer evening the Portsmouth gun booms out just as the goat-sucker begins its song. His mind, like the bird's crop that the farmer's wife found stuffed with vegetables and cooked for her dinner, has nothing but insects in it and tender green shoots. This innocent, this unconscious happiness is conveyed, not by assertion, but much more effectively by those unsought memories that come of their own accord unsought. They are all of hot summer evenings—at Oxford in Christ Church quadrangle; riding from Richmond to Sunbury with the swallows skimming the river. Even the strident voice of the cricket, so discordant to some, fills his mind "with a train of summer ideas, of everything that is rural, verdurous and joyful." There is a continuity in his happiness; the same thoughts recur on the same occasions. "I made the same remark in former years as I came the same way annually." Year after year he was thinking of the swallows.

But the landscape in which this bird roams so freely has

its hedges. They shut in, but they protect. There is what he calls, so aptly, Providence. Church spires, he remarks, "are very necessary ingredients in the landscape." Providence dwells there—inscrutable, for why does it allot so many years to Aunt Snookes' tortoise? But all-wise—consider the legs of the frog—"How wonderful is the economy of Providence with regards to the limbs of so vile an animal!" In another fifty years Providence would have been neither so inscrutable nor as wise—it would have lost its shade. But Providence about 1760 was in its prime; it sets all doubts at rest, and so leaves the mind free to question practically everything. Besides Providence there are the castles and seats of the nobility. He respects them almost equally. The old families—the Howes, the Mordaunts—know their places and keep the poor in theirs. Gilbert White is far less tender to the poor—"We abound with poor," he writes, as if the vermin were beneath his notice—than to the grasshopper whom he lifts out of its hole so carefully and once inadvertently squeezed to death. Finally, shading the landscape with its august laurel, is literature—Latin literature, naturally. His mind is haunted by the classics. He sounds a Latin phrase now and then as if to tune his English. The echo that was so famous a feature of Selborne seems of its own accord to boom out *Tityre, tu patulae recubans* . . . It was with Virgil in his mind that Gilbert White described the women making rush candles at Selborne.

So we observe through our field-glasses this very fine specimen of the eighteenth-century clerical naturalist. But just as we think to have got him named he moves. He sounds a note that is not the characteristic note of the common English clergyman. "When I hear fine music I am haunted with passages therefrom night and day; and especially at first waking, which by their importunity, give me more uneasiness than pleasure." Why does music, he asks, "so strangely affect some men, as it were by recollection, for days after a concert is over?"

It is a question that sends us baffled to his biography. But we learn only what we knew already—that his affection for Kitty Mulso was not passionate; that he was born at Selborne in 1720 and died there in 1793; and that his "days passed with scarcely any other vicissitudes than those of the seasons." But one fact is added—a negative, but a revealing fact; there is no portrait of him in existence. He has no face. That is why perhaps he escapes identification. His observation of the insect in the grass is minute; but he also raises his eyes to the horizon and looks and listens. In that moment of abstraction he fears sounds that make him uneasy in the early morning; he escapes from Selborne, from his own age, and comes winging his way to us in the dusk along the hedgerows. A clerical owl? A parson with the wings of a bird? A hybrid? But his own description fits him best. "The kestrel or wind-hover," he says, "has a peculiar mode of hanging in the air in one place, his wings all the time being briskly agitated."

Life Itself [1]

ONE could wish that the psycho-analysts would go into the question of diary keeping. For often it is the one mysterious fact in a life otherwise as clear as the sky and as candid as the dawn. Parson Woodforde is a case in point—his diary is the only mystery about him. For forty-three years he sat down almost daily to record what he did on Monday and what he had for dinner on Tuesday; but for whom he wrote or why he wrote it is impossible to say. He does not unburden his soul in his diary; yet it is no mere record of engagements and expenses. As for literary fame, there is no sign that he ever thought of it, and finally, though the man himself is peaceable above all things, there are little indiscretions and criticisms which would have got him into trouble and hurt the feelings of his friends had they read them. What purpose, then, did the sixty-eight little books fulfil? Perhaps it was the desire for intimacy. When James Woodforde opened one of his neat manuscript books, he entered into conversation with a second James Woodforde, who was not quite the same as the reverend gentleman who visited the poor and preached in the church. These two friends said much that all the world might hear; but they had a few secrets which they shared with each other only. It was a great comfort, for example, that Christmas when Nancy, Betsy, and Mr.

[1] Written in 1927. Copyright 1927 by Editorial Publications, Inc. (*New Republic*).

21

Walker seemed to be in conspiracy against him, to exclaim in the diary: "The treatment I meet with for my Civility this Christmas is to me abominable." The second James Woodforde sympathized and agreed. Again, when a stranger abused his hospitality it was a relief to inform the other self who lived in the little book that he had put him to sleep in the attic story "and I treated him as one that would be too free if treated kindly." It is easy to understand why in the quiet life of a country parish these two bachelor friends became in time inseparable. An essential part of him would have died had he been forbidden to keep his diary. And as we read—if reading is the word for it—we seem to be listening to someone who is murmuring over the events of the day to himself in the quiet space which precedes sleep. It is not writing, and to speak the truth it is not reading. It is slipping through half a dozen pages and strolling to the window and looking out. It is going on thinking about the Woodfordes while we watch the people in the street below. It is taking a walk and making up the life and character of James Woodforde as we make up our friends' characters, turning over something they have said, pondering the meaning of something they have done, remembering how they looked one day when they thought themselves unobserved. It is not reading; it is ruminating.

James Woodforde, then, was one of those smooth-cheeked, steady-eyed men, demure to look at, whom we can never imagine except in the prime of life. He was of an equable temper, with only such acerbities and touchinesses as are generally to be found in those who have had a love affair in their youth and remained, as they fancy, unwed because of it. The Parson's love affair, however, was nothing very tremendous. Once when he was a young man in Somerset he liked to walk over to Shepton and to visit a certain "sweet-tempered" Betsy White who lived there. He had a great mind "to make a bold stroke" and ask her to marry him. He went so far, indeed, as to propose marriage "when opportunity served" and Betsy was willing. But he delayed; time passed; four years passed, indeed, and Betsy went to Devonshire, met a Mr. Webster who had five hundred pounds a year, and married him. When James Woodforde met them in the turnpike road, he could say little, "being shy," but to his diary he remarked—and this no doubt was his private version of the affair ever after—"she has proved herself to me a mere jilt."

But he was a young man then, and as time went on we cannot help suspecting that he was glad to consider the question of marriage shelved once and for all, so that he might settle down with his niece Nancy at Weston Longueville and give himself simply and solely, every day and all day, to the great business of living. What else to call it we do not know. It seems to be life itself.

For James Woodforde was nothing in particular. Life had it all her own way with him. He had no special gift; he had no oddity or infirmity. It is idle to pretend that he was a zealous priest. God in Heaven was much the same to him as King George upon the throne—a kindly monarch, that is to say, whose festivals one kept by preaching a sermon on Sunday much as one kept the royal birthday by firing a blunderbuss and drinking a toast at dinner. Should anything untoward happen, like the death of a boy who was dragged and killed by a horse, he would instantly, but rather perfunctorily, exclaim: "I hope to God the Poor

Boy is happy," and add: "We all came home singing";
just as when Justice Creed's peacock spread its tail—"and
most noble it is"—he would exclaim: "How wonderful are
Thy Works O God in every Being." But there was no
fanaticism, no enthusiasm, no lyric impulse about James
Woodforde. In all these pages, indeed, each so neatly divided into compartments, and each of those again filled, as
the days themselves were, so quietly and fully in a hand
like the pacing of a well-tempered nag, one can only call
to mind a single poetic phrase about the transit of Venus,
how "It appeared as a black patch upon a fair Lady's
face." The words themselves are mild enough, but they
hang over the undulating expanse of the Parson's prose
with the resplendence of the star itself. So in the fen
country a barn or a tree appears twice its natural size
against the surrounding flats. But what led him to this
palpable excess that summer's night we do not know. It
cannot have been that he was drunk. He spoke out too
roundly against such failings in his brother Jack to have
been guilty himself. Jack was the wild one of the family.
Jack drank at the "Catherine Wheel." Jack came home
and had the impudence to defend suicide to his old father.
James himself drank his pint of port, but he was a man
who liked his meat. When we think of the Woodfordes,
uncle and niece, we think of them as often as not waiting
with some impatience for their dinner. They gravely watch
the joint set upon the table; they swiftly get their knives
and forks to work upon the succulent leg or loin, and
without much comment, unless a word is passed about the
gravy or the stuffing, go on eating. They munch, day
after day, year after year, until they have devoured herds
of sheep and oxen, flocks of poultry, an odd dozen or so

of swans and cygnets, bushels of apples and plums, while the pastries and the jellies crumble and squash beneath their spoons in mountains, in pyramids, in pagodas. Never was there a book so stuffed with food as this one is. To read the bill of fare respectfully and punctually set forth gives one a sense of repletion. It is as if one had lunched at Simpsons daily for a week. Trout and chicken, mutton and peas, pork and apple sauce—so the joints succeed each other at dinner; and there is supper with more joints still to come, all, no doubt, home grown, and of the juiciest and sweetest; all cooked, often by the mistress herself, in the plainest English way, save when the dinner was at Weston Hall and Mrs. Custance surprised them with a London dainty—a pyramid of jelly, that is to say, with a "landscape appearing through it." Then Mrs. Custance, for whom James Woodforde had a chivalrous devotion, would play the "Sticcardi Pastorale" and make "very soft music indeed"; or would get out her work-box and show them how neatly contrived it was, unless indeed Mrs. Custance were giving birth to another child upstairs, whom the Parson would baptize and very frequently bury. The Parson had a deep respect for the Custances. They were all that country gentry should be—a little given to the habit of keeping mistresses, perhaps, but that peccadillo could be forgiven them in view of their generosity to the poor, the kindness they showed to Nancy, and their condescension in asking the Parson to dinner when they had great people staying with them. Yet great people were not much to James's liking. Deeply though he respected the nobility, "one must confess," he said, "that being with our equals is much more agreeable."

He was too fond of his ease and too shrewd a judge of

the values of things to be much troubled with snobbery; he much preferred the quiet of his own fireside to adventuring after dissipation abroad. If an old man brought a Madagascar monkey to the door, or a Polish dwarf or a balloon was being shown at Norwich, the Parson would go and have a look at them, and be free with his shillings, but he was a quiet man, a man without ambition, and it is more than likely that his niece found him a little dull. It is the niece Nancy, to speak plainly, who makes us uneasy. There are the seeds of domestic disaster in her character, unless we mistake. It is true that on the afternoon of April 27th, 1780, she expressed a wish to read Aristotle's philosophy, which Miss Millard had got of a married woman, but she is a stolid girl; she eats too much, she grumbles too much, and she takes too much to heart the loss of her red box. No doubt she was sensible enough; we will not blame her for being pert and saucy, or for losing her temper at cards, or even for hiding the parcel that came by post when her uncle longed to know what was in it, and had never done such a thing by her. But when we compare her with Betsy Davy, we realize that one human being has only to come into the room to raise our spirits, and another sets us on edge merely by the way she blows her nose. Betsy, the daughter of that frivolous wanton Mrs. Davy (who fell downstairs the day Miss Donne swallowed the barleycorn with its stalk), Betsy the shy little girl, Betsy livening up and playing with the Parson's wig, Betsy falling in love with Mr. Walker, Betsy receiving the present of a fox's brush from him, Betsy compromising her reputation with a scamp, Betsy bereaved of him—for Mr. Walker died at the age of twenty-three and was buried in a plain coffin—Betsy left, it is to feared, in a very scandalous condition—Betsy always

charms; we forgive Betsy anything. The trouble with
Nancy is that she is beginning to find Weston dull. No
suitor has yet appeared. It is but too likely that the ten
years of Parson Woodforde's life that still remain will
often have to record how Nancy teased him with her
grumbling.

The ten years that remain—one knows, of course, that
it must come to an end. Already the Custances have gone
to Bath; the Parson has had a touch of gout; far away,
with a sound like distant thunder, we hear the guns of the
French Revolution. But it is comforting to observe that
the imprisonment of the French king and queen, and the
anarchy and confusion in Paris, are only mentioned after
it has been recorded that Thomas Ram has lost his cow
and that Parson Woodforde has "brewed another Barrell
of Table Beer today." We have a notion, indeed—and here
it must be confessed that we have given up reading Parson
Woodforde altogether, and merely tell over the story on
a stroll through fields where the hares are scampering and
the rooks rising above the elm trees—we have a notion that
Parson Woodforde does not die. Parson Woodforde goes
on. It is we who change and perish. It is the kings and
queens who lie in prison. It is the great towns that are
ravaged with anarchy and confusion. But the river Wen-
sum still flows; Mrs. Custance is brought to bed of yet
another baby; there is the first swallow of the year. The
spring comes, and summer with its hay and its straw-
berries; then autumn, when the walnuts are exceptionally
fine, though the pears are poor; so we lapse into winter,
which is indeed boisterous, but the house, thank God,
withstands the storm; and then again there is the first
swallow, and Parson Woodforde takes his greyhounds
out a-coursing.

Crabbe

NOTHING is more remarkable in reading the life of Crabbe than his passion for weeds. After his wife's death—she was mad for the last years of her life, alternately melancholic and exalted—he gave up weed collecting and took to fossils. But he always went fossilizing alone; though if children insisted upon coming he suffered them. "Playing with fossils," he called it. When he went to stay with his son George he went off, always alone, to grout for fossils in the blue lias quarries; "stopping to cut up any herb not quite common that grew in his path"; and he would return loaded with them. "The dirty fossils were placed in our best bedroom, to the great diversion of the female part of my family, the herbs stuck in the borders, among my choice flowers, that he might see them when he came again. I never displaced one of them." This gnarled and sea-salted man was no smug clergyman underneath. He had a passion for the rejected and injured, the stunted, the hardy, the wild self-grown, self-supported unsightly weed. He was himself a weed. His birth and breeding had been the weeds—at Aldborough, where he was born on Christmas Eve, 1754. His father was a warehouse keeper, and rose to be collector of Salt Duties, or Salt Master, in that miserable dull sea village, the sound of whose waves never went out of George's ears, even at Belvoir or Trowbridge. His mother had kept a public house, and his father, a short powerful man, who used sometimes to read poetry—Milton or Young—to his children but was fondest of mathematics, became, owing to the death of his only daughter, violent sometimes; her "untimely death drew from him those gloomy and savage tokens of misery, which haunted, fifty years after, the memory of his gentler son." His mother was pious, resigned, and dropsical.

Such, then, was his original weedlike life, on the quays rolling casks, waiting for a signal from the offing. And nothing is more remarkable than that this pale boy should have raised himself once and for all, by the force of one letter to Burke, into a luxurious, educated, cushioned career for life. Nothing of the kind would now be possible. Burke has been supplanted by the elementary school and scholarships.

Then there were his amorous propensities. This has to be referred to by the most respectful of sons—did he not let his father's weeds grow among his own choice flowers?— because "These things were so well-known among the circle of which at this period he formed the delight and ornament that I have thought it absurd not to dwell on them." He suffered at the age of sixty-four more acutely from love and jealousy than most young men of twenty. Crabbe's nature, indeed, included more than one full-grown human being. He could shine—witness his diary, brief, pointed—in the very highest society. He had admirable manners, but, though he always gave way, yet always expected to be given way to. Moreover he was untidy in the extreme. His study table was notorious. And he was genial; called his sons "old fellows" and liked to offer his friends good claret. He tipped servants, gave presents, was loved and plundered by the poor, who pestered him for shillings so that his birthday was a kind of levée for the whole neighbourhood. As a preacher too he was unconventional, and would stand in a seat near the window to finish reading his sermon in the dark. And he took opium, with very good results, in a constant and slightly increasing dose. He would wander with his children in the fields at Glemham till the moon rose, reading aloud from some novel as he walked, while the boys chased moths, filled their caps with glow worms, and the nightingales sang. He wrote innumerable books which he afterwards burnt in his garden, the children stirring up the fire and flinging on it fresh manuscripts. Thus was burnt his *Essay on Botany* because it was in English and his friend, Mr. Davies of Trinity College, Cambridge, "could not stomach the notion of degrading such a science by treating of it in a modern language." For this reason he missed the honour of being known as the discoverer of the humble trefoil now known as Trifolium Suffocatum. And in 1787 he was seized one fine summer's day with so intense a longing for the sea that he mounted his horse, rode alone to the coast of Lincolnshire sixty miles from his home, dipped in the waves that washed the beach of Aldborough, and returned home to sit in his untidy study, arranging minerals, shells, and insects.

Selina Trimmer[1]

THE gardens at Chatsworth which contained so many strange exotic plants brought by the great gardener Paxton from foreign lands, could boast, too, of one modest daisy whose surname was Trimmer and whose Christian name was Selina. She was a governess of course, and when we think what it meant to Charlotte Brontë and to Miss Weeton to be a governess in a middle-class family, the life of Selina Trimmer redounds more to the credit of the Cavendishes than all the splendours of Chatsworth, Devonshire House and Hardwick Hall. She was a governess; yet her pupil Lady Harriet wrote to her when she became engaged, "I send you the enclosed bracelet. . . . I often think of all your past conduct to me with affection and gratitude not to be expressed. God bless you, my dearest friend."

Selina sheds light upon the Cavendishes, but outside that radiance little is known of her. Her life must begin with a negative—she was not her sister-in-law, the famous Mrs. Trimmer of the *Tales*. She had a brother who lived at Brentford. From Brentford then, about 1790, came Selina, up the great marble stairs, following a footman, to be governess to the little Cavendishes in the nursery at Devonshire House. But were they all Cavendishes—the six romping, high-spirited children she found there? Three it appeared had no right to any surname at all. And who was

[1] Written in June, 1940.

31

the Lady Elizabeth Foster who lived on such intimate terms with the disagreeable Duke, and on such friendly terms with the lovely Duchess? Soon it must have dawned upon Trimmer as she sat over her Quaker discourse when her pupils were in bed that she had taken up her lodging in the abode of vice. Downstairs there was drinking and gambling; upstairs there were bastards and mistresses. According to Brentford standards she should have drawn her skirts about her and flounced out of the polluted place at once. Yet she stayed on. Far from being vicious, the Devonshire House family was healthy and in its own way virtuous. No more devoted family existed. The children adored their mother. They were on the best of terms with one another. If the Duke was an indifferent father, his daughters were as dutiful as the daughters of any country parson. One person, it is true, all the children hated, and that was Lady Liz. But they hated her not because she was their father's mistress, but because she was corrupt; whining and cooing, false and spiteful. Could it be possible, then, that an absence of conventional morality brings into being a real morality? Were not the little girls, Georgiana and Hary-o,[1] who knew from childhood all the facts that are concealed from female Trimmers till they were married women, far less sentimental, less prudish and silly, infinitely more honest, sensible and downright than the middle-class girls whose virtue was so carefully shielded at Brentford?

These were questions that Trimmer must have pondered as she walked with her dubious brood in Hyde Park or

[1] *Hary-o.* The Letters of Lady Harriet Cavendish, 1796-1809. Edited by her grandson Sir George Leveson-Gower, K.B.E., and his daughter Iris Palmer.

escorted them to parties. They were asked everywhere. The courtyard at Devonshire House was full of coaches by day and by night. Nobody looked askance at them. So, while she taught the little Cavendishes their sums and their pothooks, they taught her; they enlarged her mind. They laughed at her and teased her and vowed that she was carrying on a love affair with Bob Adair. But for all that they treated her as if she were a woman of flesh and blood. There was only one class for the Cavendish children, and that was their own. Whatever their faults, and Hary-o always overslept, and could never read only one book at a time, the Cavendishes were the least snobbish of people. They treated her as an equal; they accepted her as part of their pagan and classless society. When the girls began to go out into the world they wrote as frankly and freely to their "dearest Selina" about their parties and their partners as they wrote to each other.

By the time they were going out into the great world, Trimmer was well aware of its dangers. She could take comfort in the fact that Georgiana and Hary-o were spared at least one temptation—they had not their mother's beauty. "I am delighted to be reckoned like mama," Hary-o wrote. "'A very bad edition though,' as an honest man said of me at Mrs. Somebody's party." They were short, fat, and rather heavy featured. But by way of compensation they had excellent brains. Their little eyes were extremely shrewd; in mind they were precocious and caustic. Hary-o could dash off a description of her fox-hunting cousin Althorp with a vivacity that any novelist might have envied, and with a worldly wisdom that would have done credit to a dowager.

Althorp as he might have been, no reasonable woman could refuse or help loving and respecting. Althorp as he is, no reasonable woman can for a moment think of but as an eager huntsman. He has no more importance in society *now* (as he is, remember) than the chairs and tables. . . . Evenings and Sundays are to him a visible penance. . . . But when he appears at breakfast in his red jacket and jockey cap, it is a sort of intoxicating delight that must be seen to seem credible, and one feels the same sort of good-natured pleasure as at seeing a Newfoundland dog splash into the water, a goldfinch out of his cage, or a mouse run out of his trap. This is the man that I cannot wish to marry. . . .

Shocked, puzzled yet charmed, Selina stayed on. But she preserved her own standards. In that intimate society where every lord and lady had a nickname, Trimmer had hers. She was called Raison Sévère, Triste Raison, Vent de Bise. Lady Bessborough lamented ". . . rigidly right, she forgets that one may do right without making oneself disagreeable to everyone around." And Bess, Lady Elizabeth Foster, shivered in her presence. "Bess . . . says she always affects her like a North-East wind." Trimmer was no sycophant. By degrees she assumed the part that is so often played by the humble retainer; from governess she became confidante. In that wild whirling life of incessant love-making and intrigue she represented reason, morality— something that Hary-o as she grew up missed in her mother and needed. Mama, she owned to her sister when Duncannon pestered her, was "not prudent"; mama did not mind putting her daughter into a "most awkward situation." But Selina, on the other hand, "gave me a most furious lecture that my coquetry was dreadful, and that, without caring for my cousin, I had made him fall in love with me." It was "merely to enjoy the triumph of supplanting Lady E.," Trimmer said. Lady Harriet was angry at Trimmer's plain speaking, but she respected her for it nevertheless.

More and more, as Hary-o grew older, the extraordinary complications of Devonshire House morality involved her in tortures of doubt—what was her duty to her father, what, after her mother's death, to his mistress, and what did she owe to society? Ought she to allow Lady Liz to drag her into the company of the abandoned Mrs. Fitzherbert? "And yet I have no right to be nice about the company I go into; or rather no power, for I think no blame can be attached to me for that I so reluctantly live in." Strangely, it was not to the Bessboroughs or to the Melbournes that Hary-o turned in her dilemma; it was to Trimmer. Though companion now to old Lady Spencer, Trimmer came back to bear Harriet company at Devonshire House when Lady Liz was queening it there, saying "we" and "us" all the time, and fondling the Duke's spotted and speckled puppies in her shawl. Trimmer alone had the courage to show that the dogs bored her. Trimmer compelled the Duke and George Lamb to talk about "the Quaker persuasion and Mr. Boreham's scruples about giving the oath." In those tortured days Trimmer, "arch advocate of reason," was the greatest blessing to her distracted pupil. And it was finally to Trimmer that Harriet turned when the crucial question of her life had to be decided. Was she to marry her aunt's lover, Lord Granville? He had two children by Lady Bessborough. They had always been in league against her. She had hated him; yet there had come over her the spell of his wonderful almond-shaped eyes, and it would mean escape—from Lady Liz, from the ignominies and insults that her father's mistress put upon her. What was she to do? What she did was to marry Granville—"Adored Granville, who would make a barren desert smile." And it proved, on the face of it, an ideal union. Lord Granville became a model of the domestic virtues. Harriet developed into the most respectable of Victorian matrons, wearing a large black bonnet, setting up old orange women with baskets of trifles, illuminating book markers with texts, and attending church assiduously. She survived till 1862. But did Trimmer suffer a Victorian change? Or did Trimmer remain immutably herself? There was something hardy and perennial about Trimmer. One can imagine her grown very old and very gaunt, dwindling out her declining years in discreet obscurity. But what tales she could have told had she liked—about the lovely Duchess and the foolish Caro Ponsonby, and the Melbournes and the Bessboroughs—all vanished, all changed. The only relic of that wild world that remained was the bracelet on her wrist. It recalled much that had better be forgotten, and yet, as Trimmer looked at it, how happy she had been in Devonshire House with Hary-o, her dearest friend.

The Captain's Death Bed[1]

THE Captain lay dying on a mattress stretched on the floor of the boudoir room; a room whose ceiling had been painted to imitate the sky, and whose walls were painted with trellis work covered with roses upon which birds were perching. Mirrors had been let into the doors, so that the village people called the room the "Room of a Thousand Pillars" because of its reflections. It was an August morning as he lay dying; his daughter had brought him a bunch of his favourite flowers—clove pinks and moss roses; and he asked her to take down some words at his dictation:—

'Tis a lovely day [he dictated] and Augusta has just brought me three pinks and three roses, and the bouquet is charming. I have opened the windows and the air is delightful. It is now exactly nine o'clock in the morning, and I am lying on a bed in a place called Langham, two miles from the sea, on the coast of Norfolk. . . . To use the common sense of the word [he went on] I am happy. I have no sense of hunger whatever, or of thirst; my taste is not impaired. . . . After years of casual, and, latterly, months of intense thought, I feel convinced that Christianity is true . . . and that God is love. . . . It is now half-past nine o'clock. World, adieu.

Early in the morning of August 9th, 1848, just about dawn he died.

But who was the dying man whose thoughts turned to love and roses as he lay among his looking-glasses and his

[1] Written in September, 1935.

painted birds? Singularly enough, it was a sea captain; and still more singularly it was a sea captain who had been through the multitudinous engagements of the Napoleonic wars, who had lived a crowded life on shore, and who had written a long shelf of books of adventure, full of battle and murder and conquest. His name was Frederick Marryat. Who then was Augusta, the daughter who brought him the flowers? She was one of his eleven children; but of her the only fact that is now known to the public is that once she went ratting with her father and seized an enormous rat—"You must know that our Norfolk rats are quite as large as well-grown guinea pigs"—and held on to him with her bare hands, much to the amazement of the onlookers and, we may guess, to the admiration of her father, who remarked that his daughters were "true game." Then, again, what was Langham? Langham was an estate in Norfolk for which Captain Marryat had exchanged Sussex House over a glass of champagne. And Sussex House was a house at Hammersmith in which he lived while he was equerry to the Duke of Sussex. But here certainty begins to falter. Why he quarrelled with the Duke of Sussex and ceased to be his equerry; why, after an apparently pacific interview with Lord Auckland at the Admiralty he was in such a rage that he broke a blood vessel; why, after having eleven children by his wife, he left her; why, being possessed of a house in the country, he lived in London; why, being the centre of a gay and brilliant society he suddenly shut himself up in the country and refused to budge; why Mrs. B—— refused his love and what were his relations with Mrs. S——; these are questions that we may ask, but that we must ask in vain. For the two little volumes with very large print and very small pages in which his daughter

Florence wrote his life refuse to tell us. One of the most active, odd and adventurous lives that any English novelist has ever lived is also one of the most obscure.

Some of the reasons for this obscurity lie on the surface. In the first place there was too much to tell. The Captain began his life as a midshipman in Lord Cochrane's ship the *Impérieuse* in the year 1806. He was then aged fourteen. And here are a few extracts from a private log that he kept in July, 1808, when he was sixteen:—

——24th. Taking guns from the batteries.
——25th. Burning bridges and dismantling batteries to impede the French.
August 1st. Taking the brass guns from the batteries.
——15th. Took a French despatch boat off Cette.
——18th. Took and destroyed a signal post.
——19th. Blew up a signal post.

So it goes on. Every other day he was cutting out a brig, taking a tower, engaging gunboats, seizing prize ships or being chased by the French. In the first three years of his life at sea he had been in fifty fights; times out of number he jumped into the sea and rescued a drowning man. Once much against his will, for he could swim like a fish, he was rescued by an old bumboat woman who could also swim like a fish. Later he engaged with so much success in the Burmese War that he was allowed to bear a Burmese gilt war-boat on his arms. Clearly if the extracts from the private log had been expanded it would have swollen to a row of volumes; but how was the private log to be expanded by a lady who had presumably never burnt a bridge, dismantled a battery, or blown out a Frenchman's brains in her life? Very wisely she had recourse to Marshall's Naval Biography and to the Gazette. "Gazette details," she remarked, "are proverbially dry, but they are trustworthy." Therefore the public life is dealt with dryly, if trustworthily.

The private life however remained; and the private life, if we may judge from the names of the friends he had and the money he spent and the quarrels he waged, was as violent and various in its way as the other. But here again reticence prevailed. It was partly that his daughter delayed; almost twenty-four years had passed before she wrote and friends were dead and letters destroyed; and it was partly that she was his daughter, imbued with filial reverence and with the belief also that "a biographer has no business to meddle with any facts below the surface." The famous statesman Sir R—— P—— therefore is Sir R—— P——; and Mrs. S—— is Mrs. S——. It is only now and then, almost by accident, that we are startled by a sudden groan—"I have had my swing, tried and tasted everything, and I find that it is vanity"; "I have been in a peck of troubles—domestic, agricultural, legal and pecuniary"; or just for a moment we are allowed to glance at a scene, "You reposing on the sofa, C—— sitting by you and I on the footstool" which "is constantly recurring to my memory as a picture" and has crept into one of the letters. But, as the Captain adds, "It has all vanished like 'air, thin air.'" It has all, or almost all, vanished; and if posterity wants to know about the Captain it must read his books.

That the public still wishes to read his books is proved by the fact that the best known of them, *Peter Simple* and *Jacob Faithful*, were reprinted a few years ago in a handsome big edition, with introductions by Professor Saintsbury and Mr. Michael Sadleir. And the books are quite capable of being read, though nobody is going to pretend that they are among the masterpieces. They have not struck out any immortal scene or character; they are far from marking an epoch in the history of the novel. The critic with an eye for pedigree can trace the influence of Defoe, Fielding, and Smollett naturally asserting itself in their straightforward pages. It may well be that we are drawn to them for reasons that seem far enough from literature. The sun on the cornfield; the gull following the plough; the simple speech of country people leaning over gates, breeds the desire to cast the skin of a century and revert to those simpler days. But no living writer, try though he may, can bring the past back again, because no living writer can bring back the ordinary day. He sees it through a glass, sentimentally, romantically; it is either too pretty or too brutal; it lacks ordinariness. But the world of 1806 was to Captain Marryat what the world of 1935 is to us at this moment, a middling sort of a place, where there is nothing particular to stare at in the street or to listen to in the language. So to Captain Marryat there was nothing out of the way in a sailor with a pigtail or in a bumboat woman volleying hoarse English. Therefore the world of 1806 is real to us and ordinary, yet sharp-edged and peculiar. And when the delight of looking at a day that was the ordinary day a century ago is exhausted, we are kept reading by the fact that our critical faculties enjoy whetting themselves upon a book which is not among the classics. When the artist's imagination is working at high pressure it leaves very little trace of his effort; we have to go gingerly on tip-toe among the invisible joins and complete marriages that take place in those high regions. Here it is easier going. Here in these cruder books we get closer to the art of fiction; we see the bones and the muscles and the arteries clearly marked. It is a good exercise in criticism to follow a sound craftsman, not marvellously but sufficiently endowed at his work. And as we read *Peter Simple* and *Jacob Faithful* there can be no doubt that Captain Marryat had in embryo at least most of the gifts that go to make a master. Do we think of him as a mere storyteller for boys? Here is a passage which shows that he could use language with the suggestiveness of a poet; though to get the full effect, as always in fiction, it must be read up to through the emotions of the characters. Jacob is alone after his father's death on the Thames lighter at dawn:—

I looked around me—the mist of the morning was hanging over the river. . . . As the sun rose, the mist gradually cleared away; trees, houses and green fields, other barges coming up with the tide, boats passing and repassing, the barking of dogs, the smoke issuing from the various chimneys, all broke upon me by degrees; and I was recalled to the sense that I was in a busy world, and had my own task to perform.

Then if we want a proof that the Captain, for all his sturdiness, had that verbal sensibility which at the touch of a congenial thought lets fly a rocket, here we have a discourse on a nose.

It was not an aquiline nose, nor was it an aquiline nose reversed. It was not a nose snubbed at the extremity, gross, heavy, or carbuncled, or fluting. In all its magnitude of proportions it was an intellectual nose. It was thin, horny, transparent, and sonorous. Its snuffle was consequential, and its sneeze oracular. The very sight of it was impressive; its sound when blown in school hours was ominous.

Such was the nose that Jacob saw looming over him when he woke from his fever to hear the Dominie breathing those strange words, "Earth, lay light upon the lighter-boy—the lotus, the water-lily, that hath been cast on shore to die." And for pages at a time he writes that terse springy prose which is the natural speech of a school of writers trained to the business of moving a large company briskly from one incident to another over the solid earth. Further, he can create a world; he has the power to set us in the midst of ships and men and sea and sky all vivid, credible, authentic, as we are made suddenly aware when Peter quotes a letter from home and the other side of the scene appears; the solid land, England, the England of Jane Austen, with its parsonages, its country houses, its young women staying at home, its young men gone to sea; and for a moment the two worlds, that are so opposite and yet so closely allied, come together. But perhaps the Captain's greatest gift was his power of drawing character. His pages are full of marked faces. There is Captain Kearney, the magnificent liar; and Captain Horton, who lay in bed all day long; and Mr. Chucks, and Mrs. Trotter who cadges eleven pairs of cotton stockings—they are all drawn vigorously, decisively, from the living face, just as the Captain's pen, we are told, used to dash off caricatures upon a sheet of notepaper.

With all these qualities, then, what was there stunted in his equipment? Why does the attention slip and the eye merely register printed words? One reason, of course, is that there are no heights in this level world. Violent and agitated as it is, as full of fights and escapes as Captain Marryat's private log, yet there comes a sense of monotony; the same emotion is repeated; we never feel that we are approaching anything; the end is never a consummation. Again, emphatic and trenchant as his characters are, not one of them rounds and fills to his full size, because some of the elements that go to make character are lacking. A chance sentence suggests why this should be so. "After this we had a conversation of two hours; but what lovers say is very silly, except to themselves, and the reader need not be troubled with it." The intenser emotions of the human race are kept out. Love is banished; and when love is banished, other valuable emotions that are allied to her are apt to go too. Humour has to have a dash of passion in it; death has to have something that makes us ponder. But here there is a kind of bright hardness. Though he has a curious love of what is physically disgusting—the face of a child nibbled by fish, a woman's body bloated with gin— he is sexually not so much chaste as prudish, and his morality has the glib slickness of a schoolmaster preaching down to small boys. In short, after a fine burst of pleasure there comes a time when the spell that Captain Marryat lays upon us wears thin, and we see through the veil of fiction facts—facts, it is true, that are interesting in themselves; facts about yawls and jolly boats and how boats going into action are "fitted to pull with grummets upon iron thole pins"; but their interest is another kind of interest, and as much out of harmony with imagination as a bedroom cupboard is with the dream of someone waking from sleep.

Often in a shallow book, when we wake, we wake to nothing at all; but here when we wake, we wake to the presence of a personage—a retired naval officer with an active mind and a caustic tongue, who as he trundles his wife and family across the Continent in the year 1835 is forced to give expression to his opinions in a diary. Sick though he was of story-writing and bored by a literary life—"If I were not rather in want of money," he tells his mother, "I certainly would not write any more"—he must express his mind somehow; and his mind was a courageous mind, an unconventional mind. The Press-gang, he thought an abomination. Why, he asked, do English philanthropists bother about slaves in Africa when English children are working seventeen hours a day in factories? The Game Laws are, in his opinion, a source of much misery to the poor; the law of primogeniture should be altered, and there is something to be said for the Roman Catholic religion. Every kind of topic—politics, science, religion, history— comes into view, but only for a fleeting glance. Whether the diary form was to blame or the jolting of a stage coach, or whether lack of book learning and a youth spent in cutting out brigs is a bad training for the reflective powers, the Captain's mind, as he remarked when he stopped for two hours and had a look at it, "is like a kaleidoscope." But no, he added with just self-analysis, it was not like a kaleidoscope; "for the patterns of kaleidoscopes are regular, and there is very little regularity in my brain, at all events." He hops from thing to thing. Now he rattles off the history of Liége; next moment he discourses upon reason and instinct; then he considers what degree of pain is inflicted upon fish by taking them with the hook; and then, taking a walk through the streets, it strikes him how very seldom you now meet with a name beginning with X. "Rest!" he exclaims with reason; "no, the wheels of a carriage may rest, even the body for a time may rest, but the mind will not." And so, in an excess of restlessness, he is off to America.

Nor do we catch sight of him again—for the six volumes in which he recorded his opinion of America, though they got him into trouble with the inhabitants, now throw light upon nothing in particular—until his daughter, having shut up her Dictionaries and Gazettes, bethinks her of a few "vague remembrances." They are only trifles, she admits, and put together in a very random way, but still she remembers him very vividly. He was five foot ten and weighed fourteen stone, she remembers; he had a deep dimple in his chin, and one of his eyebrows was higher than the other, so that he always wore a look of inquiry. Indeed, he was a very restless man. He would break into his brother's room and wake him in the middle of the night to suggest that they should start at once to Austria and buy a château in Hungary and make their fortunes. But, alas! he never did make his fortune, she recalls. What with his building at Langham, and the great decoy which he had made on his best grazing land, and other extravagances not easy for a daughter to specify, he left little wealth behind him. He had to keep hard at his writing. He wrote his books sitting at a table in the dining-room, from which he could see the lawn and his favourite bull Ben Brace grazing there. And he wrote so small a hand that the copyist had to stick a pin in to mark the place. Also he was wonderfully neat in his dress, and would have nothing but white china on his breakfast table, and kept sixteen clocks and liked to hear them all strike at once. His children called him "Baby," though he was a man of violent passions, dangerous to thwart, and often "very grave" at home.

"These trifles put on paper look sadly insignificant," she concludes. Yet as she rambles on they do in their butterfly way bring back the summer morning and the dying Captain after all his voyages stretched on the mattress in the boudoir room dictating those last words to his daughter about love and roses. "The more fancifully they were tied together, the better he liked it," she says. Indeed, after his death a bunch of pinks and roses was "found pressed between his body and the mattress."

Ruskin

WHAT did our fathers of the nineteenth century do to deserve so much scolding? That is a question which we find ourselves asking sometimes as we dip here and there into the long row of volumes which bear the names of Carlyle and Ruskin. And if we also dip into the lives of those great men we shall find evidence that our fathers were a good deal responsible for the tone which their teachers adopted towards them. There can be no doubt that they liked their great men to be isolated from the rest of the world. Genius was nearly as antisocial and demanded almost as drastic a separation from the ordinary works and duties of mankind as insanity. Accordingly, the great man of that age had much temptation to withdraw to his pinnacle and become a prophet, denouncing a generation from whose normal activities he was secluded. When Carlyle expressed his readiness to work somewhere in a public office, no such place was found for him, and for the rest of his life he was left to grind out book after book with a bitter consciousness within him that such was not the most venerable of lives. All the worship that was offered could not sweeten what wiser treatment might have entirely blotted out. Ruskin started from the opposite pole as far as circumstances were concerned, but he too drifted into the same isolation, and he leaves us convinced that of the two, his was the sadder life.

Yet if all the fairies had conspired together at his birth

to protect this man of genius and foster him to the utmost, what more could they have done? He had wealth and comfort and opportunity from the very first. While he was still a boy his genius was recognized, and he had only to publish his first book to become one of the most famous men of the day at the age of twenty-four. But the fairies after all did not give him the gifts he wanted. If one had seen Ruskin about the year 1869, according to Professor Norton, "you would tell me that you had never seen so sad a man, never one whose nature seemed to have been so sensitized to pain by the experience of life." This surpassing gift of eloquence, in the first place, brought him far more of evil than of good. Still, after sixty years or so, the style in which page after page of *Modern Painters* is written takes our breath away. We find ourselves marvelling at the words, as if all the fountains of the English language had been set playing in the sunlight for our pleasure, but it seems scarcely fitting to ask what meaning they have for us. After a time, falling into a passion with this indolent pleasure-loving temper in his readers, Ruskin checked his fountains, and curbed his speech to the very spirited, free, and almost colloquial English in which *Fors Clavigera* and *Praeterita* are written. In these changes, and in the restless play of his mind upon one subject after another, there is something, we scarcely know how to define it, of the wealthy and cultivated amateur, full of fire and generosity and brilliance, who would give all he possesses of wealth and brilliance to be taken seriously, but who is fated to remain for ever an outsider. As we read these outbursts of rather petulant eloquence, we find ourselves remembering the sheltered and luxurious life, and even when we are very ignorant of the subject, the tremendous arrogance and self-confidence seem to result not from knowledge, but from a tossing and splendid impatience of spirit which is not to be broken into the drudgery of learning. We remember how for years after most men are forced to match themselves with the real world "he was living in a world of his own," to quote Professor Norton again, and losing the chance of gaining that experience with practical life, that self-control, and that development of reason which he more than most men required. If we reflect, too, that from his childhood, when he stood up among the cushions and preached, "People, be good," the passion of his life was to teach and reform, it is easy to understand how terribly and, as it must have seemed sometimes, how futilely "he hurt himself against life and the world."

But we do him much wrong if we take him merely as a prophet—a proceeding that is rather forced upon one by his followers, and forget to read his books. For if anyone is able to make his readers feel that he is alive, wrong headed, intemperate, interesting, and lovable, that writer is Ruskin. His eagerness about everything in the world is perhaps as valuable as the concentration which in another sphere produced the works of Darwin, or the *Decline and Fall of the Roman Empire*. It may be that, if we submitted his works on art to a modern art critic, or his works on economy to a modern economist, we should find that there is very little in them which is accepted by the present generation. Even an unprofessional reader, who picks up *Modern Painters* attracted very much by the bright patches of eloquence, is fairly startled by some of the statements concerning art and morality which are laid down with the usual air of infallibility and the usual array of polysyllables. Nor is it easy for one reading industriously in the six volumes of *Fors Clavigera* to find out precisely how it is that we are to save ourselves, though it is plain enough that we are all damned. Nevertheless, though his æsthetics may be wrong and his economics amateurish, you have to reckon with a force which is not to be suppressed by a whole pyramid of faults. That is why perhaps people in his life time got into the habit of calling him Master. He was possessed by a spirit of enthusiasm which compels those who are without it either to attack or to applaud; but beneath its influence they cannot remain merely passive. Even now the straight free lashing of *Fors Clavigera* seems to descend far too often for our comfort upon the skin of our own backs.

It is hard not to regret that so much of his force went into satire and attempts at reformation for which, as he knew well, he was not well-equipped by nature. It is hard too not to wish that he had lived in an age which did not isolate its great men with adulation, but encouraged them to use the best of their powers. As it is, if we want to get unalloyed good from Ruskin, we take down not *Modern Painters*, or the *Stones of Venice*, or *Sesame and Lilies*, but *Praeterita*. There he has ceased to preach or to teach or to scourge. He is writing for the last time before he enters the prolonged season of death, and his mood is still perfectly clear, more sustained than usual, and unfailingly benignant. Compared with much of his writing, it is extremely simple in style; but the simplicity is the flower of perfect skill. The words lie like a transparent veil upon his meaning. And the passage with which the book ends, though it was written when he could hardly write, is surely more beautiful than those more elaborate and gilded ones which we are apt to cut out and admire:

Fonte Branda I last saw with Charles Norton under the same arches where Dante saw it. We drank of it together, and walked together that evening in the hills above, where the fireflies among the scented thickets shone fitfully in the still undarkened air. *How* they shone! moving like fine-broken starlight through the purple leaves. How they shone! through the sunset that faded into thunderous night as I entered Siena three days before, the white edges of the mountainous clouds still lighted from the west, and the openly golden sky calm behind the Gate of Siena's heart, with its still golden words, *Cor magis tibi Sena pandit*, and the fireflies everywhere in sky or cloud rising and falling, mixed with the lightning, and more intense than the stars.

The Novels of Turgenev[1]

RATHER more than fifty years ago Turgenev died in France and was buried in Russia, appropriately it may seem, if we remember how much he owed to France and yet how profoundly he belonged to his own land. The influence of both countries is to be felt if we look at his photograph for a moment before reading his books. The magnificent figure in the frock coat of Parisian civilization seems to be gazing over the houses far away at some wider view. He has the air of a wild beast who is captive but remembers whence he came. "C'est un colosse charmant, un doux géant aux cheveux blancs, qui a l'air du bienveillant génie d'une montagne ou d'une forêt" the brothers Goncourt wrote when they met him at dinner in 1863. "Il est beau, grandement beau, énormément beau, avec du bleu du ciel dans les yeux, avec le charme du chantonnement de l'accent russe, de cette cantilène où il y a un rien de l'enfant et du nègre." And Henry James noted later the great physical splendour, the Slav languor and "the air of neglected strength, as if it had been part of his modesty never to remind himself that he was strong. He used sometimes to blush like a boy of sixteen." Perhaps something of the same combination of qualities is to be found if we turn to his books.

At first, after years of absence it may be, they seem to

[1] Written in November, 1933. Copyright 1933 by Yale University Press (*The Yale Review*).

us a little thin, slight and sketchlike in texture. Take *Rudin*, for instance—the reader will place it among the French school, among the copies rather than the originals, with the feeling that the writer has set himself an admirable model, but in following it has sacrificed something of his own character and force. But the superficial impression deepens and sharpens itself as the pages are turned. The scene has a size out of all proportion to its length. It expands in the mind and lies there giving off fresh ideas, emotions, and pictures much as a moment in real life will sometimes only yield its meaning long after it has passed. We notice that though the people talk in the most natural speaking voices, what they say is always unexpected; the meaning goes on after the sound has stopped. Moreover, they do not have to speak in order to make us feel their presence; "Volintsev started and raised his head, as though he had just waked up"—we had felt him there though he had not spoken. And when in some pause we look out of the window, the emotion is returned to us, deepened, because it is given through another medium, by the trees or the clouds, by the barking of a dog, or the song of a nightingale. Thus we are surrounded on all sides—by the talk, by the silence, by the look of things. The scene is extraordinarily complete.

It is easy to say that in order to gain a simplicity so complex Turgenev has gone through a long struggle of elimination beforehand. He knows all about his people, so that when he writes he chooses only what is most salient without apparent effort. But when we have finished *Rudin*, *Fathers and Children*, *Smoke*, *On the Eve* and the others many questions suggest themselves to which it is not so easy to find an answer. They are so short and yet they hold so much. The emotion is so intense and yet so calm. The form is in one sense so perfect, in another so broken. They are about Russia in the fifties and sixties of the last century, and yet they are about ourselves at the present moment. Can we then find out from Turgenev himself what principles guided him—had he, for all his seeming ease and lightness, some drastic theory of art? A novelist, of course, lives so much deeper down than a critic that his statements are apt to be contradictory and confusing; they seem to break in process of coming to the surface, and do not hold together in the light of reason. Still, Turgenev was much interested in the art of fiction, and one or two of his sayings may help us to clarify our impressions of the famous novels. Once, for example, a young writer brought him the manuscript of a novel to criticize. Turgenev objected that he had made his heroine say the wrong thing. "What then ought she to have said?" the author asked. Turgenev exploded. "Trouver l'expression propre, c'est votre affaire!" But, the youth objected, he could not find it. "Eh bien! vous devez la trouver. . . . Ne pensez pas que je sais l'expression et que je ne veux pas vous la dire. Trouver, en la cherchant, une expression *propre* est impossible: elle doit couler de source. Quelquefois même, il faut créer l'expression ou le mot." And he advised him to put away his manuscript for a month or so, when the expression might come to him. If not—"Si vous n'y arrivez pas, cela voudra dire que vous ne ferez jamais rien qui vaille." From this it would seem that Turgenev is among those who hold that the right expression, which is of the utmost importance, is not to be had by observation, but comes from the depths unconsciously. You cannot find by looking. But then again he speaks of the novelist's art, and now he lays the greatest emphasis upon the need of observation. The novelist must observe everything exactly, in himself and in others. "La douleur passera et la page excellente reste." He must observe perpetually, impersonally, impartially. And still he is only at the beginning. ". . . il faut encore lire, toujours étudier, approfondir tout ce qui entoure, non seulement tâcher de saisir la vie dans toutes les manifestations, mais encore la comprendre, comprendre les lois d'après lesquelles elle se meut et qui ne se montrent pas toujours . . ." That was how he himself worked before he grew old and lazy, he said. But one has need of strong muscles to do it, he added; nor if we consider what he is asking can we accuse him of exaggeration.

For he is asking the novelist not only to do many things but some that seem incompatible. He has to observe facts impartially, yet he must also interpret them. Many novelists do the one; many do the other—we have the photograph and the poem. But few combine the fact and the vision; and the rare quality that we find in Turgenev is the result of this double process. For in these short chapters he is doing two very different things at the same time. With his infallible eye he observes everything accurately. Solomin picks up a pair of gloves; they were "white chamois-leather gloves, recently washed, every finger of which had stretched at the tip and looked like a finger-biscuit." But he stops when he has shown us the glove exactly; the interpreter is at his elbow to insist that even a glove must be relevant to the character, or to the idea. But the idea alone is not enough; the interpreter is never allowed to mount unchecked into the realms of imagination; again the observer pulls him back and reminds him of the other truth, the truth of fact. Even Bazarov, the heroic, packed his best trousers at the top of his bag when he wanted to impress a lady. The two partners work in closest alliance. We look at the same thing from different angles, and that is one reason why the short chapters hold so much; they contain so many contrasts. On one and the same page we have irony and passion; the poetic and the commonplace; a tap drips and a nightingale sings. And yet, though the scene is made up of contrasts, it remains the same scene; our impressions are all relevant to each other.

Such a balance, of course, between two very different faculties is extremely rare, especially in English fiction, and demands some sacrifices. The great characters, with whom we are so familiar in our literature, the Micawbers, the Pecksniffs, the Becky Sharps, will not flourish under such supervision; they need, it seems, more licence; they must be allowed to dominate and perhaps to destroy other competitors. With the possible exception of Bazarov and of Harlov in *A Lear of the Steppes* no one character in Turgenev's novels stands out above and beyond the rest so that we remember him apart from the book. The Rudins, the Lavretskys, the Litvinovs, the Elenas, the Lisas, the Mariannas shade off into each other, making, with all their variations, one subtle and profound type rather than several distinct and highly individualized men and women. Then, again, the poet novelists like Emily Brontë, Hardy, or Melville, to whom facts are symbols, certainly give us a more overwhelming and passionate experience in *Wuthering Heights* or *The Return of the Native* or *Moby Dick* than any that Turgenev offers us. And yet what Turgenev offers us not only often affects us as poetry, but his books are perhaps more completely satisfying than the others.

57

They are curiously of our own time, undecayed, and complete in themselves.

For the other quality that Turgenev possesses in so great a degree is the rare gift of symmetry, of balance. He gives us, in comparison with other novelists, a generalized and harmonized picture of life. And this is not only because his scope is wide—he shows us different societies, the peasant's, the intellectual's, the aristocrat's, the merchant's—but we are conscious of some further control and order. Yet such symmetry, as we are reminded, perhaps, by reading *A House of Gentlefolk*, is not the result of a supreme gift for storytelling. Turgenev, on the contrary, often tells a story very badly. There are loops and circumlocutions in his narrative—". . . we must ask the reader's permission to break off the thread of our story for a time," he will say. And then for fifty pages or so we are involved in great-grandfathers and great-grandmothers, much to our confusion, until we are back with Lavretsky at O—— "where we parted from him, and whither we will now ask the indulgent reader to return with us." The good storyteller, who sees his book as a succession of events, would never have suffered that interruption. But Turgenev did not see his books as a succession of events; he saw them as a succession of emotions radiating from some character at the centre. A Bazarov, a Harlov seen in the flesh, perhaps, once in the corner of a railway carriage, becomes of paramount importance and acts as a magnet which has the power to draw things mysteriously belonging, though apparently incongruous, together. The connexion is not of events but of emotions, and if at the end of the book we feel a sense of completeness, it must be that in spite of his defects as a storyteller Turgenev's ear for emotion was so fine that even if he uses an abrupt contrast, or passes away from his people to a description of the sky or of the forest, all is held together by the truth of his insight. He never distracts us with the real incongruity—the introduction of an emotion that is false, or a transition that is arbitrary.

It is for this reason that his novels are not merely symmetrical but make us feel so intensely. His heroes and heroines are among the few fictitious characters of whose love we are convinced. It is a passion of extraordinary purity and intensity. The love of Elena for Insarov, her anguish when he fails to come, her despair when she seeks refuge in the chapel in the rain; the death of Bazarov and the sorrow of his old father and mother remain in the mind like actual experiences. And yet, strangely enough, the individual never dominates; many other things seem to be going on at the same time. We hear the hum of life in the fields; a horse champs his bit; a butterfly circles and settles. And as we notice, without seeming to notice, life going on, we feel more intensely for the men and women themselves because they are not the whole of life, but only part of the whole. Something of this, of course, is due to the fact that Turgenev's people are profoundly conscious of their relation to things outside themselves. "What is my youth for, what am I living for, why have I a soul, what is it all for?" Elena asks in her diary. The question is always on their lips.

It lends a profundity to talk that is otherwise light, amusing, full of exact observation. Turgenev is never, as in England he might have been, merely the brilliant historian of manners. But not only do they question the aim of their own lives but they brood over the question of Russia. The intellectuals are always working for Russia; they sit up arguing about the future of Russia till the dawn rises over the eternal samovar. "They worry and worry away at that unlucky subject, as children chew away at a bit of india-rubber," Potugin remarks in *Smoke*. Turgenev, exiled in body, cannot absent himself from Russia—he has the almost morbid sensibility that comes from a feeling of inferiority and suppression. And yet he never allows himself to become a partisan, a mouthpiece. Irony never deserts him; there is always the other side, the contrast. In the midst of political ardour we are shown Fomushka and Fimushka, "chubby, spruce little things, a perfect pair of little poll-parrots," who manage to exist very happily singing glees in spite of their country. Also it is a difficult business, he reminds us, to know the peasants, not merely to study them. "I could not *simplify* myself," wrote Nezhdanov, the intellectual, before he killed himself. Moreover though Turgenev could have said with Marianna ". . . I suffer for all the oppressed, the poor, the wretched in Russia," it was for the good of the cause, just as it was for the good of his art, not to expatiate, not to explain. "Non, quand tu as énoncé le fait, n'insiste pas. Que le lecteur le discute et le comprenne lui-même. Croyez-moi, c'est mieux dans l'intérêt même des idées qui vous sont chères." He compelled himself to stand outside; he laughed at the intellectuals; he showed up the windiness of their arguments, the sublime folly of their attempts. But his emotion, and their failure, affect us all the more powerfully now because of that aloofness. Yet if this method was partly the result of discipline and theory, no theory, as Turgenev's novels abundantly prove, is able to go to the root of the matter and eliminate the artist himself; his temperament remains ineradicable. Nobody, we say over and over again as we read him, even in a translation, could have written this except Turgenev. His birth, his race, the impressions of his childhood, pervade everything that he wrote.

But, though temperament is fated and inevitable, the writer has a choice, and a very important one, in the use he makes of it. "I" he must be; but there are many different "I's" in the same person. Shall he be the "I" who has suffered this slight, that injury, who desires to impose his own personality, to win popularity and power for himself and his views; or shall he suppress that "I" in favour of the one who sees as far as he can impartially and honestly, without wishing to plead a cause or to justify himself? Turgenev had no doubt about his choice; he refused to write "élégamment et chaudement ce que vous ressentez à l'aspect de cette chose ou de cet homme." He used the other self, the self which has been so rid of superfluities that it is almost impersonal in its intense individuality; the self which he defines in speaking of the actress Violetta:—

She had thrown aside everything subsidiary, everything superfluous, and *found herself;* a rare, a lofty delight for an artist! She had suddenly crossed the limit, which it is impossible to define, beyond which is the abiding place of beauty.

That is why his novels are still so much of our own time; no hot and personal emotion has made them local and transitory; the man who speaks is not a prophet clothed with thunder but a seer who tries to understand. Of course there are weaknesses; one grows old and lazy as he said; sometimes his books are slight, confused, and perhaps sentimental. But they dwell in "the abiding place of beauty" because he chose to write with the most fundamental part of his being as a writer; nor, for all his irony and aloofness, do we ever doubt the depth of his feeling.

Half of Thomas Hardy[1]

THOMAS HARDY, it is not surprising to learn, had not sufficient admiration for himself to record his recollections and not enough interest in himself to brood over his own character. "A naturalist's interest in the hatching of a queer egg or germ is the utmost introspective consideration you should allow yourself," he wrote, and the observation was made in a pocket-book which nobody but himself was to read. Hence, though he was forced to agree that a life of him must be written, it is by his wish a life so devoid of artifice, so simple in its structure that it resembles nothing so much as the talk of an old man over the fire about his past.[2] Much of it indeed was written down by Mrs. Hardy as he spoke it. Many of the phrases are unmistakably his own. And whatever it may lack in substance or in symmetry is more than made up for by the sound of the speaking voice and the suggestiveness which it carries with it. Indeed, by no other method could Mrs. Hardy have kept so close to her husband's spirit.

For Hardy was the last person to be subjected to the rigours of biography. Never was anyone less stereotyped, less formalized, less flattened out by the burden of fame and the weight of old age. He sprang up effortlessly, unconsciously, like a heather root under a stone, not by im-

[1] Written in 1928. Copyright 1928 by Editorial Publications, Inc. (*New Republic*).
[2] *The Early Life of Thomas Hardy*. By Florence Emily Hardy.

posing his views or by impressing his personality, but by being simply and consistently himself. Everything he wrote—it is a quality that makes up for a thousand faults—had this integrity ingrained in it. One finds it again pervading his life. Fantastic as it sounds, one can scarcely help fancying that it was Hardy who imagined it all—the fiddling father, the mother who loved reading, the house "between woodland and heathland"; the old English family, with its legends of Monmouth and Sedgemoor, and its "spent social energies," who had come down in the world—"So we go down, down, down," said Hardy, meeting the head of his family trudging beside a common spring trap in the road. Everything takes on the colour of his own temperament. His memories have the quality of moments of vision. He could remember coming home at three in the morning from fiddling with his father—for the Hardys had fiddled in church and farm for generations without taking a penny for it, and little Tom was a dancer and a fiddler from his birth—and seeing "a white human figure without a head" in the hedge—a man almost frozen to death. He could remember the farm-women at the harvest supper "sitting on a bench against the wall in the barn and leaning against each other as they warbled,

> 'Lie there, lie there, thou false-hearted man,
> Lie there instead o' me.' "

He could remember how his father, the music-loving builder, would stroll on to the heath alone with the telescope that had belonged to some sea-faring Hardy and "stay peering out into the distance by the half-hour." He could remember how he had once stood on the heath and put that same brass telescope to his eye and seen a man in

white fustian on the gallows at Dorchester. At that moment the figure "dropped downward and the faint note of
the town clock struck eight," and he seemed alone on the
heath with the hanged man. But more distinctly than anything else he could remember lying on his back as a small
boy and thinking how useless he was and how he did not
wish to grow up—"he did not want at all to be a man, or
to possess things, but to remain as he was in the same spot,
and to know no more people than he already knew (about
half a dozen). Yet . . . he was in perfect health and
happy circumstances."

So the memories succeed each other, like poems, visualized and complete. It was thus, perhaps, that Hardy's
mind worked when it was most at its ease, flashing its light
fitfully and capriciously like a lantern swinging in a hand,
now on a rose-bush, now on a tramp frozen in the hedge.
He has none of that steady and remorseless purpose that
people would attribute to him. It was by chance that he
saw things, not by design. He puts the telescope to his eye
and there is a man on the gallows. He walks in Dorchester
High Street and sees the gipsy girls with their big brass
earrings in the light from a silversmith's shop. At once
these sights shape themselves into poems and set themselves
to some old tune that has been running in his mind. He
stops to muse upon their meaning. He cannot hold firmly
on his way. Indeed, he "cared for life only as an emotion
and not as a scientific game"; he did not want to grow up
and possess things. Hence the doubts and the fluctuations
of his career. He might have gone to Cambridge had he
chosen, but he did not make the effort. He fumbled about
with architecture, pulled down the old churches that he
loved and built new ones. Now he was going to devote

himself to poetry, now to fiction. One result of this vacil-
lation seems to have been that he lay singularly open to
influence. He wrote a satirical novel in the manner of
Defoe, and because Meredith advised him to write another
with a more complicated plot, he sat down and wrote
Desperate Remedies with a plot as complicated as a
mediæval mouse-trap. When *The Spectator* said that the
novel (because there is a rich spinster in it with an illegiti-
mate child) was rightly anonymous, for even a *nom-de-
plume* might "at some future time disgrace the family
name, and still more the Christian name, of a repentant
and remorseful novelist," Hardy sat on a stile and wished
himself dead. It was in deference to another critic John
Morley, that he wrote *Under the Greenwood Tree* in the
pastoral manner; and it was in reply to the jibes of the
journalists, who said that he was a house decorator, that
he put aside the first version of *The Woodlanders* and
proved his sophistication by writing *The Hand of Ethel-
berta.*

All this deference to authority, which contrasts so
queerly with the perfectly uncompromising character of
his genius, comes no doubt from some inertness of temper
in the descendant of a spent race; but it rose, too, from a
fact which Hardy himself noticed, that he came to ma-
turity much later than most men. His gifts lay hidden far
longer than is usual. Poems dropped now and again into
a drawer. But the desire to write poetry seems to have
been fitful and dubious even when he was at the most
poetic age. Bread and butter had to be earned, however,
and therefore reluctantly and hesitatingly, without the
illusions or the hot-headedness of the born novelist he
stumbled into a calling for which he had little respect, and

for which, if he had magnificent gifts, he had also great disabilities.

For though it was all very well to write novels like *Far from the Madding Crowd* upon chips of wood or white leaves or even upon flat stones out-of-doors, he was persuaded that a novelist, to be successful, must describe manners and customs. He must live in town. He must frequent dinners, and clubs and crushes. He must keep a notebook. And so, though Hardy could not bear the touch of an arm upon his shoulder, and a note-book in his pocket made him "barren as the Sahara," he faced the position squarely; rented a house in Upper Tooting, bought a notebook, and dined out nightly. "Certainly," exclaimed Miss Thackeray, when he consulted her, "a novelist must necessarily like society!"

Society seen from Upper Tooting looked a little queer. He put the brass telescope to his eye and saw the strangest sights. Men and women were being hung even in the gayest streets. He mused upon the passions and sorrows that raged in the breasts of the crowd at the Marble Arch. He lay in bed at Upper Tooting and could not sleep because he lay so close "to a monster who had four heads and eight million eyes." He sat next Lady Camperdown at dinner "and could not get rid of the feeling that I was close to a great naval engagement." But he also noted down the correct things. He met Matthew Arnold, who "had a manner of having made up his mind upon everything years ago," and Henry James, "who has a ponderously warm manner of saying nothing in infinite sentences"; and old Mrs. Proctor, "who swam about through the crowd like a swan"; and Byron's Ianthe, "a feeble beldame muffled up in black and furs"; and the Carnarvons and the Salisburys and the Portsmouths—and of all this he took note as a novelist should. Moreover, when the books were finished he did whatever the editors required him to do to make them salable. Book after book appeared in magazines with passages cut out or with incidents put in to please the British public. For if the whole thing—in this case the whole thing was *The Mayor of Casterbridge*—was "mere journey work," did it very much matter what compromise he made? Fiction was a trade like another—off he went to the Crawford-Dilke case, note-book in hand. Yet now and then the note-book would record a state of mind or a thought that was quite unsuitable for fiction. For instance: ". . . when I enter into a room to pay a simple morning call I have unconsciously the habit of regarding the scene as if I were a spectre not solid enough to influence my environment; only fit to behold and say, as another spectre said, 'Peace be unto you.'" Or again he mused, "people are somnambulists—the material is not the real—only the visible, the real being invisible optically."

For while with one-half of his mind Hardy noted down what a successful novelist ought to observe, the other half remorselessly saw through these observations and turned them to moonshine. Hardy, of course, might have suppressed the second half; he might have succeeded in writing agreeable cynical novels of London life like any other. But that obstinate conviction that made him for all his efforts an outsider, that faculty for putting the telescope to his eye and seeing strange, grim pictures—if he went to a First-Aid lecture he saw children in the street behind a skeleton, if he went to a French play he saw a cemetery behind the players' heads—all this fecundity and pressure of the imagination brought about at last not a compromise but a solution. Why run about with note-books observing manners and customs when his mind involuntarily flooded itself with strange imaginations and sung itself scraps of old ballads? Why not simplify, make abstract, give the whole rather than the detail? Again the note-book records certain ideas that would be out of place in a novel. "The 'simply natural' is interesting no longer. The much decried, mad, late-Turner rendering is now necessary to create my interest. The exact truth as to material fact ceases to be of importance in art—I want to see the deeper reality underlying the scenic, the expression of what are sometimes called abstract imaginings." But it was a question how far abstract imagination could be expressed in a novel. Would not realities fatally conflict with that observation of manners and customs which Hardy, so simply and so modestly, had accepted as the staple of the novelist's trade?

The first half of Hardy's life ends with that note of interrogation. We have reached the year 1891. He has written *Tess of the D'Urbervilles*. It has appeared in *The Graphic*. At the editor's request, Hardy has omitted the christening scene; he has allowed the milkmaids to be wheeled across the lane in a wheelbarrow instead of being carried in Clare's arms; and, although one father of daughters still objects that the bloodstain on the ceiling is indecent—"Hardy could never understand why"—the book is a great success. But, we ask ourselves, what is going to happen next?

Leslie Stephen [1]

BY the time that his children were growing up the great days of my father's life were over. His feats on the river and on the mountains had been won before they were born. Relics of them were to be found lying about the house—the silver cup on the study mantelpiece; the rusty alpenstocks that leant against the bookcase in the corner; and to the end of his days he would speak of great climbers and explorers with a peculiar mixture of admiration and envy. But his own years of activity were over, and my father had to content himself with pottering about the Swiss valleys or taking a stroll across the Cornish moors.

That to potter and to stroll meant more on his lips than on other people's is becoming obvious now that some of his friends have given their own version of those expeditions. He would start off after breakfast alone, or with one companion. Shortly before dinner he would return. If the walk had been successful, he would have out his great map and commemorate a new short cut in red ink. And he was quite capable, it appears, of striding all day across the moors without speaking more than a word or two to his companion. By that time, too, he had written the *History of English Thought in the Eighteenth Century*, which is said by some to be his masterpiece; and the *Science of Ethics*—the book which interested him most; and *The*

[1] Written in 1932.

69

Playground of Europe, in which is to be found "The Sunset on Mont Blanc"—in his opinion the best thing he ever wrote.

He still wrote daily and methodically, though never for long at a time. In London he wrote in the large room with three long windows at the top of the house. He wrote lying almost recumbent in a low rocking chair which he tipped to and fro as he wrote, like a cradle, and as he wrote he smoked a short clay pipe, and he scattered books round him in a circle. The thud of a book dropped on the floor could be heard in the room beneath. And often as he mounted the stairs to his study with his firm, regular tread he would burst, not into song, for he was entirely unmusical, but into a strange rhythmical chant, for verse of all kinds, both "utter trash," as he called it, and the most sublime words of Milton and Wordsworth stuck in his memory, and the act of walking or climbing seemed to inspire him to recite whichever it was that came uppermost or suited his mood.

But it was his dexterity with his fingers that delighted his children before they could potter along the lanes at his heels or read his books. He would twist a sheet of paper beneath a pair of scissors and out would drop an elephant, a stag, or a monkey with trunks, horns, and tails delicately and exactly formed. Or, taking a pencil, he would draw beast after beast—an art that he practised almost unconsciously as he read, so that the fly-leaves of his books swarm with owls and donkeys as if to illustrate the "Oh, you ass!" or "Conceited dunce," that he was wont to scribble impatiently in the margin. Such brief comments, in which one may find the germ of the more temperate statements of his essays, recall some of the characteristics of his talk. He could be very silent, as his friends have testified. But his remarks, made suddenly in a low voice between the puffs of his pipe, were extremely effective. Sometimes with one word—but his one word was accompanied by a gesture of the hand—he would dispose of the tissue of exaggerations which his own sobriety seemed to provoke. "There are 40,000,000 unmarried women in London alone!" Lady Ritchie once informed him. "Oh, Annie, Annie!" my father exclaimed in tones of horrified but affectionate rebuke. But Lady Ritchie, as if she enjoyed being rebuked, would pile it up even higher next time she came.

The stories he told to amuse his children of adventures in the Alps—but accidents only happened, he would explain, if you were so foolish as to disobey your guides— or of those long walks, after one of which, from Cambridge to London on a hot day, "I drank, I am sorry to say, rather more than was good for me," were told very briefly, but with a curious power to impress the scene. The things that he did not say were always there in the background. So, too, though he seldom told anecdotes, and his memory for facts was bad, when he described a person—and he had known many people, both famous and obscure—he would convey exactly what he thought of him in two or three words. And what he thought might be the opposite of what other people thought. He had a way of upsetting established reputations and disregarding conventional values that could be disconcerting, and sometimes perhaps wounding, though no one was more respectful of any feeling that seemed to him genuine. But when, suddenly opening his bright blue eyes, and rousing himself from what had seemed complete abstraction, he gave his opinion, it was difficult to disregard it. It was a habit, especially when deafness made him unaware that this opinion could be heard, that had its inconveniences.

"I am the most easily bored of men," he wrote, truthfully as usual: and when, as was inevitable in a large family, some visitor threatened to stay not merely for tea but also for dinner, my father would express his anguish at first by twisting and untwisting a certain lock of hair. Then he would burst out, half to himself, half to the powers above, but quite audibly, "Why can't he go? Why can't he go?" Yet such is the charm of simplicity—and did he not say, also truthfully, that "bores are the salt of the earth"?—that the bores seldom went, or, if they did, forgave him and came again.

Too much, perhaps, has been said of his silence; too much stress has been laid upon his reserve. He loved clear thinking; he hated sentimentality and gush; but this by no means meant that he was cold and unemotional, perpetually critical and condemnatory in daily life. On the contrary, it was his power of feeling strongly and of expressing his feeling with vigour that made him sometimes so alarming as a companion. A lady, for instance, complained of the wet summer that was spoiling her tour in Cornwall. But to my father, though he never called himself a democrat, the rain meant that the corn was being laid; some poor man was being ruined; and the energy with which he expressed his sympathy—not with the lady—left her discomfited. He had something of the same respect for farmers and fishermen that he had for climbers and explorers. So, too, he talked little of patriotism, but during the South African War—and all wars were hateful to him—he lay awake thinking that he heard the guns on the battlefield. Again, neither his reason nor his cold common sense helped to convince him that a child could be late for dinner without having been maimed or killed in an accident. And not all his mathematics together with a bank balance which he insisted must be ample in the extreme, could persuade him, when it came to signing a cheque, that the whole family was not "shooting Niagara to ruin," as he put it. The pictures that he would draw of old age and the bankruptcy court, of ruined men of letters who have to support large families in small houses at Wimbledon (he owned a very small house at Wimbledon) might have convinced those who complain of his under-statements that hyperbole was well within his reach had he chosen.

Yet the unreasonable mood was superficial, as the rapidity with which it vanished would prove. The cheque-book was shut; Wimbledon and the workhouse were forgotten. Some thought of a humorous kind made him chuckle. Taking his hat and his stick, calling for his dog and his daughter, he would stride off into Kensington Gardens, where he had walked as a little boy, where his brother Fitzjames and he had made beautiful bows to young Queen Victoria and she had swept them a curtsey, and so, round the Serpentine, to Hyde Park Corner, where he had once saluted the great Duke himself; and so home. He was not then in the least "alarming"; he was very simple, very confiding; and his silence, though one might last unbroken from the Round Pond to the Marble Arch, was curiously full of meaning, as if he were thinking half aloud, about poetry and philosophy and people he had known.

He himself was the most abstemious of men. He smoked a pipe perpetually, but never a cigar. He wore his clothes until they were too shabby to be tolerable; and he held old-fashioned and rather puritanical views as to the vice of luxury and the sin of idleness. The relations between parents and children today have a freedom that would have been impossible with my father. He expected a certain standard of behaviour, even of ceremony, in family life. Yet if freedom means the right to think one's own thoughts and to follow one's own pursuits, then no one respected and indeed insisted upon freedom more completely than he did. His sons, with the exception of the Army and Navy, should follow whatever professions they chose; his daughters, though he cared little enough for the higher education of women, should have the same liberty. If at one moment he rebuked a daughter sharply for smoking a cigarette—smoking was not in his opinion a nice habit in the other sex—she had only to ask him if she might become a painter, and he assured her that so long as she took her work seriously he would give her all the help he could. He had no special love for painting; but he kept his word. Freedom of that sort was worth thousands of cigarettes.

It was the same with the perhaps more difficult problem of literature. Even today there may be parents who would doubt the wisdom of allowing a girl of fifteen the free run of a large and quite unexpurgated library. But my father allowed it. There were certain facts—very briefly, very shyly he referred to them. Yet "Read what you like," he said, and all his books, "mangy and worthless," as he called them, but certainly they were many and various, were to be had without asking. To read what one liked because one liked it, never to pretend to admire what one did not—that was his only lesson in the art of reading. To write in the fewest possible words, as clearly as possible, exactly what one meant—that was his only lesson in the art of writing. All the rest must be learnt for oneself. Yet a child must have been childish in the extreme not to feel that such was the teaching of a man of great learning and wide experience, though he would never impose his own views or parade his own knowledge. For, as his tailor remarked when he saw my father walk past his shop up Bond Street, "There goes a gentleman that wears good clothes without knowing it."

In those last years, grown solitary and very deaf, he would sometimes call himself a failure as a writer; he had been "jack of all trades, and master of none." But whether he failed or succeeded as a writer, it is permissible to believe that he left a distinct impression of himself on the minds of his friends. Meredith saw him as "Phoebus Apollo turned fasting friar" in his earlier days; Thomas Hardy, years later, looked at the "spare and desolate figure" of the Schreckhorn and thought of

him,
Who scaled its horn with ventured life and limb,
Drawn on by vague imaginings, maybe,
Of semblance to his personality
In its quaint glooms, keen lights, and rugged trim.

But the praise he would have valued most, for though he was an agnostic nobody believed more profoundly in the worth of human relationships, was Meredith's tribute after his death: "He was the one man to my knowledge worthy to have married your mother." And Lowell, when he called him "L.S., the most lovable of men," has best described the quality that makes him, after all these years, unforgettable.

Mr. Conrad: A Conversation[1]

THE Otways, perhaps, inherited their love of reading from the ancient dramatist whose name they share, whether they descend from him (as they like to think) or not. Penelope, the oldest unmarried daughter, a small dark woman turned forty, her complexion a little roughened by country life, her eyes brown and bright, yet subject to strange long stares of meditation or vacancy, had always, since the age of seven, been engaged in reading the classics. Her father's library, though strong chiefly in the literature of the East, had its Popes, its Drydens, its Shakespeares, in various stages of splendour and decay; and if his daughters chose to amuse themselves by reading what they liked, certainly it was a method of education which, since it spared his purse, deserved his benediction.

That education it could be called, no one nowadays would admit. All that can be said in its favour was that Penelope Otway was never dull, gallantly ambitious of surmounting small hillocks of learning, and of an enthusiasm which greater knowledge might perhaps have stinted or have diverted less fortunately into the creation of books of her own. As it was, she was content to read and to talk, reading in the intervals of household business, and talking when she could find company, on Sundays for the most part, when visitors came down, and sat on fine summer days under the splendid yew tree on the lawn.

[1] Written in 1923.

On this occasion, a hot morning in August, her old friend David Lowe was distressed, but hardly surprised, to find five magnificent volumes lying on the grass by her chair, while Penelope acknowledged his presence by putting her fingers between the pages of a sixth and looking at the sky.

"Joseph Conrad," he said, lifting the admirable books—solid, stately, good-looking, yet meant for a long life-time of repeated re-reading—on to his knee. "So I see you have made up your mind. Mr. Conrad is a classic."

"Not in your opinion," she replied; "I remember the bitter letters you wrote me when you read *The Arrow of Gold* and *The Rescue*. You compared him to an elderly and disillusioned nightingale singing over and over, but hopelessly out of tune, the one song he had learned in his youth."

"I had forgotten," said David, "but it is true. The books puzzled me after those early novels, *Youth, Lord Jim, The Nigger of the Narcissus*, which we thought so magnificent. I said to myself perhaps it is because he is a foreigner. He can understand us perfectly when we talk slowly, but not when we are excited or when we are at our ease. There is nothing colloquial in Conrad; nothing intimate; and no humour, at least of the English kind. And those are great drawbacks for a novelist, you will admit. Then, of course, it goes without saying that he is a romantic. No one objects to that. But it entails a terrible penalty—death at the age of forty—death or disillusionment. If your romantic persists in living, he must face his disillusionment. He must make his music out of contrasts. But Conrad has never faced his disillusionment. He goes on singing the same songs about sea captains and the sea, beautiful, noble,

77

and monotonous; but now I think with a crack in the flawless strain of his youth. It is a mind of one fact; and such a mind can never be among the classics."

"But he is a great writer! A great writer!" cried Penelope, gripping the arms of her chair. "How shall I prove it to you? Admit, in the first place, that your views are partial. You have skipped; you have sipped; you have tasted. From *The Nigger of the Narcissus* you have leapt to *The Arrow of Gold*. Your gimcrack theory is a confection of cobwebs spun while you shave, chiefly with a view to saving yourself the trouble of investigating and possibly admiring the work of a living writer in your own tongue. You are a surly watch-dog; but Conrad you will have to admit."

"My ears are pricked," said David; "explain your theory."

"My theory is made of cobwebs, no doubt, like your own. But of this I am certain. Conrad is not one and simple; no, he is many and complex. That is a common case among modern writers, as we have often agreed. And it is when they bring these selves into relation—when they simplify, when they reconcile their opposites—that they bring off (generally late in life) those complete books which for that reason we call their masterpieces. And Mr. Conrad's selves are particularly opposite. He is composed of two people who have nothing whatever in common. He is your sea captain, simple, faithful, obscure; and he is Marlow, subtle, psychological, loquacious. In the early books the Captain dominates; in the later it is Marlow at least who does all the talking. The union of these two very different men makes for all sorts of queer effects. You must have noticed the sudden silences, the awkward colli-

sions, the immense lethargy which threatens at every moment to descend. All this, I think, must be the result of
that internal conflict. For while Marlow would like to
track every motive, explore every shadow, his companion
the sea captain is for ever at his elbow saying '. . . the
world, the temporal world, rests on a very few simple
ideas; so simple that they must be as old as the hills.' Then
again, Marlow is a man of words; they are all dear to him,
appealing, seductive. But the sea captain cuts him short.
'The gift of words,' he says, 'is no great matter.' And it is
the sea captain who triumphs. In Conrad's novels personal
relations are never final. Men are tested by their attitude
to august abstractions. Are they faithful, are they honourable, are they courageous? The men he loves are reserved
for death in the bosom of the sea. Their elegy is Milton's
'Nothing is here to wail . . . nothing but what may quiet
us in a death so noble'—an elegy which you could never
possibly speak over the body of any of Henry James'
characters, whose intimacies have been personal—with
each other."

"Pardon me," said David, "an apparent rudeness. Your
theory may be a good one, but the moment you quote
Conrad himself theories turn to moonshine. Unfortunate
art of criticism, which only shines in the absence of the
sun! I had forgotten the spell of Conrad's prose. It must
be of extraordinary strength, since the few words you
have quoted rouse in me an overpowering hunger for
more." He opened *The Nigger of the Narcissus* and read:
"On men reprieved by its disdainful mercy the immortal
sea confers in its justice the full privilege of desired unrest . . ." "The men turned in wet and turned out stiff
to face the redeeming and ruthless exactions of their ob-

79

scure fate." "It is not fair," he said, "to quote such scraps, but even from them I get an extreme satisfaction."

"Yes," said Penelope, "they're fine in the grand deliberate manner which has in it the seeds of pomposity and monotony. But I almost prefer his sudden direct pounce right across the room like a cat on a mouse. There's Mrs. Schomberg, for instance, 'a scraggy little woman with long ringlets and a blue tooth,' or a dying man's voice 'like the rustle of a single dry leaf driven along the smooth sand of a beach.' He sees once and he sees for ever. His books are full of moments of vision. They light up a whole character in a flash. Perhaps I prefer Marlow the instinctive to Captain Whalley the moralist. But the peculiar beauty is the product of the two together. The beauty of surface has always a fibre of morality within. I seem to see each of the sentences you have read advancing with resolute bearing and a calm which they have won in strenuous conflict, against the forces of falsehood, sentimentality, and slovenliness. He could not write badly, one feels, to save his life. He had his duty to letters as sailors have theirs to their ships. And indeed he praises those inveterate landlubbers, Henry James and Anatole France, as though they were bluff sea dogs who had brought their books to port without compasses in a gale of wind."

"Certainly he was a strange apparition to descend upon these shores in the last part of the nineteenth century—an artist, an aristocrat, a Pole," said David. "For after all these years I cannot think of him as an English writer. He is too formal, too courteous, too scrupulous in the use of a language which is not his own. Then of course he is an aristocrat to the backbone. His humour is aristocratic—ironic, sardonic, never broad and free like the common

English humour which descends from Falstaff. He is infinitely reserved. And the lack of intimacy which I complain of may perhaps be due, not merely to those 'august
abstractions' as you call them, but to the fact that there
are no women in his books."

"There are the ships, the beautiful ships," said Penelope.
"They are more feminine than his women, who are either
mountains of marble or the dreams of a charming boy over
the photograph of an actress. But surely a great novel can
be made out of a man and a ship, a man and a storm, a
man and death and dishonour?"

"Ah, we are back at the question of greatness," said
David. "Which, then, is the great book, where, as you say,
the complex vision becomes simple, and Marlow and the
sea captain combine to produce a world at once exquisitely subtle, psychologically profound, yet based upon a
very few simple ideas 'so simple that they must be as old
as the hills'?"

"I have just read *Chance*," said Penelope. "It is a great
book, I think. But now you will have to read it yourself,
for you are not going to accept my word, especially when
it is a word which I cannot define. It is a great book, a
great book," she repeated.

81

The Cosmos[1]

" 'AND what is Cosmos, Mr. Sanderson?' asks Sister Edith.
'What is the meaning of the word?' And then I go off like
a rocket and explode in stars in the empyrean." These two
large volumes[2] are full of the sparks that fell from that
constantly recurring explosion. For Mr. Cobden-Sanderson
was always trying to explain to somebody—it might be
Professor Tyndall ("I gave him my own view of human
destiny, namely, the ultimate coalescence of the human
intellect in knowledge with its other self, the Universe"),
it might be Mr. Churchill, it might be a strange lady
whose motor-car had broken down on the road near Mal-
vern—what the word Cosmos meant. He had learned gradually and painfully himself. For at first the world seemed
to him to have no order whatsoever. Everything was
wrong. It was wrong for him to become a clergyman; it
was wrong to take a degree; it was wrong to remain at
the Bar. It was wrong that he, who had three dress-suits
already, should order another from Poole and pay for it
with his wife's money. But what then was right? That was
by no means so apparent. "What was I to do?" he asked
himself at three o'clock in the morning in the year 1882,
"aching with exhaustion and nervous horror." Ought he
to live in Poplar and work among the poor? Ought he to
devote his life to the work of the Charity Organization

[1] Written in 1926.
[2] *The Journals of Thomas James Cobden-Sanderson*, 1879-1922.

Society? What ought he to give in return for all that he received? For some time—and the candour with which these private struggles are laid bare is no small part of the deep interest of these diaries—he vacillated and procrastinated and drank beef-tea at eleven o'clock in the morning. Lady Carlisle accused him of "dreamy egotism." His doctor laughed at his concern for his health. His father was deeply disappointed that he should give up the Bar—and for what? His wife confessed that when she read "what I wrote about the mountains, and repeated little phrases, she thought me, and had always thought me at such moments, quite a lunatic!" But once in his early distress he had found that life became suddenly "rounded off and whole" by a very simple expedient; he had bought a gridiron and cooked a chop. Now, several years later, relief began to filter through from the same channels. Since he enjoyed using his hands, said Mrs. Morris when he consulted her, why should he not learn to bind books? He took lessons at once, and became, with a speed which astonished him, capable of making "something beautiful and as far as human things can be, permanent." It was an astonishing relief from attending to the affairs of the London and North Western Railway Company. But the Book Beautiful, as he called it, though tooled magnificently and bound in rose-red morocco, was not an end in itself. It was only a humble beginning—something well-made which served to put his own mind and body in order and so in harmony with the greater order which he was beginning, as he pared and gilded, to perceive transcending all human affairs. For there was a unity of the whole in which the virtues and even the vices of mankind were caught up and put to their proper uses. Once attain to that vision, and

all things fell into their places. From that vantage ground
the white butterfly caught in the spider's net was "all in
the world's plan" and Englishmen and Germans blowing
each other's heads off in the trenches were "brothers not
enemies" conspiring to "create the great emotions which
in turn create the greater creation." To envisage this whole
and to make the binding of books and the printing of
books and everything one did and said and felt further this
end was work enough for one lifetime.

But in addition, Mr. Cobden-Sanderson felt the inevitable desire to explain the meaning of the word Cosmos to
all and sundry, to Sister Edith and to Professor Tyndall.
The volumes are full of attempts at explanation. He was
not quite certain what he meant; nevertheless he must
"repeat and repeat" and so "get relief." He laboured, too,
under a groundless fear that he might catch the contagion
of Jane Austen's style. Instead of becoming clearer, therefore, the vision, iterated and reiterated, becomes more and
more nebulous, until after two volumes of explanation we
are left asking, with Sister Edith, "But, Mr. Sanderson,
how does one 'fly to the great Rhythm'? What is the
extraordinary ring of harmony within harmony that en-
circles us; what reason is there to suppose that a mountain
wishes us well or that a lake has a profound moral meaning to impart? What, in short, does the word Cosmos
mean?" Whereupon the rocket explodes, and the red and
gold showers descend, and we look on with sympathy, but
feel a little chill about the feet and not very clear as to
the direction of the road.

But the man himself, who sent his rockets soaring into
such incongruous places (he would write a letter about the
Ideal to *The Times*) is neither vapid nor insipid nor

wrapped round, as so many idealists tend to become, in comfortable cotton wool. On the contrary, he was for ever being stung and taunted, as he carried on his business of bookbinder and printer, by the uncompromising creature who was perched upon his shoulders. There were days when the gold would not stick on his lettering; days when on "turning the leather down at the headband I found it too short." Then he flew into a passion of rage, "tore the leather off the board, and cut it, and cut it, and slashed it with a knife." *I* did this, he reflected the next moment, I who have seen the vision can yet fall into ecstasies of vulgar anger! The vision forced him to test everything by its light, no matter what the effort, the unpopularity, the despondency it caused. What did the Coronation mean? he asked. What did the Boer War mean? Nothing could be taken for granted.

But by degrees the ideal got the upper hand. The sense of reality grew fainter. Often he seemed to be passing out of the body into a trance of thought. "I think I am more related to the hills and the streams . . . than to men and women," he wrote. He roamed off among the mountains to dream and worship. He felt that his part was no longer among the fighters but among the dreamers. Now and then, chiefly in the Swiss chalet of Lady Russell, he came down to dinner dressed in a dressing-gown, with a brush and comb bag on his head, housemaid's gloves on his hands, holding a fan, and was "very merry." But his sense of humour seems to have been suffocated by the effort which he made persistently to "overcome the ordinariness of ordinary life." The cat was wonderful, and the moon; the charwoman and the oak tree; the bread and the butter; the night and the stars. Everything seems to suffer a curious magnification. Nothing exists in itself but only as a means to something else. The solid objects of daily life become rimmed with high purposes, significant, symbolical. The people who drift through these diaries—even Swinburne and Morris—have become curiously thin; we see the stars shining through their backbones. It is in no way incongruous or surprising then to find him in his old age slipping off secretly on dark nights to the river. In his hand he carried a mysterious box swathed round with tape. Looking round him to see that he was not observed, he pitched his burden over the parapet into the water. It was thus that he bequeathed the Doves Type to the river; thus that he saved the ideal from desecration. But one night he missed his aim. Two pages wrapped in white paper lodged upon a ledge above the stream. He could see them, but he could not reach them. What was he to do? he asked himself, in bewilderment and amazement. The authorities might send for him; he might be cross-examined. Well, so be it. If they asked him to explain himself he would "take refuge in the infinitudes." "My idea was magnificent; the act was ridiculous," he said. "Besides," he reflected, "nothing was explicable." And perhaps he was right.

Walter Raleigh

ON a certain Wednesday in March, 1889, Walter Raleigh, then aged twenty-eight, gave his first lecture upon English literature in Manchester. It was not his first lecture by any means, for he had already lectured the natives of India on the same subject for two years. After Manchester came Liverpool; after Liverpool, Glasgow; after Glasgow, Oxford. At all these places he lectured incessantly upon English literature. Once he lectured three times a day. He became, indeed, such an adept at the art of lecturing that towards the end "sometimes he would prepare what he had to say in his half-hour's walk from his home at Ferry Hinksey." People who heard him said that his lectures stimulated them, opened their eyes, made them think for themselves. " 'Raleigh's not always at his best, but when he's good nobody can touch him'—that was the general verdict." Nevertheless, in the course of two large volumes filled with delightful and often brilliant letters it would be difficult to find a single remark of any interest whatsoever about English literature.

There is necessarily a great deal of talk about the profession of teaching literature, and the profession of writing literary text books, of "doing Chaucer in six chapters and Wordsworth, better known as Daddy, also in six chapters." But when one looks for the unprofessional talk, the talk which is talked among friends when business hours are over, one is bewildered and disappointed. Is this all that the Professor of English literature has to say? "Scott tomorrow—not a poet I think but fine old man. Good old Scott." "The weak point in William [Blake] is not his Reason, which is A.1, but his imagination . . . Wonderful things the inspired old bustard said from time to time in conversation." "As for old Bill Wordsworth he is the same old stick-in-the-mud as ever . . . He gets praised chiefly for his celebrated imitation of Shakespeare (which is really very good) and for his admirable reproduction of a bleat. But he has a turn of his own, if only he would do it and be damned to him." Any clever man at a dinner party anxious not to scare the rowing blue or the city magnate who happens to be within earshot would have talked about books exactly as Raleigh wrote about them at his leisure. There is nothing to suggest that literature was a matter of profound interest to him when he was not lecturing about it. When we read the letters of Keats, the diary of the Goncourts, the letters of Lamb, the casual remarks of that unfashionable poet Tennyson, we feel that, waking or sleeping, these men never stopped thinking about literature. It is kneaded into the stuff of their brains. Their fingers are dyed in it. Whatever they touch is stained with it. Whatever they are doing their minds fill up involuntarily with some aspect of the absorbing question. Nor does it seem to have occurred to them to wonder what the rowing blue will think of them for talking seriously about books. "I think poetry should surprise by a fine excess and not by singularity; it should strike the reader as a wording of his own highest thoughts and appear almost a remembrance," wrote Keats, and there is not a damn in the sentence. But the Professor of English literature could scarcely open his lips without dropping into

slang; he could never mention Bill Blake or Bill Shakespeare or old Bill Wordsworth without seeming to apolo-
gize for bringing books into the talk at all. Yet there is no
doubt, Walter Raleigh was one of the best Professors of
Literature of our time; he did brilliantly whatever it is
that Professors are supposed to do. How then shall we
compose the difference—solve the discrepancy?

In the first place the Professor of English Literature is not
there to teach people how to write; he is there to teach
them how to read. Moreover, those people include city
magnates, politicians, schoolmistresses, soldiers, scientists,
mothers of families, country clergymen in embryo. Many
of them have never opened a book before. Many will
seldom get a chance of opening a book again. They have
to be taught—but what? Raleigh himself had no doubts on
this point. His business was "only to get people to love
the poets." "To make people old or young," he wrote,
"care for say the principal English poets as much or half
as much as I do—that would, I am vain enough to think,
be something—if it can be done." He obstinately refused
to stuff his pupils with facts. "The facts, it is true, tell in
examinations. But you will none of you be any nearer
Heaven ten years hence for having taken a B.A. degree,
while for a love and understanding of Keats you may
raise yourself several inches." He had himself spent no
time scraping away the moss, repairing the broken noses
on the fabric of English literature; and he did not press
that pursuit upon his pupils. He talked his lectures almost
out of his head. He joked, he told stories. He made the
undergraduates rock with laughter. He drew them in
crowds to his lecture room. And they went away loving
something or other. Perhaps it was Keats. Perhaps it was

the British Empire. Certainly it was Walter Raleigh. But we should be much surprised if anybody went away loving poetry, loving the art of letters.

Nor is it difficult to find the reason. It is written large over Walter Raleigh's books—the English Novel, Style, Shakespeare and the rest. They have every virtue; they are readable, just, acute, stimulating, and packed with information; they are as firm in style and hard in substance as a macadamised road. But the man who wrote them had no generous measure of the gifts of a writer. The maker of these rather tight, highly academic books had never been outside the critical fence. No novel, no poem, no play had ever lured him away from his prefaces, his summings up, his surveys. The excitement, the adventure, the turmoil of creation were unknown to him. But the critic who makes us love poetry is always sufficiently gifted to have had experiences of his own. He feels his way along a line spun by his own failures and successes. He may stumble; he may stammer; he may be incapable of orderly survey. But it is the Keats, the Coleridge, the Lamb, the Flaubert who get to the heart of the matter. It is in the toil and strife of writing that they have forced the door open and gone within and told us what they have seen there. When Walter Raleigh held a pen in his hand it behaved with the utmost propriety. He never wrote a bad sentence; but he never wrote a sentence which broke down barriers. He never pressed on over the ruins of his own culture to the discovery of something better. He remained trim and detached on the high road, a perfect example of the Professor of Literature who has no influence whatever upon the art of writing. Soon, therefore, for he was by temperament highly adventurous, he began to find literature a little dull.

He began to separate literature from life. He began to cry out upon "culture" and "culture bugs." He began to despise critics and criticism. "I can't help feeling that critical admiration for what another man has written is an emotion for spinsters," he wrote. He really believed, he said, "not in refinement and scholarly elegance, those are only a game; but in blood feuds, and the chase of wild beasts and marriage by capture." In short, being incapable of humbug, a man of entire sincerity and great vitality, Walter Raleigh ceased to profess literature and became instead a Professor of Life.

There is ample evidence in the letters alone that he had a remarkable aptitude for this branch of learning. He seems never to have been bored, never to have been doubtful, never to have been sentimental. He laid hold on things with enviable directness. The whole force of his being seems to have played spontaneously upon whatever he wished and yet to have been controlled by an unerring sense that some things matter and some things do not. His equilibrium was perfect. Whether he was set down in India or Oxford, among the simple or the learned, the aristocrats or the Dons, he found his balance at once and got the utmost out of the situation. It is easy to imagine the race and flash of his talk, and what fine unexpected things he said, and what pinnacles of fun he raised and how for all his extravagance and irresponsibility the world that his wit lit up was held steady by his fundamental sanity and good sense. He was the most enchanting of companions—upon that all are agreed.

But the difficulty remained. Once make the fatal distinction between life and letters, once exalt life and find literature an occupation for old maids, and inevitably, if one is Walter Raleigh, one becomes discontented with mere praise. Professors must talk; but the lover of life must live. Unfortunately life in the sense of "blood feuds and the chase of wild beasts, and marriage by capture" was hard to come by in the last years of the nineteenth century. Queen Victoria was on the throne, Lord Salisbury was in power, and the British Empire was growing daily more robust. A breath of fresh air blew in with the Boer War. Raleigh hailed it with a shout of relief ". . . the British officer (and man) restores one's joy in the race," he said. He was coming to feel that there is some close connexion between writing and fighting, that in an age like his when the fighter did not write and the writer did not fight the divorce was unfortunate—especially for literature. "Were it not better to seek training on a battlefield, and use the first words one learns at mess?" he asked. All his sympathies were tending towards action. He was growing more and more tired of culture and criticism, more definitely of opinion that the "learned critic is a beast," that "education has taken the fine bloom off the writing of books," less and less attracted by writing at all, until finally, in 1913, he bursts out that he "can't read Shakespeare any more. . . . Not that I think him a bad author, particularly," he adds, "but I can't bear literature." When the guns fired in August, 1914, no one saluted them more rapturously than the Professor of English Literature at Oxford. "The air is better to breathe than it has been for years," he exclaimed. "I'm glad I lived to see it, and sick that I'm not in it."

It seemed indeed as if his chance of life had come too late. He still seemed fated to praise fighting but not to fight, to lecture about life but not to live. He did what a man of his age could do. He drilled. He marched. He wrote pamphlets. He lectured more frequently than ever; he practically ceased to read. At length he was made historian of the Air Force. To his infinite satisfaction he consorted with soldiers. To his immense delight he flew to Baghdad. He died within a week or two after his return. But what did that matter? The Professor of English Literature had lived at last.

Mr. Bennett and Mrs. Brown[1]

IT seems to me possible, perhaps desirable, that I may be the only person in this room who has committed the folly of writing, trying to write, or failing to write, a novel. And when I asked myself, as your invitation to speak to you about modern fiction made me ask myself, what demon whispered in my ear and urged me to my doom, a little figure rose before me—the figure of a man, or of a woman, who said, "My name is Brown. Catch me if you can."

Most novelists have the same experience. Some Brown, Smith, or Jones comes before them and says in the most seductive and charming way in the world, "Come and catch me if you can." And so, led on by this will-o'-the-wisp, they flounder through volume after volume, spending the best years of their lives in the pursuit, and receiving for the most part very little cash in exchange. Few catch the phantom; most have to be content with a scrap of her dress or a wisp of her hair.

My belief that men and women write novels because they are lured on to create some character which has thus imposed itself upon them has the sanction of Mr. Arnold Bennett. In an article from which I will quote he says, "The foundation of good fiction is character-creating and nothing else. . . . Style counts; plot counts; originality of outlook counts. But none of these counts anything like so

[1] A paper read to the Heretics, Cambridge, on May 18, 1924.

94

much as the convincingness of the characters. If the characters are real the novel will have a chance; if they are not,
oblivion will be its portion. . . ." And he goes on to draw
the conclusion that we have no young novelists of first-
rate importance at the present moment, because they are
unable to create characters that are real, true, and convincing.

These are the questions that I want with greater boldness than discretion to discuss tonight. I want to make out
what we mean when we talk about "character" in fiction;
to say something about the question of reality which Mr.
Bennett raises; and to suggest some reasons why the
younger novelists fail to create characters, if, as Mr. Bennett asserts, it is true that fail they do. This will lead me,
I am well aware, to make some very sweeping and some
very vague assertions. For the question is an extremely
difficult one. Think how little we know about character—
think how little we know about art. But, to make a clear-
ance before I begin, I will suggest that we range Edwardians and Georgians into two camps; Mr. Wells, Mr.
Bennett, and Mr. Galsworthy I will call the Edwardians;
Mr. Forster, Mr. Lawrence, Mr. Strachey, Mr. Joyce, and
Mr. Eliot I will call the Georgians. And if I speak in the
first person, with intolerable egotism, I will ask you to
excuse me. I do not want to attribute to the world at large
the opinions of one solitary, ill-informed, and misguided
individual.

My first assertion is one that I think you will grant—
that every one in this room is a judge of character. Indeed
it would be impossible to live for a year without disaster
unless one practised character-reading and had some skill
in the art. Our marriages, our friendships depend on it;

our business largely depends on it; every day questions arise which can only be solved by its help. And now I will hazard a second assertion, which is more disputable perhaps, to the effect that on or about December, 1910, human character changed.

I am not saying that one went out, as one might into a garden, and there saw that a rose had flowered, or that a hen had laid an egg. The change was not sudden and definite like that. But a change there was, nevertheless; and, since one must be arbitrary, let us date it about the year 1910. The first signs of it are recorded in the books of Samuel Butler, in *The Way of All Flesh* in particular; the plays of Bernard Shaw continue to record it. In life one can see the change, if I may use a homely illustration, in the character of one's cook. The Victorian cook lived like a leviathan in the lower depths, formidable, silent, obscure, inscrutable; the Georgian cook is a creature of sunshine and fresh air; in and out of the drawing-room, now to borrow the *Daily Herald*, now to ask advice about a hat. Do you ask for more solemn instances of the power of the human race to change? Read the *Agamemnon*, and see whether, in process of time, your sympathies are not almost entirely with Clytemnestra. Or consider the married life of the Carlyles and bewail the waste, the futility, for him and for her, of the horrible domestic tradition which made it seemly for a woman of genius to spend her time chasing beetles, scouring saucepans, instead of writing books. All human relations have shifted—those between masters and servants, husbands and wives, parents and children. And when human relations change there is at the same time a change in religion, conduct, politics, and literature. Let us agree to place one of these changes about the year 1910.

I have said that people have to acquire a good deal of skill in character-reading if they are to live a single year of life without disaster. But it is the art of the young. In middle age and in old age the art is practised mostly for its uses, and friendships and other adventures and experiments in the art of reading character are seldom made. But novelists differ from the rest of the world because they do not cease to be interested in character when they have learnt enough about it for practical purposes. They go a step further, they feel that there is something permanently interesting in character in itself. When all the practical business of life has been discharged, there is something about people which continues to seem to them of overwhelming importance, in spite of the fact that it has no bearing whatever upon their happiness, comfort, or income. The study of character becomes to them an absorbing pursuit; to impart character an obsession. And this I find it very difficult to explain: what novelists mean when they talk about character, what the impulse is that urges them so powerfully every now and then to embody their view in writing.

So, if you will allow me, instead of analysing and abstracting, I will tell you a simple story which, however pointless, has the merit of being true, of a journey from Richmond to Waterloo, in the hope that I may show you what I mean by character in itself; that you may realize the different aspects it can wear; and the hideous perils that beset you directly you try to describe it in words.

One night some weeks ago, then, I was late for the train and jumped into the first carriage I came to. As I sat down

97

I had the strange and uncomfortable feeling that I was interrupting a conversation between two people who were already sitting there. Not that they were young or happy. Far from it. They were both elderly, the woman over sixty, the man well over forty. They were sitting opposite each other, and the man, who had been leaning over and talking emphatically to judge by his attitude and the flush on his face, sat back and became silent. I had disturbed him, and he was annoyed. The elderly lady, however, whom I will call Mrs. Brown, seemed rather relieved. She was one of those clean, threadbare old ladies whose extreme tidiness—everything buttoned, fastened, tied together, mended and brushed up—suggests more extreme poverty than rags and dirt. There was something pinched about her—a look of suffering, of apprehension, and, in addition, she was extremely small. Her feet, in their clean little boots, scarcely touched the floor. I felt that she had nobody to support her; that she had to make up her mind for herself; that, having been deserted, or left a widow, years ago, she had led an anxious, harried life, bringing up an only son, perhaps, who, as likely as not, was by this time beginning to go to the bad. All this shot through my mind as I sat down, being uncomfortable, like most people, at travelling with fellow passengers unless I have somehow or other accounted for them. Then I looked at the man. He was no relation of Mrs. Brown's I felt sure; he was of a bigger, burlier, less refined type. He was a man of business I imagined, very likely a respectable corn-chandler from the North, dressed in good blue serge with a pocket-knife and a silk handkerchief, and a stout leather bag. Obviously, however, he had an unpleasant business to settle with Mrs. Brown; a secret, perhaps sinister business, which they did not intend to discuss in my presence.

"Yes, the Crofts have had very bad luck with their servants," Mr. Smith (as I will call him) said in a considering way, going back to some earlier topic, with a view to keeping up appearances.

"Ah, poor people," said Mrs. Brown, a trifle condescendingly. "My grandmother had a maid who came when she was fifteen and stayed till she was eighty" (this was said with a kind of hurt and aggressive pride to impress us both perhaps).

"One doesn't often come across that sort of thing nowadays," said Mr. Smith in conciliatory tones.

Then they were silent.

"It's odd they don't start a golf club there—I should have thought one of the young fellows would," said Mr. Smith, for the silence obviously made him uneasy.

Mrs. Brown hardly took the trouble to answer.

"What changes they're making in this part of the world," said Mr. Smith, looking out of the window, and looking furtively at me as he did so.

It was plain, from Mrs. Brown's silence, from the uneasy affability with which Mr. Smith spoke, that he had some power over her which he was exerting disagreeably. It might have been her son's downfall, or some painful episode in her past life, or her daughter's. Perhaps she was going to London to sign some document to make over some property. Obviously against her will she was in Mr. Smith's hands. I was beginning to feel a great deal of pity for her, when she said, suddenly and inconsequently:

"Can you tell me if an oak-tree dies when the leaves

have been eaten for two years in succession by caterpillars?"

She spoke quite brightly, and rather precisely, in a cultivated, inquisitive voice.

Mr. Smith was startled, but relieved to have a safe topic
of conversation given him. He told her a great deal very
quickly about plagues of insects. He told her that he had
a brother who kept a fruit farm in Kent. He told her what
fruit farmers do every year in Kent, and so on, and so on.
While he talked a very odd thing happened. Mrs. Brown
took out her little white handkerchief and began to dab
her eyes. She was crying. But she went on listening quite
composedly to what he was saying, and he went on talking, a little louder, a little angrily, as if he had seen her cry
often before; as if it were a painful habit. At last it got
on his nerves. He stopped abruptly, looked out of the
window, then leant towards her as he had been doing when
I got in, and said in a bullying, menacing way, as if he
would not stand any more nonsense:

"So about that matter we were discussing. It'll be all
right? George will be there on Tuesday?"

"We shan't be late," said Mrs. Brown, gathering herself
together with superb dignity.

Mr. Smith said nothing. He got up, buttoned his coat,
reached his bag down, and jumped out of the train before
it had stopped at Clapham Junction. He had got what he
wanted, but he was ashamed of himself; he was glad to
get out of the old lady's sight.

Mrs. Brown and I were left alone together. She sat in her
corner opposite, very clean, very small, rather queer, and
suffering intensely. The impression she made was overwhelming. It came pouring out like a draught, like a smell

of burning. What was it composed of—that overwhelming and peculiar impression? Myriads of irrelevant and incongruous ideas crowd into one's head on such occasions; one sees the person, one sees Mrs. Brown, in the centre of all sorts of different scenes. I thought of her in a seaside house, among queer ornaments: sea-urchins, models of ships in glass cases. Her husband's medals were on the mantelpiece. She popped in and out of the room, perching on the edges of chairs, picking meals out of saucers, indulging in long, silent stares. The caterpillars and the oak-trees seemed to imply all that. And then, into this fantastic and secluded life, in broke Mr. Smith. I saw him blowing in, so to speak, on a windy day. He banged, he slammed. His dripping umbrella made a pool in the hall. They sat closeted together.

And then Mrs. Brown faced the dreadful revelation. She took her heroic decision. Early, before dawn, she packed her bag and carried it herself to the station. She would not let Smith touch it. She was wounded in her pride, unmoored from her anchorage; she came of gentlefolks who kept servants—but details could wait. The important thing was to realize her character, to steep oneself in her atmosphere. I had no time to explain why I felt it somewhat tragic, heroic, yet with a dash of the flighty and fantastic, before the train stopped, and I watched her disappear, carrying her bag, into the vast blazing station. She looked very small, very tenacious; at once very frail and very heroic. And I have never seen her again, and I shall never know what became of her.

The story ends without any point to it. But I have not told you this anecdote to illustrate either my own ingenuity or the pleasure of travelling from Richmond to

Waterloo. What I want you to see in it is this. Here is a character imposing itself upon another person. Here is Mrs. Brown making someone begin almost automatically to write a novel about her. I believe that all novels begin with an old lady in the corner opposite. I believe that all novels, that is to say, deal with character, and that it is to express character—not to preach doctrines, sing songs, or celebrate the glories of the British Empire, that the form of the novels, so clumsy, verbose, and undramatic, so rich, elastic, and alive, has been evolved. To express character, I have said; but you will at once reflect that the very widest interpretation can be put upon those words. For example, old Mrs. Brown's character will strike you very differently according to the age and country in which you happen to be born. It would be easy enough to write three different versions of that incident in the train, an English, a French, and a Russian. The English writer would make the old lady into a "character"; he would bring out her oddities and mannerisms; her buttons and wrinkles; her ribbons and warts. Her personality would dominate the book. A French writer would rub out all that; he would sacrifice the individual Mrs. Brown to give a more general view of human nature; to make a more abstract, proportioned, and harmonious whole. The Russian would pierce through the flesh; would reveal the soul—the soul alone, wandering out into the Waterloo Road, asking of life some tremendous question which would sound on and on in our ears after the book was finished. And then besides age and country there is the writer's temperament to be considered. You see one thing in character, and I another. You say it means this, and I that. And when it comes to writing each makes a further selection on principles of his own. Thus Mrs. Brown can be treated in an infinite variety of ways, according to the age, country, and temperament of the writer.

But now I must recall what Mr. Arnold Bennett says. He says that it is only if the characters are real that the novel has any chance of surviving. Otherwise, die it must. But, I ask myself, what is reality? And who are the judges of reality? A character may be real to Mr. Bennett and quite unreal to me. For instance, in this article he says that Dr. Watson in *Sherlock Holmes* is real to him: to me Dr. Watson is a sack stuffed with straw, a dummy, a figure of fun. And so it is with character after character—in book after book. There is nothing that people differ about more than the reality of characters, especially in contemporary books. But if you take a larger view I think that Mr. Bennett is perfectly right. If, that is, you think of the novels which seem to you great novels—*War and Peace, Vanity Fair, Tristram Shandy, Madame Bovary, Pride and Prejudice, The Mayor of Casterbridge, Villette*—if you think of these books, you do at once think of some character who has seemed to you so real (I do not by that mean so lifelike) that it has the power to make you think not merely of it itself, but of all sorts of things through its eyes—of religion, of love, of war, of peace, of family life, of balls in country towns, of sunsets, moonrises, the immortality of the soul. There is hardly any subject of human experience that is left out of *War and Peace* it seems to me. And in all these novels all these great novelists have brought us to see whatever they wish us to see through some character. Otherwise, they would not be novelists; but poets, historians, or pamphleteers.

But now let us examine what Mr. Bennett went on to

say—he said that there was no great novelist among the Georgian writers because they cannot create characters who are real, true, and convincing. And there I cannot agree. There are reasons, excuses, possibilities which I think put a different colour upon the case. It seems so to me at least, but I am well aware that this is a matter about which I am likely to be prejudiced, sanguine, and near-sighted. I will put my view before you in the hope that you will make it impartial, judicial, and broad-minded. Why, then, is it so hard for novelists at present to create characters which seem real, not only to Mr. Bennett, but to the world at large? Why, when October comes round, do the publishers always fail to supply us with a master-piece?

Surely one reason is that the men and women who began writing novels in 1910 or thereabouts had this great difficulty to face—that there was no English novelist living from whom they could learn their business. Mr. Conrad is a Pole; which sets him apart, and makes him, however admirable, not very helpful. Mr. Hardy has written no novel since 1895. The most prominent and successful novelists in the year 1910 were, I suppose, Mr. Wells, Mr. Bennett, and Mr. Galsworthy. Now it seems to me that to go to these men and ask them to teach you how to write a novel—how to create characters that are real—is precisely like going to a boot maker and asking him to teach you how to make a watch. Do not let me give you the impression that I do not admire and enjoy their books. They seem to me of great value, and indeed of great necessity. There are seasons when it is more important to have boots than to have watches. To drop metaphor, I think that after the creative activity of the Victorian age it was quite necessary, not only for literature but for life, that someone should write the books that Mr. Wells, Mr. Bennett, and Mr. Galsworthy have written. Yet what odd books they are! Sometimes I wonder if we are right to call them books at all. For they leave one with so strange a feeling of incompleteness and dissatisfaction. In order to complete them it seems necessary to do something—to join a society, or, more desperately, to write a cheque. That done, the restlessness is laid, the book finished; it can be put upon the shelf, and need never be read again. But with the work of other novelists it is different. *Tristram Shandy* or *Pride and Prejudice* is complete in itself; it is self-contained; it leaves one with no desire to do anything, except indeed to read the book again, and to understand it better. The difference perhaps is that both Sterne and Jane Austen were interested in things in themselves; in character, in itself; in the book in itself. Therefore everything was inside the book, nothing outside. But the Edwardians were never interested in character in itself; or in the book in itself. They were interested in something outside. Their books, then, were incomplete as books, and required that the reader should finish them, actively and practically, for himself.

Perhaps we can make this clearer if we take the liberty of imagining a little party in the railway carriage—Mr. Wells, Mr. Galsworthy, Mr. Bennett are travelling to Waterloo with Mrs. Brown. Mrs. Brown, I have said, was poorly dressed and very small. She had an anxious, harassed look. I doubt whether she was what you call an educated woman. Seizing upon all these symptoms of the unsatisfactory condition of our primary schools with a rapidity to which I can do no justice, Mr. Wells would instantly project upon the window-pane a vision of a better, breezier, jollier, happier, more adventurous and gallant world, where these musty railway carriages and fusty old women do not exist; where miraculous barges bring tropical fruit to Camberwell by eight o'clock in the morning; where there are public nurseries, fountains, and libraries, dining-rooms, drawing-rooms, and marriages; where every citizen is generous and candid, manly and magnificent, and rather like Mr. Wells himself. But nobody is in the least like Mrs. Brown. There are no Mrs. Browns in Utopia. Indeed I do not think that Mr. Wells, in his passion to make her what she ought to be, would waste a thought upon her as she is. And what would Mr. Galsworthy see? Can we doubt that the walls of Doulton's factory would take his fancy? There are women in that factory who make twenty-five dozen earthenware pots every day. There are mothers in the Mile End Road who depend upon the farthings which those women earn. But there are employers in Surrey who are even now smoking rich cigars while the nightingale sings. Burning with indignation, stuffed with information, arraigning civilization, Mr. Galsworthy would only see in Mrs. Brown a pot broken on the wheel and thrown into the corner.

Mr. Bennett, alone of the Edwardians, would keep his eyes in the carriage. He, indeed, would observe every detail with immense care. He would notice the advertisements; the pictures of Swanage and Portsmouth; the way in which the cushion bulged between the buttons; how Mrs. Brown wore a brooch which had cost three-and-ten-three at Whitworth's bazaar; and had mended both gloves—indeed the thumb of the left-hand glove had been replaced. And he would observe, at length, how this was the non-

stop train from Windsor which calls at Richmond for the
convenience of middle-class residents, who can afford to
go to the theatre but have not reached the social rank
which can afford motor-cars, though it is true, there are
occasions (he would tell us what), when they hire them
from a company (he would tell us which). And so he
would gradually sidle sedately towards Mrs. Brown, and
would remark how she had been left a little copyhold, not
freehold, property at Datchet, which, however, was mort-
gaged to Mr. Bungay the solicitor—but why should I pre-
sume to invent Mr. Bennett? Does not Mr. Bennett write
novels himself? I will open the first book that chance puts
in my way—*Hilda Lessways*. Let us see how he makes us
feel that Hilda is real, true, and convincing, as a novelist
should. She shut the door in a soft, controlled way, which
showed the constraint of her relations with her mother.
She was fond of reading *Maud;* she was endowed with
the power to feel intensely. So far, so good; in his leisurely,
surefooted way Mr. Bennett is trying in these first pages,
where every touch is important, to show us the kind of
girl she was.

But then he begins to describe, not Hilda Lessways, but
the view from her bedroom window, the excuse being that
Mr. Skellorn, the man who collects rents, is coming along
that way. Mr. Bennett proceeds:

"The bailiwick of Turnhill lay behind her; and all the
murky district of the Five Towns, of which Turnhill is
the northern outpost, lay to the south. At the foot of
Chatterley Wood the canal wound in large curves on its
way towards the undefiled plains of Cheshire and the sea.
On the canal-side, exactly opposite to Hilda's window,
was a flour-mill, that sometimes made nearly as much

smoke as the kilns and the chimneys closing the prospect
on either hand. From the flour-mill a bricked path, which
separated a considerable row of new cottages from their
appurtenant gardens, led straight into Lessways Street, in
front of Mrs. Lessway's house. By this path Mr. Skellorn
should have arrived, for he inhabited the farthest of the
cottages."

One line of insight would have done more than all those
lines of description; but let them pass as the necessary
drudgery of the novelist. And now—where is Hilda? Alas.
Hilda is still looking out of the window. Passionate and
dissatisfied as she was, she was a girl with an eye for
houses. She often compared this old Mr. Skellorn with the
villas she saw from her bedroom window. Therefore the
villas must be described. Mr. Bennett proceeds:

"The row was called Freehold Villas: a consciously
proud name in a district where much of the land was copyhold and could only change owners subject to the pay-
ment of 'fines,' and to the feudal consent of a 'court' pre-
sided over by the agent of a lord of the manor. Most of
the dwellings were owned by their occupiers, who, each
an absolute monarch of the soil, niggled in his sooty garden of an evening amid the flutter of drying shirts and
towels. Freehold Villas symbolized the final triumph of
Victorian economics, the apotheosis of the prudent and
industrious artisan. It corresponded with a Building Society Secretary's dream of paradise. And indeed it was a
very real achievement. Nevertheless, Hilda's irrational contempt would not admit this."

Heaven be praised, we cry! At last we are coming to
Hilda herself. But not so fast. Hilda may have been this,
that, and the other; but Hilda not only looked at houses,

and thought of houses; Hilda lived in a house. And what sort of a house did Hilda live in? Mr. Bennett proceeds:

"It was one of the two middle houses of a detached terrace of four houses built by her grandfather Lessways, the teapot manufacturer; it was the chief of the four, obviously the habitation of the proprietor of the terrace. One of the corner houses comprised a grocer's shop, and this house had been robbed of its just proportion of garden so that the seigneurial garden-plot might be triflingly larger than the other. The terrace was not a terrace of cottages, but of houses rated at from twenty-six to thirty-six pounds a year; beyond the means of artisans and petty insurance agents and rent-collectors. And further, it was well-built, generously built; and its architecture, though debased, showed some faint traces of Georgian amenity. It was admittedly the best row of houses in that newly-settled quarter of the town. In coming to it out of Freehold Villas Mr. Skellorn obviously came to something superior, wider, more liberal. Suddenly Hilda heard her mother's voice. . . ."

But we cannot hear her mother's voice, or Hilda's voice; we can only hear Mr. Bennett's voice telling us facts about rents and freeholds and copyholds and fines. What can Mr. Bennett be about? I have formed my own opinion of what Mr. Bennett is about—he is trying to make us imagine for him; he is trying to hypnotize us into the belief that, because he has made a house, there must be a person living there. With all his powers of observation, which are marvellous, with all his sympathy and humanity, which are great, Mr. Bennett has never once looked at Mrs. Brown in her corner. There she sits in the corner of the carriage—that carriage which is travelling, not from

Richmond to Waterloo, but from one age of English literature to the next, for Mrs. Brown is eternal, Mrs. Brown
is human nature, Mrs. Brown changes only on the surface,
it is the novelists who get in and out—there she sits and not
one of the Edwardian writers has so much as looked at her.
They have looked very powerfully, searchingly, and sym-
pathetically out of the window; at factories, at Utopias,
even at the decoration and upholstery of the carriage; but
never at her, never at life, never at human nature. And so
they have developed a technique of novel-writing which
suits their purpose; they have made tools and established
conventions which do their business. But those tools are
not our tools, and that business is not our business. For us
those conventions are ruin, those tools are death.

You may well complain of the vagueness of my language. What is a convention, a tool, you may ask, and
what do you mean by saying that Mr. Bennett's and Mr.
Wells's and Mr. Galsworthy's conventions are the wrong
conventions for the Georgian's? The question is difficult:
I will attempt a short cut. A convention in writing is not
much different from a convention in manners. Both in life
and in literature it is necessary to have some means of
bridging the gulf between the hostess and her unknown
guest on the one hand, the writer and his unknown reader
on the other. The hostess bethinks her of the weather, for
generations of hostesses have established the fact that this
is a subject of universal interest in which we all believe.
She begins by saying that we are having a wretched May,
and, having thus got into touch with her unknown guest,
proceeds to matters of greater interest. So it is in literature.
The writer must get into touch with his reader by putting
before him something which he recognizes, which there-

fore stimulates his imagination, and makes him willing to co-operate in the far more difficult business of intimacy. And it is of the highest importance that this common meeting-place should be reached easily, almost instinctively, in the dark, with one's eyes shut. Here is Mr. Bennett making use of this common ground in the passage which I have quoted. The problem before him was to make us believe in the reality of Hilda Lessways. So he began, being an Edwardian, by describing accurately and minutely the sort of house Hilda lived in, and the sort of house she saw from the window. House property was the common ground from which the Edwardians found it easy to proceed to intimacy. Indirect as it seems to us, the convention worked admirably, and thousands of Hilda Lessways were launched upon the world by this means. For that age and generation, the convention was a good one.

But now, if you will allow me to pull my own anecdote to pieces, you will see how keenly I felt the lack of a convention, and how serious a matter it is when the tools of one generation are useless for the next. The incident had made a great impression on me. But how was I to transmit it to you? All I could do was to report as accurately as I could what was said, to describe in detail what was worn, to say, despairingly, that all sorts of scenes rushed into my mind, to proceed to tumble them out pell-mell, and to describe this vivid, this overmastering impression by likening it to a draught or a smell of burning. To tell you the truth, I was also strongly tempted to manufacture a three-volume novel about the old lady's son, and his adventures crossing the Atlantic, and her daughter, and how she kept a milliner's shop in Westminster, the past life of Smith himself, and his house at Sheffield, though such stories seem to me the most dreary, irrelevant, and humbugging affairs in the world.

But if I had done that I should have escaped the appalling effort of saying what I meant. And to have got at what I meant I should have had to go back and back and back; to experiment with one thing and another; to try this sentence and that, referring each word to my vision, matching it as exactly as possible, and knowing that somehow I had to find a common ground between us, a convention which would not seem to you too odd, unreal, and far-fetched to believe in. I admit that I shirked that arduous undertaking. I let my Mrs. Brown slip through my fingers. I have told you nothing whatever about her. But that is partly the great Edwardians' fault. I asked them—they are my elders and betters—How shall I begin to describe this woman's character? And they said: "Begin by saying that her father kept a shop in Harrogate. Ascertain the rent. Ascertain the wages of shop assistants in the year 1878. Discover what her mother died of. Describe cancer. Describe calico. Describe—" But I cried: "Stop! Stop!" And I regret to say that I threw that ugly, that clumsy, that incongruous tool out of the window, for I knew that if I began describing the cancer and the calico, my Mrs. Brown, that vision to which I cling though I know no way of imparting it to you, would have been dulled and tarnished and vanished for ever.

That is what I mean by saying that the Edwardian tools are the wrong ones for us to use. They have laid an enormous stress upon the fabric of things. They have given us a house in the hope that we may be able to deduce the human beings who live there. To give them their due, they have made that house much better worth living in. But if you hold that novels are in the first place about people, and only in the second about the houses they live in, that is the wrong way to set about it. Therefore, you see, the Georgian writer had to begin by throwing away the method that was in use at the moment. He was left alone there facing Mrs. Brown without any method of conveying her to the reader. But that is inaccurate. A writer is never alone. There is always the public with him—if not on the same seat, at least in the compartment next door. Now the public is a strange travelling companion. In England it is a very suggestible and docile creature, which, once you get it to attend, will believe implicitly what it is told for a certain number of years. If you say to the public with sufficient conviction: "All women have tails, and all men humps," it will actually learn to see women with tails and men with humps, and will think it very revolutionary and probably improper if you say: "Nonsense. Monkeys have tails and camels humps. But men and women have brains, and they have hearts; they think and they feel,"—that will seem to it a bad joke, and an improper one into the bargain.

But to return. Here is the British public sitting by the writer's side and saying in its vast and unanimous way: "Old women have houses. They have fathers. They have incomes. They have servants. They have hot-water bottles. That is how we know that they are old women. Mr. Wells and Mr. Bennett and Mr. Galsworthy have always taught us that this is the way to recognize them. But now with your Mrs. Brown—how are we to believe in her? We do not even know whether her villa was called Albert or Balmoral; what she paid for her gloves; or whether her mother died of cancer or of consumption. How can she be alive? No; she is a mere figment of your imagination."

And old women of course ought to be made of freehold villas and copyhold estates, not of imagination.

The Georgian novelist, therefore, was in an awkward predicament. There was Mrs. Brown protesting that she was different, quite different, from what people made out, and luring the novelist to her rescue by the most fascinating if fleeting glimpse of her charms; there were the Edwardians handing out tools appropriate to house building and house breaking; and there was the British public asseverating that they must see the hot-water bottle first. Meanwhile the train was rushing to that station where we must all get out.

Such, I think, was the predicament in which the young Georgians found themselves about the year 1910. Many of them—I am thinking of Mr. Forster and Mr. Lawrence in particular—spoilt their early work because, instead of throwing away those tools, they tried to use them. They tried to compromise. They tried to combine their own direct sense of the oddity and significance of some character with Mr. Galsworthy's knowledge of the Factory Acts, and Mr. Bennett's knowledge of the Five Towns. They tried it, but they had too keen, too overpowering a sense of Mrs. Brown and her peculiarities to go on trying it much longer. Something had to be done. At whatever cost of life, limb, and damage to valuable property Mrs. Brown must be rescued, expressed, and set in her high relations to the world before the train stopped and she disappeared for ever. And so the smashing and the crashing began. Thus it is that we hear all round us, in poems and novels and biographies, even in newspaper articles and essays, the sound of breaking and falling, crashing and destruction. It is the prevailing sound of the Georgian age—rather a melancholy one if you think what melodious days there have been in the past, if you think of Shakespeare and Milton and Keats or even of Jane Austen and Thackeray and Dickens; if you think of the language, and the heights to which it can soar when free, and see the same eagle captive, bald, and croaking.

In view of these facts—with these sounds in my ears and these fancies in my brain—I am not going to deny that Mr. Bennett has some reason when he complains that our Georgian writers are unable to make us believe that our characters are real. I am forced to agree that they do not pour out three immortal masterpieces with Victorian regularity every autumn. But, instead of being gloomy, I am sanguine. For this state of things is, I think, inevitable whenever from hoar old age or callow youth the convention ceases to be a means of communication between writer and reader, and becomes instead an obstacle and an impediment. At the present moment we are suffering, not from decay, but from having no code of manners which writers and readers accept as a prelude to the more exciting intercourse of friendship. The literary convention of the time is so artificial—you have to talk about the weather and nothing but the weather throughout the entire visit—that, naturally, the feeble are tempted to outrage, and the strong are led to destroy the very foundations and rules of literary society. Signs of this are everywhere apparent. Grammar is violated; syntax disintegrated; as a boy staying with an aunt for the week-end rolls in the geranium bed out of sheer desperation as the solemnities of the sabbath wear on. The more adult writers do not, of course, indulge in such wanton exhibitions of spleen. Their sincerity is desperate, and their courage tremendous; it is only that they do not know which to use, a fork or their fingers. Thus, if you read Mr. Joyce and Mr. Eliot you will be struck by the indecency of the one, and the obscurity of the other. Mr. Joyce's indecency in *Ulysses* seems to me the conscious and calculated indecency of a desperate man who feels that in order to breathe he must break the windows. At moments, when the window is broken, he is magnificent. But what a waste of energy! And, after all, how dull indecency is, when it is not the overflowing of a superabundant energy or savagery, but the determined and public-spirited act of a man who needs fresh air! Again, with the obscurity of Mr. Eliot. I think that Mr. Eliot has written some of the loveliest single lines in modern poetry. But how intolerant he is of the old usages and politenesses of society—respect for the weak, consideration for the dull! As I sun myself upon the intense and ravishing beauty of one of his lines, and reflect that I must make a dizzy and dangerous leap to the next, and so on from line to line, like an acrobat flying precariously from bar to bar, I cry out, I confess, for the old decorums, and envy the indolence of my ancestors who, instead of spinning madly through mid-air, dreamt quietly in the shade with a book. Again, in Mr. Strachey's books, *Eminent Victorians* and *Queen Victoria*, the effort and strain of writing against the grain and current of the times is visible too. It is much less visible, of course, for not only is he dealing with facts, which are stubborn things, but he has fabricated, chiefly from eighteenth-century material, a very discreet code of manners of his own, which allows him to sit at table with the highest in the land and to say a great many things under cover of that exquisite apparel which, had they gone naked, would have been chased by the men-servants from the room. Still, if you compare *Eminent Victorians* with some of Lord Macaulay's essays, though you will feel that Lord Macaulay is always wrong, and Mr. Strachey always right, you will also feel a body, a sweep, a richness in Lord Macaulay's essays which show that his age was behind him; all his strength went straight into his work; none was used for purposes of concealment or of conversion. But Mr. Strachey has had to open our eyes before he made us see; he has had to search out and sew together a very artful manner of speech; and the effort, beautifully though it is concealed, has robbed his work of some of the force that should have gone into it, and limited his scope.

For these reasons, then, we must reconcile ourselves to a season of failures and fragments. We must reflect that where so much strength is spent on finding a way of telling the truth, the truth itself is bound to reach us in rather an exhausted and chaotic condition. Ulysses, Queen Victoria, Mr. Prufrock—to give Mrs. Brown some of the names she has made famous lately—is a little pale and dishevelled by the time her rescuers reach her. And it is the sound of their axes that we hear—a vigorous and stimulating sound in my ears—unless of course you wish to sleep, when, in the bounty of his concern, Providence has provided a host of writers anxious and able to satisfy your needs.

Thus I have tried, at tedious length, I fear, to answer some of the questions which I began by asking. I have given an account of some of the difficulties which in my view beset the Georgian writer in all his forms. I have sought to excuse him. May I end by venturing to remind you of the duties and responsibilities that are yours as partners in this business of writing books, as companions in the railway carriage, as fellow travellers with Mrs. Brown? For she is just as visible to you who remain silent as to us who tell stories about her. In the course of your daily life this past week you have had far stranger and more interesting experiences than the one I have tried to describe. You have overheard scraps of talk that filled you with amazement. You have gone to bed at night bewildered by the complexity of your feelings. In one day thousands of ideas have coursed through your brains; thousands of emotions have met, collided, and disappeared in astonishing disorder. Nevertheless, you allow the writers to palm off upon you a version of all this, an image of Mrs. Brown, which has no likeness to that surprising apparition whatsoever. In your modesty you seem to consider that writers are different blood and bone from yourselves; that they know more of Mrs. Brown than you do. Never was there a more fatal mistake. It is this division between reader and writer, this humility on your part, these professional airs and graces on ours, that corrupt and emasculate the books which should be the healthy offspring of a close and equal alliance between us. Hence spring those sleek, smooth novels, those portentous and ridiculous biographies, that milk and watery criticism, those poems melodiously celebrating the innocence of roses and sheep which pass so plausibly for literature at the present time.

Your part is to insist that writers shall come down off their plinths and pedestals, and describe beautifully if possible, truthfully at any rate, our Mrs. Brown. You should insist that she is an old lady of unlimited capacity and infinite variety; capable of appearing in any place; wearing any dress; saying anything and doing heaven knows what. But the things she says and the things she does and her eyes and her nose and her speech and her silence have an overwhelming fascination, for she is, of course, the spirit we live by, life itself.

But do not expect just at present a complete and satisfactory presentment of her. Tolerate the spasmodic, the obscure, the fragmentary, the failure. Your help is invoked in a good cause. For I will make one final and surpassingly rash prediction—we are trembling on the verge of one of the great ages of English literature. But it can only be reached if we are determined never, never to desert Mrs. Brown.

All About Books[1]

YOUR last letter ends with the following sentence: "The cold profile of Mont Blanc; falling snow; peasants and pine trees; a string of stout fellows roped together with alpenstocks—such is the prospect from my window; so for pity's sake draw your chair to the fire, take your pen in your hand and write me a long, long letter all about books." But you must realize that a long, long letter is apt to be exaggerated, inaccurate, and full of those irreticences and hyperboles which the voice of the speaker corrects in talk. A letter is not a review; it is not a considered judgment, but, on condition that you do not believe a word I say, I will scribble for an hour or two whatever comes into my head about books.

That it has been a very bad season goes without saying. The proof of it is that old Mr. Baddeley had read *Guy Mannering* for the fifty-eighth time. Never was Jane Austen in greater demand. Trollope, Dickens, Carlyle, and Macaulay are all providing that solace, that security, that sense that the human heart does not change which our miserable age requires and our living authors so woefully fail to provide. When, therefore, the rumour spread that the diary of an old clergyman called Cole, who had gone to Paris in the autumn of 1765, was about to be published, and that Miss Waddell had put her brilliance and her

[1] Written in January, 1931. Copyright 1931 by Editorial Publications, Inc. (*New Republic*).

erudition at our service, a purr of content and anticipation
rose from half the armchairs of England. This Cole, moreover, was not anybody's Cole; he was Horace Walpole's
Cole; nor does it need any pedantic familiarity with history to be aware that the autumn of 1765 was for one
old blind woman in Paris the most excruciating, the most
humiliating, the most ecstatic of her life. At last Horace
Walpole had come—after what snubs, what humiliations,
what bitter disappointments! At last Madame du Deffand
would—not indeed see him in the flesh, but feel him with
the spirit. He would be in the same room with her; he
would talk his broken French; she would feel come over
her that strange delight, that abasement, that ecstasy—call
it not love, for love he would not have it called—which
the presence of the elderly and elegant Horace never failed
to inspire in a heart that had long outlived any sensation
but boredom, despair and disgust. It was in that very
autumn that Cole chose to visit Paris. Cole, it seemed
probable since Walpole liked him, would have eyes in his
head; certainly he had a diary in his portmanteau. What
revelations might one not expect? What confidences from
one Englishman to another? And Horace Walpole was
willing. Every day he sent his servant to ask Cole to
dinner. And every day—it is incredible what the dead will
do, but it is true—Cole preferred to go sightseeing. He
went to Notre Dame; he went to the Sorbonne; he went
to the Convent of that Virgin, to the Cathedral of this
Saint. When he came home he sat down to digest and
methodize what he had seen. He was too tired to dine with
Mr. Walpole. So instead of revelations we have information. "On the right hand of the High Altar as one enters.
. . . The dome of this church is very beautiful. . . . Over

the door is a curious alto-relievo representing the Last Supper. . . ." That is what he writes about, and, of course, about the habits of the natives. The habits of the natives are disgusting; the women hawk on the floor; the forks are dirty; the trees are poor, the Pont Neuf is not a patch on London Bridge; the cows are skinny; morals are licentious; polish is good; cabbages cost so much; bread is made of coarse flour; Mr. Drumgold could not with patience mention the character of John James Rousseau; the Coles are distantly related to the Herberts; and a French turkey is about the size of an English hen. How natural it all is! How admirable Mr. Cole would be at home in his own parish! How gladly we will read sixteen volumes about life in Bletchley if Miss Waddell will print them! But the present volume is nothing short of torture. "Cole," one is inclined to cry, "if you don't give up sightseeing today, if you don't dine with Mr. Walpole, if you don't report every word he says, leaving Drumgold out of it altogether, if you don't turn the talk somehow upon Madame du Deffand, if you don't somehow tell us more about one of the most curious affairs of the heart that was ever transacted, or failing that, rake up a few odds and ends of interest about that amazing society that was playing spillikins on the verge of revolution, we will—" But what can we do? The dead have no sense whatever of what is due to posterity. Mr. Cole imperturbably pulls on his boots and proceeds to visit the Sorbonne.

Must one then read *Guy Mannering*, or take Jane Austen from the bookshelf? No, the advantage of belonging to a good library is that it is only upon very exceptional occasions that one need have recourse to the classics. New books, in fresh jackets, are delivered daily, and good books, too—*Things I Remember*, by the Grand Duchess Marie of Russia, for instance, a very terrible book; *The Diary of a Somersetshire Parson*—a very absorbing book; *By Guess and by God*—a very exciting yet infinitely childish book; and *Scrutinies*, a collection of critical essays by various writers. But what kind of book is *Scrutinies*? That, indeed, I cannot tell you at the moment for the good reason that I have not read it; but you can guess from the title and a glance at the table of contents that it consists of articles by the tolerably young—Messrs. Alec Brown, B. Higgins, Mary Butts, Jack Lindsay, P. Quennell, Sherard Vines, C. Saltmarshe, and so on, upon the tolerably old—Messrs. Eliot, Huxley, Joyce, Lawrence, Sitwell, Strachey, and so on. And if I hesitate to read beyond the title page at present it is for the very sound and simple reason that it is so much pleasanter to look upon the young than upon the old, the young who are fresh and pliable, who have not stood out in the storm and stiffened into attitudes and hardened into wrinkles. Beauty is theirs now, as soon the future will be theirs also. Let us, therefore, leave the figures of the elders where they stand and turn our bull's eye upon the advancing and victorious hordes of youth.

And what is our first impression as we look? A very strange one. How orderly they come! One could swear that they are all arrayed in troops, and all march in step, and all halt, charge and otherwise behave themselves under the command of officers mounted upon chargers. As far as one can see—a bull's eye, it must be admitted, is not a very steady or comprehensive weapon—there is not a single straggler or deserter among them; there is no dancing or disorder; no wild voice cries alone; no man or woman breaks the ranks and leaves the troop and takes to the wilderness stirring desire and unrest among the hearts of his companions. All is orderly, all is preconcerted. If division there is, even that is regular. Camp is opposed to camp; the hostile parties separate, form, meet, fight, leave each other for dead upon the ground; rise, form and fight again. Classic is opposed to romantic; naturalist to metaphysic. Never was there such a sight since the world began. Never—as they come nearer this too becomes certain—were the young so well-equipped as at present. No more respectable army has ever issued from the portals of the two great Universities—none more courageous, more instructed, more outspoken, more intolerant of humbug in all its forms, better fitted to deal pretence its death and falsity its finish—and yet (for all these flowers, of course, conceal a viper) there is a fatal defect; they do not lead, they follow. Where is the adventurous, the intolerant, the immensely foolish young man or woman who dares to be himself? He or she must, of course, be there. He or she will in time to come make himself known. But at present, since he always keeps the ranks, since if he fights he is careful, like Sir Walter Blunt in *Henry the Fourth*, to wear the armour of his king, there is no knowing him at present from the seven hundred and fifty-five others who are similarly disguised.

If this is true, if there is now a uniformity and a drill and a discretion unknown before, what do you think can be the reason? In one word, and I have room for one only, and that is murmured in your private ear—education. Some years since, for reasons unknown, but presumably of value, it must have occurred to someone that the arts of reading and of writing can be taught. Degrees were given at the Universities to those who showed proficiency in their native tongue. And the teachers of the living language were not old and hoary; as fitted their subject they were young and supple. Persuasion sat on their tongues, and the taught, instead of mocking, loved their teachers. And the teachers took the manuscripts of the young and drew circles of blue chalk round this adjective and circles of red chalk round that adverb. They added in purple ink what Pope would have thought and what Wordsworth would have said. And the young, since they loved their teachers, believed them. Hence it came about that, instead of knowing that the sun was in the sky and the bird on the branch, the young knew the whole course of English literature from one end to another; how one age follows another; and one influence cancels another; and one style is derived from another; and one phrase is better than another. They took service under their teachers instead of riding into battle alone. All their marriages—and what are the five years between twenty and twenty-five in the life of a writer but years of courtship and wedding, of falling in love with words and learning their nature, how to mate them by one's own decree in sentences of one's own framing?—all their marriages were arranged in public; tutors introduced the couples; lecturers supervised the amours; and examiners finally pronounced whether the fruit of the union was blessed or the reverse. Such methods, of course, produce an erudite and eugenic offspring. But, one asks, turning over the honest, the admirable, the entirely sensible and unsentimental pages, where is love? Meaning by that, where is the sound of the sea and the red of the rose; where is music, imagery, and a voice speaking from the heart?

That this is all great nonsense I am well aware. But what else can you expect in a letter? The time has come to open *Scrutinies* and begin to read—no, the time has come to rake out the cinders and go to bed.

Reviewing[1]

I

IN London there are certain shop windows that always attract a crowd. The attraction is not in the finished article but in the worn-out garments that are having patches inserted in them. The crowd is watching the women at work. There they sit in the shop window putting invisible stitches into moth-eaten trousers. And this familiar sight may serve as illustration to the following paper. So our poets, playwrights, and novelists sit in the shop window, doing their work under the curious eyes of reviewers. But the reviewers are not content, like the crowd in the street, to gaze in silence; they comment aloud upon the size of the holes, upon the skill of the workers, and advise the public which of the goods in the shop window is the best worth buying. The purpose of this paper is to rouse discussion as to the value of the reviewer's office—to the writer, to the public, to the reviewer, and to literature. But a reservation must first be made—by "the reviewer" is meant the reviewer of imaginative literature—poetry, drama, fiction; not the reviewer of history, politics, economics. His is a different office, and for reasons not to be discussed here he fulfils it in the main so adequately and indeed admirably that his value is not in question. Has the reviewer, then, of imaginative literature any value at the

[1] Written in 1939.

present time to the writer, to the public, to the reviewer, and to literature? And, if so, what? And if not, how could his function be changed, and made profitable? Let us broach these involved and complicated questions by giving one quick glance at the history of reviewing, since it may help to define the nature of a review at the present moment.

Since the review came into existence with the newspaper, that history is a brief one. *Hamlet* was not reviewed, nor *Paradise Lost*. Criticism there was but criticism conveyed by word of mouth, by the audience in the theatre, by fellow writers in taverns and private workshops. Printed criticism came into existence, presumably in a crude and primitive form, in the seventeenth century. Certainly the eighteenth century rings with the screams and catcalls of the reviewer and his victim. But towards the end of the eighteenth century there was a change—the body of criticism then seems to split into two parts. The critic and the reviewer divided the country between them. The critic—let Dr. Johnson represent him—dealt with the past and with principles; the reviewer took the measure of new books as they fell from the press. As the nineteenth century drew on, these functions became more and more distinct. There were the critics—Coleridge, Matthew Arnold—who took their time and their space; and there were the "irresponsible" and mostly anonymous reviewers who had less time and less space, and whose complex task it was partly to inform the public, partly to criticize the book, and partly to advertise its existence.

Thus, though the reviewer in the nineteenth century has much resemblance to his living representative, there were certain important differences. One difference is shown by the author of the *Times History:* "The books reviewed were fewer, but the reviews were longer than now. . . . Even a novel might get two columns and more."—he is referring to the middle of the nineteenth century. Those differences are very important as will be seen later. But it is worth while to pause for a moment to examine other results of the review which are first manifest then, though by no means easy to sum up; the effect that is to say of the review upon the author's sales and upon the author's sensibility. A review had undoubtedly a great effect upon sales. Thackeray, for instance, said that the *Times'* review of *Esmond* "absolutely stopped the sale of the book." The review also had an immense though less calculable effect upon the sensibility of the author. Upon Keats the effect is notorious; also upon the sensitive Tennyson. Not only did he alter his poems at the reviewer's bidding, but actually contemplated emigration; and was thrown, according to one biographer, into such despair by the hostility of reviewers that his state of mind for a whole decade, and thus his poetry, was changed by them. But the robust and self-confident were also affected. "How can a man like Macready," Dickens demanded, "fret and fume and chafe himself for such lice of literature as these?"—the "lice" are writers in Sunday newspapers—"rotten creatures with men's forms and devils' hearts?" Yet lice as they are, when they "discharge their pigmy arrows" even Dickens with all his genius and his magnificent vitality cannot help but mind and has to make a vow to overcome his rage and "to gain the victory by being indifferent and bidding them whistle on."

In their different ways then the great poet and the great novelist both admit the power of the nineteenth-century reviewer; and it is safe to assume that behind them stood a myriad of minor poets and minor novelists whether of the sensitive variety or of the robust who were all affected in much the same way. The way was complex; it is difficult to analyse. Tennyson and Dickens are both angry and hurt; they are also ashamed of themselves for feeling such emotions. The reviewer was a louse; his bite was contemptible; yet his bite was painful. His bite injured vanity; it injured reputation; it injured sales. Undoubtedly in the nineteenth century the reviewer was a formidable insect; he had considerable power over the author's sensibility; and upon the public taste. He could hurt the author; he could persuade the public either to buy or to refrain from buying.

2

The figures being thus set in position and their functions and powers roughly outlined, it must next be asked whether what was true then is true now. At first sight there seems to be little change. All the figures are still with us—critic; reviewer; author; public; and in much the same relations. The critic is separate from the reviewer; the function of the reviewer is partly to sort current literature; partly to advertise the author; partly to inform the public. Nevertheless there is a change; and it is a change of the highest importance. It seems to have made itself felt in the last part of the nineteenth century. It is summed up in the words of the *Times'* historian already quoted: ". . . the tendency was for reviews to grow shorter and to be less long delayed." But there was another tendency; not only did the reviews become shorter and quicker, but they increased immeasurably in number. The result of these three tendencies was of the highest importance. It was catastrophic indeed; between them they have brought about the decline and fall of reviewing. Because they were quicker, shorter, and more numerous the value of reviews for all parties concerned has dwindled until— is it too much to say until it has disappeared? But let us consider. The people concerned are the author, the reader, and the publisher. Placing them in this order let us ask first how these tendencies have affected the author—why the review has ceased to have any value for him? Let us assume, for brevity's sake, that the most important value of a review to the author was its effect upon him as a writer—that it gave him an expert opinion of his work and allowed him to judge roughly how far as an artist he had failed or succeeded. That has been destroyed almost entirely by the multiplicity of reviews. Now that he has sixty reviews where in the nineteenth century he had perhaps six, he finds that there is no such thing as "an opinion" of his work. Praise cancels blame; and blame praise. There are as many different opinions of his work as there are different reviewers. Soon he comes to discount both praise and blame; they are equally worthless. He values the review only for its effect upon his reputation and for its effect upon his sales.

The same cause has also lessened the value of the review to the reader. The reader asks the reviewer to tell him whether the poem or novel is good or bad in order that he may decide whether to buy it or not. Sixty reviewers at once assure him that it is a masterpiece—and worthless. The clash of completely contradictory opinions cancel each other out. The reader suspends judgment; waits for an opportunity of seeing the book himself; very probably forgets all about it, and keeps his seven and sixpence in his pocket.

The variety and diversity of opinion affect the publisher in the same way. Aware that the public no longer trusts either praise or blame, the publisher is reduced to printing both side by side: "This is . . . poetry that will be remembered in hundreds of years time . . ." "There are several passages that make me physically sick,"[1] to quote an actual instance; to which he adds very naturally, in his own person: "Why not read it yourself?" That question is enough by itself to show that reviewing as practised at present has failed in all its objects. Why bother to write reviews or to read them or to quote them if in the end the reader must decide the question for himself?

3

If the reviewer has ceased to have any value either to the author or to the public it seems a public duty to abolish him. And, indeed, the recent failure of certain magazines consisting largely of reviews seems to show that whatever the reason, such will be his fate. But it is worth while to look at him in being—a flutter of little reviews is still attached to the great political dailies and weeklies—before he is swept out of existence, in order to see what he is still trying to do; why it is so difficult for him to do it; and whether perhaps there is not some element of value that ought to be preserved. Let us ask the reviewer himself to throw light upon the nature of the problem as it appears to him. Nobody is better qualified to do so than Mr.

[1] *The New Statesman*, April, 1939.

Harold Nicolson. The other day[1] he dealt with the duties and the difficulties of the reviewer as they appear to him. He began by saying that the reviewer, who is "something quite different from the critic," is "hampered by the hebdomadal nature of his task,"—in other words, he has to write too often and too much. He went on to define the nature of that task. "Is he to relate every book that he reads to the eternal standards of literary excellence? Were he to do that, his reviews would be one long ululation. Is he merely to consider the library public and to tell people what it may please them to read? Were he to do that, he would be subjugating his own level of taste to a level which is not very stimulating. How does he act?" Since he cannot refer to the eternal standards of literature; since he cannot tell the library public what they would like to read—that would be "a degradation of the mind"—there is only one thing that he can do: he can hedge. "I hedge between the two extremes. I address myself to the authors of the books which I review; I want to tell them why I either like or dislike their work; and I trust that from such a dialogue the ordinary reader will derive some information."

That is an honest statement; and its honesty is illuminating. It shows that the review has become an expression of individual opinion, given without any attempt to refer to "eternal standards" by a man who is in a hurry; who is pressed for space; who is expected to cater in that little space for many different interests; who is bothered by the knowledge that he is not fulfilling his task; who is doubtful what that task is; and who, finally, is forced to hedge. Now the public though crass is not such an ass as to invest seven and sixpence on the advice of a reviewer writing

[1] *Daily Telegraph*, March, 1939.

under such conditions; and the public though dull is not such a gull as to believe in the great poets, great novelists, and epoch-making works that are weekly discovered under such conditions. Those are the conditions however; and there is good reason to think that they will become more drastic in the course of the next few years. The reviewer is already a distracted tag on the tail of the political kite. Soon he will be conditioned out of existence altogether. His work will be done—in many newspapers it is already done—by a competent official armed with scissors and paste who will be called (it may be) the Gutter. The Gutter will write out a short statement of the book; extract the plot (if it is a novel); choose a few verses (if it is a poem); quote a few anecdotes (if it is a biography). To this what is left of the reviewer—perhaps he will come to be known as the Taster—will fix a stamp—an asterisk to signify approval, a dagger to signify disapproval. This statement—this Gutter and Stamp production—will serve instead of the present discordant and distracted twitter. And there is no reason to think that it will serve two of the parties concerned worse than the present system. The library public will be told what it wishes to know—whether the book is the kind of book to order from the library; and the publisher will collect asterisks and daggers instead of going to the pains to copy out alternate phrases of praise and abuse in which neither he nor the public has any faith. Each perhaps will save a little time and a little money. There remain however, two other parties to be considered—that is the author and the reviewer. What will the Gutter and Stamp system mean to them?

To deal first with the author—his case is the more complex, for his is the more highly developed organism. Dur-

ing the two centuries or so in which he has been exposed
to reviewers he has undoubtedly developed what may be
called a reviewer consciousness. There is present in his
mind a figure who is known as "the reviewer." To Dickens
he was a louse armed with pigmy arrows, having the form
of a man and the heart of a devil. To Tennyson he was
even more formidable. It is true that the lice are so many
today and they bite so innumberably that the author is
comparatively immune from their poison—no author now
abuses reviewers as violently as Dickens or obeys them as
submissively as Tennyson. Still, there are eruptions even
now in the press which lead us to believe that the reviewer's fang is still poisoned. But what part is affected by
his bite?—what is the true nature of the emotion he causes?
That is a complex question; but perhaps we can discover
something that will serve as answer by submitting the
author to a simple test. Take a sensitive author and place
before him a hostile review. Symptoms of pain and anger
rapidly develop. Next tell him that nobody save himself
will read those abusive remarks. In five or ten minutes the
pain which, if the attack had been delivered in public,
would have lasted a week and bred bitter rancour, is completely over. The temperature falls; indifference returns.
This proves that the sensitive part is the reputation; what
the victim feared was the effect of abuse upon the opinion
that other people had of him. He is afraid, too, of the
effect of abuse upon his purse. But the purse sensibility is
in most cases far less highly-developed than the reputation
sensibility. As for the artist's sensibility—his own opinion
of his own work—that is not touched by anything good
or bad that the reviewer says about it. The reputation sensibility however is still lively; and it will thus take some

time to persuade authors that the Gutter and Stamp system is as satisfactory as the present reviewing system. They will say that they have "reputations"—bladders of opinion formed by what other people think about them; and that these bladders are inflated or deflated by what is said of them in print. Still, under present conditions the time is at hand when even the author will believe that nobody thinks the better or the worse of him because he is praised or blamed in print. Soon he will come to realize that his interests—his desire for fame and money—are as effectively catered for by the Gutter and Stamp system as by the present reviewing system.

But even when this stage is reached, the author may still have some ground for complaint. The reviewer did serve some end besides that of inflating reputations and stimulating sales. And Mr. Nicolson has put his finger on it. "I want to tell them why I either like or dislike their work." The author wants to be told why Mr. Nicolson likes or dislikes his work. This is a genuine desire. It survives the test of privacy. Shut doors and windows; pull the curtains. Ensure that no fame accrues or money; and still it is a matter of the very greatest interest to a writer to know what an honest and intelligent reader thinks about his work.

4

At this point let us turn once more to the reviewer. There can be no doubt that his position at the present moment, judging both from the outspoken remarks of Mr. Nicolson and from the internal evidence of the reviews themselves, is extremely unsatisfactory. He has to write in haste and to write shortly. Most of the books he reviews are not worth the scratch of a pen upon paper—it is futile to refer them to "eternal standards." He knows further, as Matthew Arnold has stated, that even if the conditions were favourable, it is impossible for the living to judge the works of the living. Years, many years, according to Matthew Arnold, have to pass before it is possible to deliver an opinion that is not "only personal, but personal with passion." And the reviewer has one week. And authors are not dead but living. And the living are friends or enemies; have wives and families; personalities and politics. The reviewer knows that he is hampered, distracted, and prejudiced. Yet knowing all this and having proof in the wild contradictions of contemporary opinion that it is so, he has to submit a perpetual succession of new books to a mind as incapable of taking a fresh impression or of making a dispassionate statement as an old piece of blotting paper on a post office counter. He has to review; for he has to live; and he has to live, since most reviewers come of the educated class, according to the standards of that class. Thus he has to write often, and he has to write much. There is, it seems, only one alleviation of the horror, that he enjoys telling authors why he likes or dislikes their books.

5

The one element in reviewing that is of value to the reviewer himself (independently of the money earned) is the one element that is of value to the author. The problem then is how to preserve this value—the value of the dialogue as Mr. Nicolson calls it—and to bring both parties together in a union that is profitable, to the minds and purses of both. It should not be a difficult problem to solve. The medical profession has shown the way. With some differences the medical custom might be imitated— there are many resemblances between doctor and reviewer, between patient and author. Let the reviewers then abolish themselves or what relic remains of them, as reviewers, and resurrect themselves as doctors. Another name might be chosen—consultant, expositor or expounder; some credentials might be given, the books written rather than the examinations passed; and a list of those ready and authorized to practise made public. The writer then would submit his work to the judge of his choice; an appointment would be made; an interview arranged. In strict privacy, and with some formality—the fee, however, would be enough to ensure that the interview did not degenerate into tea-table gossip—doctor and writer would meet; and for an hour they would consult upon the book in question. They would talk, seriously and privately. This privacy in the first place would be an immeasurable advantage to them both. The consultant would speak honestly and openly, because the fear of affecting sales and of hurting feelings would be removed. Privacy would lessen the shop window temptation to cut a figure, to pay off scores. The consultant would have no library public to inform and consider; no reading public to impress and amuse. He could thus concentrate upon the book itself, and upon telling the author why he likes or dislikes it. The author would profit equally. An hour's private talk with a critic of his own choosing would be incalculably more valuable than the five hundred words of criticism mixed with extraneous matter that is now allotted him. He could state his case. He could point to his difficulties. He would no longer feel, as so often at present, that the critic is talking about something that he has not written. Further, he would have the advantage of coming into touch with a well-stored mind, housing other books and even other literatures, and thus other standards; with a live human being, not with a man in a mask. Many bogeys would lose their horns. The louse would become a man. By degrees the writer's "reputation" would drop off. He would become quit of that tiresome appendage and its irritable consequences—such are a few of the obvious and indisputable advantages that privacy would ensure.

Next there is the financial question—would the profession of expositor be as profitable as the profession of reviewer? How many authors are there who would wish to have an expert opinion on their work? The answer to this is to be heard crying daily and crying loudly in any publisher's office or in any author's post bag. "Give me advice," they repeat, "give me criticism." The number of authors seeking criticism and advice genuinely, not for advertising purposes but because their need is acute, is an abundant proof of the demand. But would they pay the doctor's fee of three guineas? When they discovered, as certainly they would, how much more an hour of talk holds, even if it costs three guineas, than the hurried letter which they now extort from the harassed publisher's reader, or the five hundred words which is all they can count on from the distracted reviewer, even the indigent would think it an investment worth making. Nor is it only the young and needy who seek advice. The art of writing is difficult; at every stage the opinion of an impersonal and disinterested critic would be of the highest value.

Who would not spout the family teapot in order to talk with Keats for an hour about poetry, or with Jane Austen about the art of fiction?

6

There remains finally the most important, but the most difficult of all these questions—what effect would the abolition of the reviewer have upon literature? Some reasons for thinking that the smashing of the shop window would make for the better health of that remote goddess have already been implied. The writer would withdraw into the darkness of the workshop; he would no longer carry on his difficult and delicate task like a trouser mender in Oxford Street, with a horde of reviewers pressing their noses to the glass and commenting to a curious crowd upon each stitch. Hence his self-consciousness would diminish and his reputation would shrivel. No longer puffed this way and that, now elated, now depressed, he could attend to his work. That might make for better writing. Again the reviewer, who must now earn his pence by cutting shop window capers to amuse the public and to advertise his skill, would have only the book to think of and the writer's need. That might make for better criticism.

But there might be other and more positive advantages. The Gutter and Stamp system by eliminating what now passes for literary criticism—those few words devoted to "why I like or dislike this book"—will save space. Four or five thousand words, possibly, might be saved in the course of a month or two. And an editor with that space at his disposal might not only express his respect for literature, but actually prove it. He might spend that space, even in a political daily or weekly, not upon stars and snippets, but upon unsigned and uncommercial literature—upon essays, upon criticism. There may be a Montaigne among us—a Montaigne now severed into futile slices of one thousand to fifteen hundred words weekly. Given time and space he might revive, and with him an admirable and now almost extinct form of art. Or there may be a critic among us—a Coleridge, a Matthew Arnold. He is now frittering himself away, as Mr. Nicolson has shown, upon a miscellaneous heap of poems, plays, novels, all to be reviewed in one column by Wednesday next. Given four thousand words, even twice a year, the critic might emerge, and with him those standards, those "eternal standards," which if they are never referred to, far from being eternal cease to exist. Do we not all know that Mr. A writes better or it may be worse than Mr. B? But is that all we want to know? Is that all we ought to ask?

But to sum up, or rather to heap a little cairn of conjectures and conclusions at the end of these scattered remarks for somebody else to knock down. The review, it is contended, increases self-consciousness and diminishes strength. The shop window and the looking-glass inhibit and confine. By putting in their place discussion—fearless and disinterested discussion—the writer would gain in range, in depth, in power. And this change would tell eventually upon the public mind. Their favourite figure of fun, the author, that hybrid between the peacock and the ape, would be removed from their derision, and in his place would be an obscure workman doing his job in the darkness of the workshop and not unworthy of respect. A new relationship might come into being, less petty and less personal than the old. A new interest in literature, a new respect for literature might follow. And, financial advantages apart, what a ray of light that would bring, what a ray of pure sunlight a critical and hungry public would bring into the darkness of the workshop!

NOTE

By Leonard Woolf

This essay raises questions of considerable importance to literature, journalism, and the reading public. With many of its arguments I agree, but some of its conclusions seem to me doubtful because the meaning of certain facts has been ignored or their weight under-estimated. The object of this note is to draw attention to these facts and to suggest how they may modify the conclusions.

In the eighteenth century a revolution took place in the reading public and in the economic organization of literature as a profession. Goldsmith, who lived through the revolution, has given us a clear picture of what took place and an admirable analysis of its effects. There was an enormous expansion of the reading public. Hitherto the writer had written and the publisher published for a small, cultured, literary public. The author and publisher depended economically upon a patron or patrons, and books were luxury articles produced for a small, luxury-consuming class. The expansion of the reading public destroyed this system and substituted another. It became economically possible for the publisher to publish books for "the public"; to sell a sufficient number of copies to pay his expenses, including a living wage to the author, and make a profit for himself. This killed the patronage system and eliminated the patron. It opened the way to the cheap book, read by thousands instead of by tens. The author, if he wanted to make a living by writing, now had to write for "the public" instead of for the patron. Whether this change of system was on the whole good or bad for literature and the writer may be a subject of dispute; it is, however, to be noted that Goldsmith, who had experienced both systems and is generally considered to have produced at least one "work of art," was wholeheartedly in favour of the new. The new system inevitably produced the reviewer, just as it produced modern journalism, of which the reviewer is only a small and particular phase. As the number of readers increased and with them the number of books and writers and publishers, two things happened: writing and publishing became highly competitive trades or professions and a need arose of giving to the vast reading public information regarding the contents and quality of the books published so that each person would have something to go on in making his selection of the books to read out of the thousands published.

Modern journalism saw its opportunity to meet this demand for information about new books and invented reviewing and the reviewer. As the size, differentiation, and quality of the reading public have changed, so too have the number, variety, and quality of books changed. This has entailed, no doubt, a change in the number, the variety, and the quality of reviewers. But the function of the reviewer remains fundamentally the same: it is to give to readers a description of the book and an estimate of its quality in order that he may know whether or not it is the kind of book which he may want to read.

Reviewing is therefore quite distinct from literary criticism. The reviewer, unlike the critic, in 999 cases out of 1,000 has nothing to say to the author; he is talking to the reader. On the rare occasions when he finds that he is reviewing a real work of art, if he is honest and intelligent, he will have to warn his readers against the fact and descend or ascend for a short time into the regions of true criticism. But to assume that, because of this, the art of reviewing is easy and mechanical is a complete misapprehension. I can speak with the experience of a journalist who was responsible for years for getting reviews and reviewers on a reputable paper. Reviewing is a highly-skilled profession. There are incompetent and dishonest reviewers, just as there are incompetent and dishonest politicians, carpenters, and writers; but the standard of competence and honesty is as high in reviewing as in any other trade or profession of which I have had inside knowledge. It is not at all an easy thing to give a clear, intelligent, and honest analysis of a novel or a book of poems. The fact that in the exceptional cases in which the book reviewed may have some claims to be a new work of art two reviewers take sometimes diametrically opposite views is really irrelevant and does not alter the fact that the vast majority of reviews give an accurate and often interesting account of the book reviewed.

Literary magazines have failed because they have fallen between two stools. The modern reading public is not interested in literary criticism and you cannot sell it to them. The monthly or quarterly which hopes to print literary criticism and pay is doomed to disappointment. Most of them have therefore tried to butter the bread of criticism with reviewing. But the public which wants reviewing will not pay 2s. 6d., 3s. 6d., or 5s. for it monthly or quarterly when they can get it just as good in the dailies and weeklies.

So much for the reviewer, the reading public, and the critic. One word about the writer. The writer who wants to write works of art and make a living by doing so is in a difficult position. As an artist the critic and criticism may be of immense value or interest to him. But he has no right to complain that the reviewer does not perform the function of critic for him. If he wants criticism, he should adopt the ingenious suggestion made in this essay. But that will not make the reviewer unnecessary or unimportant to him. If he wants to sell his books to the great reading public and the circulating libraries, he will still need the reviewer—and that is why he will probably, like Tennyson and Dickens, continue to abuse the reviewer when the review is not favourable.

Modern Letters[1]

AMONG the commonplaces, this one takes a prominent place—that the art of letter writing is dead; that it flourished in the days of the frank, dwindled under the penny post, and was dealt its death blow by the telephone—now it lies feebly expiring. Once in a way it might be well to look into this truism, to examine the day's post, to compare the flimsy sheets of today, rapidly written over in such various hands with those statelier compositions that were a week, or perhaps a month, on the road, and were, therefore, written in much better hands upon paper that still lies crisp between thumb and finger.

There, of course, lie some of the chief distinctions between the old letters and the new, more care, more time went to their composition. But need we take it for granted that care and time are wholly to the good? A letter then was written to be read and not by one person only. It was a composition that did its best to deserve the expense it cost. The arrival of the post was an occasion. The sheets were not for the waste-paper basket in five minutes, but for handing round, and reading aloud and then for deposit in some family casket as a record. These undoubtedly were inducements to careful composition, to the finishing of sentences, the artful disposition of trifles, the polish of phrases, the elaboration of arguments and the arts of the writing master. But whether Sir William Temple, who

[1] Written in 1930.

wished to know if Dorothy was well and happy and to be assured that she loved him, enjoyed her letters as much as we enjoy them is perhaps doubtful. Sir Horace Mann or West or Gray did not, one guesses, break the seals of Walpole's thick packets in a hurry. One can imagine that they waited for a good fire, and a bottle of wine, and a group of friends and then read the witty and delightful pages aloud, in perfect confidence that nothing was going to be said that was too private for another ear—indeed, the very opposite was the case—such wit, such polish, such a budget of news was too good for a single person and demanded to be shared with others. Often, more often than not, the great letter writers were suppressed novelists, frustrated essayists born before their time. In our day, Dorothy Osborne would have been an admirable biographer, and Walpole one of our most distinguished and prolific journalists—whether to the profit or loss of the world it is impossible to say. Indisputably they practised to perfection a peculiar art, born of special circumstances, but to go on, as we in our rash condemnatory mood so often do, to say that their art was the art of letter writing and that we have lost it, and that our art, because it differs from theirs, is no art at all, seems an unnecessary act of pessimism and self-depreciation.

Here, of course, there should be laid down once and for all the principles of letter writing. But since Aristotle never got so far and since the art has always been an anonymous and hand-to-mouth practice, whose chief adepts would have been scandalized had they been convicted of design or intention, it will be more convenient to leave those principles obscure. Let us turn, therefore, without a yard measure to examine the morning's post,

and those posts of other mornings that have been thrust
pell-mell into old drawers more from laziness than from
any desire to preserve a record for posterity. These pages
came by post, were addressed by one person to one person,
fell into the letter-box, and were laid on the breakfast
table—that is all. In the first place, they are very badly
written. Whether the invention of the fountain pen is to
blame, certainly a well-formed handwriting is now the
rarest of happy discoveries. Moreover, no common style
of writing prevails. Here it slants, here it bends back; it is
rapid, and running in almost every case. The paper too is
of all sizes and coloured blue, green, yellow; much of it
is shoddy enough, and coated with some smooth glaze
which will no doubt turn traitor before fifty years are
passed. This haphazard harum-scarum individuality is reflected in the style. There is none at first showing—each
writer makes his own. Urgent need is the begetter of most
of these pages. The writers have forgotten, or want to
know, or wish to be sure, or must remind one. A sentence
about the weather may be thrown in as makeweight; an
initial is scrawled, the stamp stuck on upside down, and
so off it goes. The whole affair is purely utilitarian.

Besides these, however, though not so common, are letters written mostly from abroad with the old wish to get
into touch with a friend, to give news, to communicate
in short what would be said in a private conversation. A
friend marooned in a Spanish inn, one travelling in Italy,
one who has taken up his residence in India, these are now
the nearest representatives of Cowper at Olney writing to
Lady Hesketh at Bath. But with what a difference! In the
first place nobody would be so rash as to read a modern
letter, even from Rangoon, in mixed company. One does

not know what is coming next. Modern letter writers are highly indiscreet. Almost certainly there is some phrase that will cause pain. Very careful editing is needed before a letter can be read aloud to friends. And then our conventions allow of so much freedom of speech—language is so colloquial, slap dash, and unpruned that the presence of someone of another generation would be a grave deterrent. What is sincerity might be mistaken for coarseness. Further, the modern letter writer is so casual, and so careless of the forms and ceremonies of literature, that the pages do not stand the ordeal of reading aloud well. But then, on the other hand, the privacy, the intimacy of these letters make them far more immediately interesting and exciting than the old letters. There is no news for the whole world in them, because newspapers have made that unneeded. Only one person is written to, and the writer had some reason for wishing to write to him or her in particular. Its meaning is private, its news intimate. For these reasons it is a rash incriminating document and the proper place for it is not between the pages of the family Bible but in a drawer with a key.

There then, pell-mell, with all their imperfections thick upon them, they are stuffed—today's post on top of yesterday's post and so on, undocketed, unsorted, as they came. And as the years pass so they accumulate. The drawers are almost bursting with letters; some of the writers are dead, others have vanished; others write no more. What is to be done with them? Let us look quickly through them and see whether the time has not come to burn them. But once begin dipping and diving, reading this and reading that, and what to do with them is completely forgotten. Page after page is turned. Here are invitations to parties ten years old. Here are postcards demanding the return of lost umbrellas. Here are childish sheets thanking for boxes of water-colour paints. Here are calculations about the cost of building a house. Here are long, wild, profuse letters, all about somebody who did not want, it seems, to marry somebody else. The effect is indescribable. One could swear one heard certain voices, smelt certain flowers, was in Italy, was in Spain, was horribly bored, terribly unhappy, tremendously excited all over again. If the art of letter writing consists in exciting the emotions, in bringing back the past, in reviving a day, a moment, nay a very second, of past time, then these obscure correspondents, with their hasty haphazard ways, their gibes and flings, their irreverence and mockery, their careful totting up of days and dates, their general absorption in the moment and entire carelessness what posterity will think of them, beat Cowper, Walpole, and Edward Fitzgerald hollow. Yes, but what to do with them? The question remains, for as one reads it becomes perfectly plain that the art of letter writing has now reached a stage, thanks to the penny post and telephone, where it is not dead—that is the last word to apply to it—but so much alive as to be quite unprintable. The best letters of our time are precisely those that can never be published.

Reading

WHY did they choose this particular spot to build the house on? For the sake of the view perhaps. Not, I suppose, that they looked at views as we look at them, but rather as an incentive to ambition, as a proof of power. For in time they were lords of that valley, green with trees, and owned at least all that part of the moor that lies on the right-hand side of the road. At any rate the house was built here, here a stop was put to trees and ferns; here one room was laid upon another, and down some feet into the earth foundations were thrust and deep cool cellars hollowed out.

The house had its library; a long low room, lined with little burnished books, folios, and stout blocks of divinity. The cases were carved with birds pecking at clusters of wooden fruit. A sallow priest tended them, dusting the books and the carved birds at the same time. Here they all are; Homer and Euripides; Chaucer; then Shakespeare; and the Elizabethans, and following come the plays of the Restoration, more handled these, and greased as if from midnight reading, and so down to our time or very near it, Cowper, Burns, Scott, Wordsworth and the rest. I liked that room. I liked the view across country that one had from the window, and the blue line between the gap of the trees on the moor was the North Sea. I liked to read there. One drew the pale armchair to the window, and so the light fell over the shoulder upon the page. The shadow of the gardener mowing the lawn sometimes crossed it, as he led his pony in rubber shoes up and down, the machine giving a little creak, which seemed the very voice of summer, as it turned and drew another broad belt of green by the side of the one just cut. Like the wake of ships I used to think them, especially when they curved round the flower beds for islands, and the fuchsias might be lighthouses, and the geraniums, by some freak of fancy, were Gibraltar; there were the red coats of the invincible British soldiers upon the rock.

Then tall ladies used to come out of the house and go down the grass drives to be met by the gentlemen of those days, carrying racquets and white balls which I could just see, through the bushes that hid the tennis lawn, bounding over the net, and the figures of the players passed to and fro. But they did not distract me from my book; any more than the butterflies visiting the flowers, or the bees doing their more serious business on the same blossoms, or the thrushes hopping lightly from the low branches of the sycamore to the turf, taking two steps in the direction of some slug or fly, and then hopping, with light decision, back to the low branch again. None of these things distracted me in those days; and somehow or another, the windows being open, and the book held so that it rested upon a background of escallonia hedges and distant blue, instead of being a book it seemed as if what I read was laid upon the landscape not printed, bound, or sewn up, but somehow the product of trees and fields and the hot summer sky, like the air which swam, on fine mornings, round the outlines of things.

These were circumstances, perhaps, to turn one's mind to the past. Always behind the voice, the figure, the fountain there seemed to stretch an immeasurable avenue, that ran to a point of other voices, figures, fountains which tapered out indistinguishably upon the furthest horizon. If I looked down at my book I could see Keats and Pope behind him, and then Dryden and Sir Thomas Browne— hosts of them merging in the mass of Shakespeare, behind whom, if one peered long enough, some shapes of men in pilgrims' dress emerged, Chaucer perhaps, and again—who was it? some uncouth poet scarcely able to syllable his words; and so they died away.

But, as I say, even the gardener leading his pony was part of the book, and, straying from the actual page, the eye rested upon his face, as if one reached it through a great depth of time. That accounted for the soft swarthy tint of the cheeks, and the lines of his body, scarcely disguised by the coarse brown stuff of his coat, might have belonged to any labouring man in any age, for the clothing of the field labourer has changed little since Saxon days, and a half-shut eye can people a field much as it was before the Norman conquest. This man took his place naturally by the side of those dead poets. He ploughed; he sowed; he drank; he marched in battle sometimes; he sang his song; he came courting and went underground raising only a green wave in the turf of the churchyard, but leaving boys and girls behind him to continue his name and lead the pony across the lawn, these hot summer mornings.

Through that same layer of time one could see, with equal clearness, the more splendid figures of knights and ladies. One could see them; that is true. The ripe apricot of the ladies' dress, the gilt crimson of the knights set floating coloured images in the dark ripples of the lake water. In the church too you see them laid out as if in triumphant repose, their hands folded, their eyes shut, their favourite hounds at their feet, and all the shields of their ancestors, faintly touched still with blue and red, supporting them. Thus garnished and made ready they seem to await, to expect, in confidence. The day of judgment dawns. His eyes open, his hand seeks hers, he leads her forth through the opened doors and the lines of angels with their trumpets, to some smoother lawn, more regal residence and mansions of whiter masonry. Meanwhile, the silence is scarcely broken by a word. It is, after all, a question of seeing them.

For the art of speech came late to England. These Fanshawes and Leghs, Verneys, Pastons, and Hutchinsons, all well endowed by birth and nature and leaving behind them such a treasure of inlaid wood and old furniture, things curiously made and delicately figured, left with it only a very broken message or one so stiff that the ink seems to have dried as it traced the words. Did they, then, enjoy these possessions in silence, or was the business of life transacted in a stately way to match these stiff polysyllables and branching periods? Or, like children on a Sunday, did they compose themselves and cease their chatter when they sat down to write what would pass from hand to hand, serve for winter gossip round a dozen firesides, and be laid up at length with other documents of importance in the dry room above the kitchen fireplace?

"In October, as I told you," wrote Lady Fanshawe some time about the year 1601, "my husband and I went into France by way of Portsmouth where, walking by the seaside . . . two ships of the Dutch shot bullets at us, so near that we heard them whiz by us: at which I called my husband to make haste back, and began to run. But he altered not his pace, saying, if we must be killed, it were as good to be killed walking as running." There, surely, it is the spirit of dignity that controls her. The bullets whiz across the sand, but Sir Richard walks no faster, and summons up his idea of death—death visible, tangible, an enemy, but an enemy of flesh and blood to be met courageously with drawn sword like a gentleman—which temper she (poor woman) admires, though she cannot, on the beach at Portsmouth, altogether imitate. Dignity, loyalty, magnanimity—such are the virtues she would commend, and frame her speech to, checking it from its natural slips and trifles, and making believe that life for people of gentle birth and high morality was thus decorous and sublime. The pen, too, when the small shot of daily life came whizzing about her—eighteen children in twenty-one years she bore and buried the greater part—must curb itself to walk slowly, not to run. Writing is with them, as it can no longer be with us, making; making something that will endure and wear a brave face in the eyes of posterity. For posterity is the judge of these ideals, and it is for that distant and impartial public that Lady Fanshawe writes and Lucy Hutchinson, and not for John in London or Elizabeth married and gone to live in Sussex; there is no daily post for children and friends bringing to the breakfast table not only news of crops and servants, visitors and bad weather, but the subtler narrative of love and coldness, affection waning or carried on secure; there is no language it seems for that frail burden. Horace Walpole, Jane Carlyle, Edward Fitzgerald are ghosts on the very outskirts of time. Thus these ancestors of ours, though stately and fair to look upon, are silent; they move through galleries and parks in the midst of a little oasis of silence which holds the intruding modern spirit at bay. Here, again, are the Leghs; generations upon generations of them, all red haired, all living at Lyme, which has been building these three centuries and more, all men of education, character, and opportunity, and all, by modern standards, dumb. They will write of a fox hunt and how afterward "a Bowle of Hott Punch with ye Fox's foot stew'd in it" was drunk, and how "Sir Willm drunk pretty plentifully, and just at last perceiv'd he should be fuddled, 'but,' quoth he, 'I care not if I am, I have kill'd a fox today.'" But having killed their fox, drunk their punch, raced their horses, fought their cocks, and toasted, discreetly, the King over the water, or, more openly, "A Fresh Earth and High Metaled Terrier," their lips shut, their eyes close; they have nothing more to say to us. Taciturn or crass as we may think them, dull men inheriting their red hair and very little brain beneath it, nevertheless more business was discharged by them, more of life took its mould from them than we can measure, or, indeed, dispense with. If Lyme had been blotted out and the thousand other houses of equal importance which lay about England like little fortresses of civilization, where you could read books, act plays, make laws, meet your neighbours, and talk with strangers from abroad, if these spaces won from the encroaching barbarity had not persisted till the foothold was firm and the swamp withheld, how would our more delicate spirits have fared—our writers, thinkers, musicians, artists—without a wall to shelter under, or flowers upon which to sun their wings? Waging war year after year upon winter and rough weather, needing all their faculties to keep the roof sound, the larder full, the children taught and clothed, dependents cared for, naturally our ancestors appear in their spare time rather surly and silent—as plough-boys after a long day's work scrape the mud from their boots, stretch the cramped muscles of their backs, and stumble off to bed without thought of book or pen or evening paper. The little language of affection and intimacy which we seek in vain necessitates soft pillows, easy chairs, silver forks, private rooms; it must have at its command a store of little words, nimble and domesticated, coming at the call of the lightest occasion, refining themselves to the faintest shadow. Above all perhaps, good roads and carriages, frequent meetings, partings, festivities, alliances, and ruptures are needed to break up the splendid sentences; easy chairs it may be were the death of English prose. The annals of an old and obscure family like the Leghs show clearly enough how the slow process of furnishing the bare rooms and taking coach for London, as a matter of course, abolish its isolation, merge the dialect of the district into the common speech of the land, and teach, by degrees, a uniform method of spelling. One can see in fancy the face itself changing, and the manner of father to son, mother to daughter, losing what must have been their tremendous formality, their unquestioned authority. But what dignity, what beauty broods over it all!

It's a hot summer morning. The sun has browned the outermost leaves of the elm trees, and already, since the gale, one or two lie on the grass, having completed the whole range of existence from bud to withered fibre and become nothing but leaves to be swept up for the autumn bonfires. Through the green arches the eye with a curious desire seeks the blue which it knows to be the blue of the sea; and knowing it can somehow set the mind off upon

a voyage, can somehow encircle all this substantial earth
with the flowing and the unpossessed. The sea—the sea—I
must drop my book, the pious Mrs. Hutchinson, and leave
her to make what terms she can with Margaret, Duchess
of Newcastle. There's a sweeter air outside—how spicy,
even on a still day, after the house!—and bushes of verbena
and southernwood yield a leaf as one passes to be crushed
and smelt. If we could see also what we can smell—if, at
this moment crushing the southernwood, I could go back
through the long corridor of sunny mornings, boring my
way through hundreds of Augusts, I should come in the
end, passing a host of less-important figures, to no less a
person than Queen Elizabeth herself. Whether some tinted
wax-work is the foundation of my view, I do not know;
but she always appears very distinctly in the same guise.
She flaunts across the terrace superbly and a little stiffly
like the peacock spreading its tail. She seems slightly infirm, so that one is half inclined to smile; and then she raps
out her favourite oath as Lord Herbert of Cherbury heard
it, as he bowed his knee among the courtiers, when, far
from being infirm, she shows a masculine and rather repul-
sive vigour. Perhaps, under all that stiff brocade, she has
not washed her shrivelled old body? She breakfasts off beer
and meat and handles the bones with fingers rough with
rubies. It may be so, yet Elizabeth, of all our kings and
queens, seems most fit for that gesture which bids the great
sailors farewell, or welcomes them home to her presence
again, her imagination still lusting for the strange tales
they bring her, her imagination still young in its wrinkled
and fantastic casket. It is their youth; it is their immense
fund of credulity; their minds still unwritten over and
capable of such enormous designs as the American forests

cast upon them, or the Spanish ships, or the savages, or the soul of man—this is what makes it impossible, walking the terrace, not to look upon the blue sea line, and think of their ships. The ships, Froude says, were no bigger than a modern English yacht. As they shrink and assume the romantic proportions of the Elizabethan ship, so the sea runs enormously larger and freer and with bigger waves upon it than the sea of our time. The summons to explore, to bring back dyes and roots and oil, and find a market for wool and iron and cloth has been heard in the villages of the West. The little company gathers together somewhere off Greenwich. The courtiers come running to the palace windows; the Privy Councillors press their faces to the panes. The guns are shot off in salute, and then, as the ships swing down the tide, one sailor after another walks the hatches, climbs the shrouds, stands upon the mainyards to wave his friends a last farewell. For directly England and the coast of France are beneath the horizon, the ships swim into the unfamiliar, the air has its voices, the sea its lions and serpents, evaporations of fire and tumultuous whirlpools. The clouds but sparely hide the Divinity; the limbs of Satan are almost visible. Riding in company through the storm, suddenly one light disappears; Sir Humfrey Gilbert has gone beneath the waves: when morning comes they seek his ship in vain. Sir Hugh Willoughby sails to discover the North-West passage, and makes no return. Sometimes, a ragged and worn-out man comes knocking at the door, and claims to be the boy who went years ago to sea and is now come back to his father's house. "Sir William his father and my lady his mother knew him not to be their son, until they found a secret mark, which was a wart upon one of his knees."

But he brings with him a black stone, veined with gold, or an ivory tusk, or a lamp of silver, and stories of how such stones are strewn about to be picked up off the ground as you will. What if the passage to the fabled land of uncounted riches lay only a little further up the coast? What if the known world was only the prelude to some more splendid panorama? When, after the long voyage, the ships dropped anchor in the great river of the Plate and the men went exploring through the undulating lands, startling the grazing herds of deer and glimpsing between the trees the dusky limbs of savages, they filled their pockets with pebbles that might be emeralds, or rubies, or sand that might be gold. Sometimes, rounding a headland, they saw far off a string of savages slowly descending to the beach bearing on their heads and linking their shoulders together with heavy burdens for the Spanish king.

These are the fine stories, used effectively all through the West Country to decoy the strong men lounging by the harbour side to leave their nets and fish for gold. Less glorious but more urgent, considering the state of the country, was the summons of the more serious-minded to set on foot some intercourse between the merchants of England and the merchants of the East. For lack of work, this staid observer wrote, the poor of England were driven to crime and "daily consumed with the gallows." Wool they had in plenty, fine, soft, strong, and durable; but no market for it and few dyes. Gradually owing to the boldness of private travellers, the native stock had been improved and embellished. Beasts and plants had been imported; and along with them the seeds of all our roses. Gradually little groups of merchant men settled here and there on the borders of the unexplored, and through their

fingers the precious stream of coloured and rare and curious things begins slowly and precariously to flow towards
London; our fields are sown with new flowers. In the
south and west, in America and the East Indies, the life
was pleasanter and success more splendid; yet in the land
of long winters and squat-faced savages the very darkness and strangeness draw the imagination. Here they are,
three or four men from the west of England set down in
the white landscape with only the huts of savages near
them, and left to make what bargains they can and pick
up what knowledge they can, until the little ships, no
bigger than yachts, appear at the mouth of the bay next
summer. Strange must have been their thoughts; strange
the sense of the unknown; and of themselves, the isolated
English, burning on the very rim of the dark, and the dark
full of unseen splendours. One of them, carrying a charter
from his company in London, went inland as far as
Moscow, and there saw the Emperor, "sitting in his chair
of estate, with his crown on his head, and a staff of goldsmith work in his left hand." All the ceremony that he
saw is carefully written out, and the sight upon which the
English merchant, the vanguard of civilization, first set
eyes has the brilliancy still of a Roman vase or other shining ornament dug up and stood for a moment in the sun
before, exposed to the air, seen by millions of eyes, it dulls
and crumbles away. There, all these centuries, the glories
of Moscow, the glories of Constantinople, have flowered
unseen. Many are preserved as if under shades of glass.
The Englishman, however, is bravely dressed for the occasion, leads in his hand, perhaps, "three fair mastiffs in
coats of red cloth" and carries a letter from Elizabeth "the

paper whereof did smell most fragrantly of camphor and ambergris, and the ink of perfect musk."

Yet if by means of these old records, courts and palaces and Sultans' presence chambers are once more displayed, stranger still are the little disks of light calling out of obscurity for a second some unadorned savage, falling like lantern light upon moving figures. Here is a story of the savage caught somewhere off the coast of Labrador, taken to England and shown about like a wild beast. Next year they bring him back and fetch a woman savage on board to keep him company. When they see each other they blush; they blush profoundly; the sailor notices it but knows not why it is. And later the two savages set up house together on board ship, she attending to his wants, he nursing her in sickness, but living, as the sailors note, in perfect chastity. The erratic searchlight cast by these records falling for a second upon those blushing cheeks three hundred years ago, among the snow, sets up that sense of communication which we are apt to get only from fiction. We seem able to guess why they blushed; the Elizabethans would notice it, but it has waited over three hundred years for us to interpret it.

There are not perhaps enough blushes to keep the attention fixed upon the broad yellow-tinged pages of Hakluyt's book. The attention wanders. Still if it wanders, it wanders in the green shade of forests. It floats far out at sea. It is soothed almost to sleep by the sweet-toned voices of pious men talking the melodious language, much broader and more sonorous sounding than our own, of the Elizabethan age. They are men of fine limbs, arched brows, beneath which the oval eyes are full and luminous, and thin golden rings are in their ears. What need have they of blushes? What meeting would rouse such emotions in them? Why should they whittle down feelings and thoughts so as to cause embarrassment and bring lines between the eyes and perplex them, so that it is no longer a ship or a man that comes before them, but some thing doubtful as a phantom, and more of a symbol than a fact? If one tires of the long dangerous and memorable voyages of M. Ralph Fitch, M. Roger Bodenham, M. Anthony Jenkinson, M. John Lok, the Earl of Cumberland and others, to Pegu and Siam, Candia and Chio, Aleppo and Muscovy, it is for the perhaps unsatisfactory reason that they make no mention of oneself; seem altogether oblivious of such an organism; and manage to exist in comfort and opulence nevertheless. For simplicity of speech by no means implies rudeness or emptiness. Indeed this free-flowing, equable narrative, though now occupied merely with the toils and adventures of ordinary ships' companies, has its own true balance, owing to the poise of brain and body arrived at by the union of adventure and physical exertion with minds still tranquil and unstirred as the summer sea.

In all this there is no doubt much exaggeration, much misunderstanding. One is tempted to impute to the dead the qualities we find lacking in ourselves. There is balm for our restlessness in conjuring up visions of Elizabethan magnanimity; the very flow and fall of the sentences lulls us asleep, or carries us along as upon the back of a large, smooth-paced cart horse, through green pastures. It is the pleasantest atmosphere on a hot summer's day. They talk of their commodities and there you see them; more clearly and separately in bulk, colour, and variety than the goods brought by steamer and piled upon docks; they talk of fruit; the red and yellow globes hang unpicked on virgin trees; so with the lands they sight; the morning mist is only just now lifting and not a flower has been plucked. The grass has long whitened tracks upon it for the first time. With the towns too discovered for the first time it is the same thing. And so, as you read on across the broad pages with as many slips and somnolences as you like, the illusion rises and holds you of banks slipping by on either side, of glades opening out, of white towers revealed, of gilt domes and ivory minarets. It is, indeed, an atmosphere, not only soft and fine, but rich, too, with more than one can grasp at any single reading.

So that, if at last I shut the book, it was only that my mind was sated, not the treasure exhausted. Moreover, what with reading and ceasing to read, taking a few steps this way and then pausing to look at the view, that same view had lost its colours, and the yellow page was almost too dim to decipher. So the book must be stood in its place, to deepen the brown line of shadow which the folios made on the wall. The books gently swelled neath my hand as I drew it across them in the dark. Travels, histories, memoirs, the fruit of innumerable lives. The dusk was brown with them. Even the hand thus sliding seemed to feel beneath its palm fulness and ripeness. Standing at the window and looking out into the garden, the lives of all these books filled the room behind with a soft murmur. Truly, a deep sea, the past, a tide which will overtake and overflow us. Yes, the tennis players looked half transparent already, as they came up the grass lawn to the house, the game being over. The tall lady stooped and picked a pallid rose; and the balls which the gentleman kept dancing up and down upon his racquet, as he walked beside her, were dim little spheres against the deep green hedge. Then, as they passed inside, the moths came out, the swift grey moths of the dusk, that only visit flowers for a second, never settling, but hanging an inch or two above the yellow of the Evening Primroses, vibrating to a blur. It was, I supposed, nearly time to go into the woods.

About an hour previously, several pieces of flannel soaked in rum and sugar had been pinned to a number of trees. The business of dinner now engrossing the grown-up people we made ready our lantern, our poison jar, and took our butterfly nets in our hands. The road that skirted the wood was so pale that its hardness grated upon our boots unexpectedly. It was the last strip of reality, how-ever, off which we stepped into the gloom of the unknown. The lantern shoved its wedge of light through the dark, as though the air were a fine black snow piling itself up in banks on either side of the yellow beam. The direction of the trees was known to the leader of the party, who walked ahead, and seemed to draw us, unheeding darkness or fear, further and further into the unknown world. Not only has the dark the power to extinguish light, but it also buries under it a great part of the human spirit. We hardly spoke, and then only in low voices which made little head-way against the thoughts that filled us. The little irregular beam of light seemed the only thing that kept us together, and like a rope prevented us from falling asunder and being engulfed. It went on indefatigably all the time, mak-ing tree and bush stand forth, in their strange night-dress of paler green. Then we were told to halt while the leader went forward to ascertain which of the trees had been prepared, since it was necessary to approach gradually lest the moths should be startled by the light and fly off. We waited in a group, and the little circle of forest where we stood became as if we saw it through the lens of a very powerful magnifying glass. Every blade of grass looked larger than by day, and the crevices in the bark much more sharply cut. Our faces showed pale and as if detached in a circle. The lantern had not stood upon the ground for ten seconds before we heard (the sense of hearing too was much more acute) little crackling sounds which seemed connected with a slight waving and bending in the surrounding grass. Then there emerged here a grasshopper, there a beetle, and here again a daddy longlegs, awkwardly making his way from blade to blade. Their movements were all so awkward that they made one think of sea creatures crawling on the floor of the sea. They went straight, as if by common consent, to the lantern, and were beginning to slide or clamber up the glass panes when a shout from the leader told us to advance. The light was turned very cautiously towards the tree; first it rested upon the grass at the foot; then it mounted a few inches of the trunk; as it mounted our excitement became more and more intense; then it gradually enveloped the flannel and the cataracts of falling treacle. As it did so, several wings flitted round us. The light was covered. Once more it was cautiously turned on. There were no whirring wings this time, but here and there, dotted about on the veins of sweet stuff, were soft brown lumps. These lumps seemed unspeakably precious, too deeply attached to the liquid to be disturbed. Their probosces were deep plunged, and as they drew in the sweetness, their wings quivered slightly as if in ecstasy. Even when the light was full upon them they could not tear themselves away, but sat there, quivering a little more uneasily perhaps, but allowing us to examine the tracery on the upperwing, those stains, spots, and veinings by which we decided their fate. Now and again a large moth dashed through the light. This served to increase our excitement. After taking those we wanted and gently tapping the unneeded on the nose so that they dropped off and began crawling through the grass in the direction of their sugar, we went on to the next tree. Cautiously shielding the light, we saw from far off the glow of two red lamps which faded as the light turned upon them; and there emerged the splendid body which wore those two red lamps at its head. Great underwings of glowing crimson were displayed. He was almost still, as if he had alighted with his wing open and had fallen into a trance of pleasure. He seemed to stretch across the tree, and beside him other moths looked only like little lumps and knobs on the bark. He was so splendid to look upon and so immobile that perhaps we were reluctant to end him; and yet when, as if guessing our intention and resuming a flight that had been temporarily interrupted, he roamed away, it seemed as if we had lost a possession of infinite value. Somebody cried out sharply. The lantern bearer flashed his light in the direction which the moth had taken. The space surrounding us seemed vast. Then we stood the light upon the ground, and once more after a few seconds, the grass bent, and the insects came scrambling from all quarters, greedy and yet awkward in their desire to partake of the light. Just as the eyes grow used to dimness and make out shapes where none were visible before, so sitting on the ground we felt we were surrounded by life, innumerable creatures were stirring among the trees; some creeping through the grass, others roaming through the air. It was a very still night, and the leaves intercepted any light from the young moon. Now and again a deep sigh seemed to breathe from somewhere near us, succeeded by sighs less deep, more wavering and in rapid succession, after which there was profound stillness. Perhaps it was alarming to have these evidences of unseen lives. It needed great resolution and the fear of appearing a coward to take up the light and penetrate still further into the depths of the wood. Somehow this world of night seemed hostile to us. Cold, alien, and unyielding, as if pre-occupied with matters in which human beings could have no part. But the most distant tree still remained to be visited. The leader advanced unrelentingly. The white strip of road upon which our boots had grated now seemed for ever lost. We had left that world of lights and homes hours ago. So we pressed on to this remote tree in the most dense part of the forest. It stood there as if upon the very verge of the world. No moth could have come as far as this. Yet as the trunk was revealed, what did we see? The scarlet underwing was already there, immobile as before, astride a vein of sweetness, drinking deep. With-out waiting a second this time the poison pot was un-covered and adroitly manœuvred so that as he sat there the moth was covered and escape cut off. There was a flash of scarlet within the glass. Then he composed himself with folded wings. He did not move again.

The glory of the moment was great. Our boldness in coming so far was rewarded, and at the same time it seemed as though we had proved our skill against the hos-tile and alien force. Now we could go back to bed and to the safe house. And then, standing there with the moth safely in our hands, suddenly a volley of shot rang out, a hollow rattle of sound in the deep silence of the wood which had I know not what of mournful and ominous about it. It waned and spread through the forest: it died away, then another of those deep sighs arose. An enormous silence succeeded. "A tree," we said at last. A tree had fallen.

What is it that happens between the hour of midnight and dawn, the little shock, the queer uneasy moment, as of eyes half open to the light, after which sleep is never so sound again? Is it experience, perhaps—repeated shocks, each unfelt at the time, suddenly loosening the fabric? breaking something away? Only this image suggests collapse and disintegration, whereas the process I have in mind is just the opposite. It is not destructive whatever it may be, one might say that it was rather of a creative character.

Something definitely happens. The garden, the butterflies, the morning sounds, trees, apples, human voices have emerged, stated themselves. As with a rod of light order has been imposed upon tumult; form upon chaos. Perhaps it would be simpler to say that one wakes, after Heaven knows what internal process, with a sense of mastery. Familiar people approach all sharply outlined in morning light. Through the tremor and vibration of daily custom one discerns bone and form, endurance and permanence. Sorrow will have the power to effect this sudden arrest of the fluidity of life, and joy will have the same power. Or it may come without apparent cause, imperceptibly, much as some bud feels a sudden release in the night and is found in the morning with all its petals shaken free. At any rate the voyages and memoirs, all the lumber and wreckage and accumulation of time which has deposited itself so thickly upon our shelves and grows like a moss at the foot of literature, is no longer definite enough for our needs. Another sort of reading matches better with the morning hours. This is not the time for foraging and rummaging, for half-closed eyes and gliding voyages. We want something that has been shaped and clarified, cut to catch the light, hard as gem or rock with the seal of human experience in it, and yet sheltering as in a clear gem the flame which burns now so high and now sinks so low in our own hearts. We want what is timeless and contemporary. But one might exhaust all images, and run words through one's fingers like water and yet not say why it is that on such a morning one wakes with a desire for poetry.

There is no difficulty in finding poetry in England. Every English home is full of it. Even the Russians have not a deeper fountain of spiritual life. With us it is, of course, sunk very deep; hidden beneath the heaviest and dampest deposit of hymn books and ledgers. Yet equally familiar, and strangely persistent in the most diverse conditions of travel and climate, is the loveliness of the hurrying clouds, of the sun-stained green, of the rapid watery atmosphere, in which clouds have been crumbled with colour until the ocean of air is at once confused and profound. There will certainly be a copy of Shakespeare in such a house, another Paradise Lost, and a little volume of George Herbert. There may be almost as probably, though perhaps more strangely, *Vulgar Errors* and the *Religio Medici*. For some reason the folios of Sir Thomas Browne are to be found on the lowest shelf of libraries in other respects entirely humdrum and utilitarian. His popularity in the small country house rests perhaps chiefly upon the fact that the *Vulgar Errors* treats largely of animals. Books with pictures of malformed elephants, baboons of grotesque and indecent appearance, tigers, deer, and so on, all distorted and with a queer facial likeness to human beings, are always popular among people who care nothing for literature. The text of *Vulgar Errors* has something of the same fascination as these woodcuts. And then it may not be fanciful to suppose that even in the year nineteen hundred and nineteen a great number of minds are still only partially lit up by the cold light of knowledge. It is the most capricious illuminant. They are still apt to ruminate, without an overpowering bias to the truth, whether a kingfisher's body shows which way the wind blows; whether an ostrich digests iron; whether owls and ravens herald ill-fortune; and the spilling of salt bad luck; what the tingling of ears forebodes, and even to toy pleasantly with more curious speculations as to the joints of elephants and the politics of storks, which came within the province of the more fertile and better-informed brain of the author. The English mind is naturally prone to take its ease and pleasure in the loosest whimsies and humours. Sir Thomas ministers to the kind of wisdom that farmers talk over their ale, and housewives over their tea cups, proving himself much more sagacious and better informed than the rest of the company, but still with the door of his mind wide open for any curious thing that chooses to enter in. For all his learning, the doctor will consider what we have to say seriously and in good faith. He will perhaps give our modest question a turn that sends it spinning among the stars. How charming, for example, to have found a flower on a walk, or a chip of pottery or a stone, that might equally well have been thunderbolt, or cannon ball, and to have gone straightway to knock upon the doctor's door with a question. No business would have had precedence over such a matter as this, unless indeed someone had been dying or coming into the world. For the doctor was evidently a humane man, and one good to have at the bedside, imperturbable, yet sympathetic. His consolations must have been sublime; his presence full of composure; and then, if something took his fancy, what enlivening speculations he must have poured forth, talking, one guesses, mostly in soliloquy, with the strangest sequences, in a rapt pondering manner, as if not expecting an answer, and more to himself than to a second person.

What second person, indeed, could answer him? At Montpellier and Padua he had learnt, but learning, instead of settling his questions, had, it seems, greatly increased his capacity for asking them. The door of his mind opened more and more widely. In comparison with other men he was indeed learned; he knew six languages; he knew the laws, customs, and policies of several states, the names of all the constellations, and most of the plants of his country; and yet—must one not always break off thus?—"yet methinks, I do not know so many as when I did but know a hundred, and had scarcely ever simpled further than Cheapside." Suppose indeed that certainty had been attainable; it had been proved to be so, and so it must be; nothing would have been more intolerable to him. His imagination was made to carry pyramids. "Methinks there be not impossibilities enough in religion for an active faith." But then the grain of dust was a pyramid. There was nothing plain in a world of mystery. Consider the body. Some men are surprised by sickness. Sir Thomas can only "wonder that we are not always so"; he sees the thousand doors that lead to death; and in addition—so he likes to speculate and fantastically accumulate considerations—"it is in the power of every hand to destroy us, and we are beholden unto everyone we meet, he doth not kill us." What, one asks, as considerations accumulate, is ever to stop the course of such a mind, unroofed and open to the sky? Unfortunately, there was the Deity. His faith shut in his horizon. Sir Thomas himself resolutely drew that blind. His desire for knowledge, his eager ingenuity, his anticipations of truth, must submit, shut their eyes, and go to sleep. Doubts he calls them. "More of these no man hath known than myself; which I confess I conquered, not in a martial posture, but on my knees." So lively a curiosity deserved a better fate. It would have delighted us to feed what Sir Thomas calls his doubts upon a liberal diet of modern certainties, but not if by so doing we had changed him, but that is the tribute of our gratitude. For is he not, among a variety of other things, one of the first of our writers to be definitely himself? His appearance has been recorded—his height moderate, his eyes large and luminous, his skin dark, and constantly suffused with blushes. But it is the more splendid picture of his soul that we feast upon. In that dark world, he was one of the explorers; the first to talk of himself, he broaches the subject with an immense gusto. He returns to it again and again, as if the soul were a wondrous disease and its symptoms not yet recorded. "The world that I regard is myself; it is the microcosm of my own frame that I cast mine eye on: for the other I use it but like my globe, and turn it round sometimes for my recreation." Sometimes, he notes, and he seems to take a pride in the strange gloomy confession, he has wished for death. "I feel sometimes a hell within myself; Lucifer keeps his court in my breast; Legion is revived in me." The strangest ideas and emotions have play in him, as he goes about his work, outwardly the most sober of mankind, and esteemed the greatest physician in Norwich. Yet, if his friends could see into his mind! But they cannot. "I am in the dark to all the world, and my nearest friends behold me but in a cloud." Strange beyond belief are the capacities that he detects in himself, profound the meditation into which the commonest sight will plunge him, while the rest of the world passes by and sees nothing to wonder at. The tavern music, the Ave Mary Bell, the broken pot that the workman has dug out of the field—at the sight and sound of them he stops dead, as if transfixed by the astonishing vista. "And surely it is not a melancholy conceit to think we are all asleep in this world, and that the conceits of this life are as mere dreams—" No one so raises the vault of the mind, and, admitting conjecture after conjecture, positively makes us stand still in amazement, unable to bring ourselves to move on.

With such a conviction of the mystery and miracle of things, he is unable to reject, disposed to tolerate and contemplate without end. In the grossest superstition there is something of devotion; in tavern music something of divinity: in the little world of man something "that was before the elements and owes no homage unto the sun." He is hospitable to everything and tastes freely of whatever is set before him. For upon this sublime prospect of time and eternity the cloudy vapours which his imagination conjures up, there is cast the figure of the author. It is not merely life in general that fills him with amazement, but his own life in particular, "which to relate were not a history, but a piece of poetry, and would sound to common ears like a fable." The littleness of egotism has not as yet

attacked the health of his interest in himself. I am chari-
table, I am brave, I am averse from nothing, I am full
of feeling for others, I am merciless upon myself, "For
my conversation, it is like the sun's, with all men, and
with a friendly aspect to good and bad"; I, I, I—how we
have lost the secret of saying that!

In short Sir Thomas Browne brings in the whole question, which is afterwards to become of such importance,
of knowing one's author. Somewhere, everywhere, now
hidden, now apparent in whatever is written down is the
form of a human being. If we seek to know him, are we
idly occupied, as when, listening to a speaker, we begin
to speculate about his age and habits, whether he is married, has children, and lives in Hampstead? It is a question to be asked, and not one to be answered. It will be
answered, that is to say, in an instinctive and irrational
manner, as our disposition inclines us. Only one must
note that Sir Thomas is the first English writer to rouse
this particular confusion with any briskness. Chaucer—but
Chaucer's spelling is against him. Marlowe then, Spencer,
Webster, Ben Jonson? The truth is the question never presents itself quite so acutely in the case of a poet. It scarcely
presents itself at all in the case of the Greeks and Latins.
The poet gives us his essence, but prose takes the mould
of the body and mind entire.

Could one not deduce from reading his books that Sir
Thomas Browne, humane and tolerant in almost every
respect, was nevertheless capable of a mood of dark superstition in which he would pronounce that two old women
were witches and must be put to death? Some of his ped-
antries have the very clink of the thumbscrew: the heart-
less ingenuity of a spirit still cramped and fettered by the

bonds of the Middle Ages. There were impulses of cruelty
in him as in all people forced by their ignorance or weak-
ness to live in a state of servility to man or nature. There
were moments, brief but intense, in which his serene and
magnanimous mind contracted in a spasm of terror. More
often by far he is, as all great men are, a little dull. Yet the
dullness of the great is distinct from the dullness of the
little. It is perhaps more profound. We enter into their
shades acquiescent and hopeful, convinced that if light is
lacking the fault is ours. A sense of guilt, as the horror
increases, mingles itself with our protest and increases the
gloom. Surely, we must have missed the way? If one
stitched together the passages in Wordsworth, Shakespeare,
Milton, every great writer in short who has left more than
a song or two behind him, where the light has failed us,
and we have only gone on because of the habit of obedience, they would make a formidable volume—the dullest
book in the world.

Don Quixote is very dull too. But his dullness, instead
of having that lethargy as of a somnolent beast which is
characteristic of great people's dullness—"After my enormous labours, I'm asleep and intend to snore if I like," they
seem to say—instead of this dullness Don Quixote has
another variety. He is telling stories to children. There
they sit round the fire on a winter's night, grown-up children, women at their spinning, men relaxed and sleepy
after the day's sport, "Tell us a story—something to make
us laugh—something gallant, too—about people like ourselves only more unhappy and a great deal happier." Obe-
dient to this demand, Cervantes, a kind accommodating
man, spun them stories, about princesses lost and amorous
knights, much to their taste, very tedious to ours. Let him

but get back to Don Quixote and Sancho Panza and all is well, for him, we cannot help thinking, as for us. Yet what with our natural reverence and inevitable servility, we seldom make our position, as modern readers of old writers, plain. Undoubtedly all writers are immensely influenced by the people who read them. Thus, take Cervantes and his audience—we, coming four centuries later, have a sense of breaking into a happy family party. Compare that group with the group (only there are no groups now since we have become educated and isolated and read our books by our own firesides in our own copies) but compare the readers of Cera Cervantes with the readers of Thomas Hardy. Hardy whiles away no firelit hour with tales of lost princesses and amorous knights—refuses more and more sternly to make things up for our entertainment. As we read him separately so he speaks to us separately, as if we were individual men and women, rather than groups sharing the same tastes. That, too, must be taken into account. The reader of today, accustomed to find himself in direct communication with the writer, is constantly out of touch with Cervantes. How far did he himself know what he was about—how far again do we over-interpret, misinterpret, read into Don Quixote a meaning compounded of our own experience, as an elder person might read a meaning into a child's story and doubt whether the child himself was aware of it? If Cervantes had felt the tragedy and the satire as we feel them, could he have foreborne as he does to stress them—could he have been as callous as he seems? Yet Shakespeare dismissed Falstaff callously enough. The great writers have this large way with them, nature's way; which we who are further from nature call cruel, since we suffer more from the effects of cruelty, or at any rate judge our suffering of greater importance, than they did. None of this, however, impairs the main pleasure of the jolly, delightful, plain-spoken book built up, foaming up, round the magnificent conception of the Knight and the world which, however people may change, must remain for ever an unassailable statement of man and the world. That will always be in existence. And as for knowing himself what he was about—perhaps great writers never do. Perhaps that is why later ages find what they seek.

But to return to the dullest book in the world. To this volume Sir Thomas has added certainly one or two pages. Yet should one desire a loophole to escape it is always possible to find one in the chance that the book is difficult, not dull. Accustomed as we are to strip a whole page of its sentences and crush their meaning out in one grasp, the obstinate resistance which a page of *Urn Burial* offers at first trips us and blinds us. "Though if *Adam* were made out of an extract of the Earth, all parts might challenge a restitution, yet few have returned their bones farre lower than they might receive them"—We must stop, go back, try out this way and that, and proceed at a foot's pace. Reading has been made so easy in our days that to go back to these crabbed sentences is like mounting only a solemn and obstinate donkey instead of going up to town by an electric train. Dilatory, capricious, governed by no consideration save his own wish, Sir Thomas seems scarcely to be writing in the sense that Froude wrote or Matthew Arnold. A page of print now fulfills a different office. Is it not almost servile in the assiduity with which it helps us on our way, making only the standard charge on our attention and in return for that giving us the full measure, but not an ounce over or under our due? In Sir Thomas

Browne's days weights and measures were in a primitive condition, if they had any existence at all. One is conscious all the time that Sir Thomas was never paid a penny for his prose. He is free since it is the offering of his own bounty to give us as little or as much as he chooses. He is an amateur; it is the work of his leisure and pleasure; he makes no bargain with us. Therefore, as Sir Thomas has no call to conciliate his reader, these short books of his are dull if he chooses, difficult if he likes, beautiful beyond measure if he has a mind that way. Here we approach the doubtful region—the region of beauty. Are we not already lost or sunk or enticed with the very first words? "When the Funeral pyre was out, and the last valediction over, men took a lasting adieu to their interred Friends." But why beauty should have the effect upon us that it does, the strange serene confidence that it inspires in us, none can say. Most people have tried and perhaps one of the invariable properties of beauty is that it leaves in the mind a desire to impart. Some offering we must make; some act we must dedicate, if only to move across the room and turn the rose in the jar, which, by the way, has dropped its petals.

The Cinema[1]

PEOPLE say that the savage no longer exists in us, that we are at the fag-end of civilization, that everything has been said already, and that it is too late to be ambitious. But these philosophers have presumably forgotten the movies. They have never seen the savages of the twentieth-century watching the pictures. They have never sat themselves in front of the screen and thought how for all the clothes on their backs and the carpets at their feet, no great distance separates them from those bright-eyed naked men who knocked two bars of iron together and heard in that clangour a foretaste of the music of Mozart.

The bars in this case, of course, are so highly wrought and so covered over with accretions of alien matter that it is extremely difficult to hear anything distinctly. All is hubble-bubble, swarm and chaos. We are peering over the edge of a cauldron in which fragments of all shapes and savours seem to simmer; now and again some vast form heaves itself up and seems about to haul itself out of chaos. Yet at first sight the art of the cinema seems simple, even stupid. There is the king shaking hands with a football team; there is Sir Thomas Lipton's yacht; there is Jack Horner winning the Grand National. The eye licks it all up instantaneously, and the brain, agreeably titillated, settles down to watch things happening without bestirring itself to think. For the ordinary eye, the English unæsthetic

[1] Written in 1926.

eye, is a simple mechanism which takes care that the body does not fall down coal-holes, provides the brain with toys and sweetmeats to keep it quiet, and can be trusted to go on behaving like a competent nursemaid until the brain comes to the conclusion that it is time to wake up. What is its purpose, then, to be roused suddenly in the midst of its agreeable somnolence and asked for help? The eye is in difficulties. The eye wants help. The eye says to the brain, "Something is happening which I do not in the least understand. You are needed." Together they look at the king, the boat, the horse, and the brain sees at once that they have taken on a quality which does not belong to the simple photograph of real life. They have become not more beautiful in the sense in which pictures are beautiful, but shall we call it (our vocabulary is miserably insufficient) more real, or real with a different reality from that which we perceive in daily life? We behold them as they are when we are not there. We see life as it is when we have no part in it. As we gaze we seem to be removed from the pettiness of actual existence. The horse will not knock us down. The king will not grasp our hands. The wave will not wet our feet. From this point of vantage, as we watch the antics of our kind, we have time to feel pity and amusement, to generalize, to endow one man with the attributes of the race. Watching the boat sail and the wave break, we have time to open our minds wide to beauty, and register on top of it the queer sensation—this beauty will continue, and this beauty will flourish whether we behold it or not. Further, all this happened ten years ago, we are told. We are beholding a world which has gone beneath the waves. Brides are emerging from the abbey—they are now mothers; ushers are ardent—they are now silent; mothers are tearful; guests are joyful; this has been won and that has been lost, and it is over and done with. The war sprung its chasm at the feet of all this innocence and ignorance but it was thus that we danced and pirouetted, toiled and desired, thus that the sun shone and the clouds scudded, up to the very end.

But the picture-makers seem dissatisfied with such obvious sources of interest as the passage of time and the suggestiveness of reality. They despise the flight of gulls, ships on the Thames, the Prince of Wales, the Mile End Road, Piccadilly Circus. They want to be improving, altering, making an art of their own—naturally, for so much seems to be within their scope. So many arts seemed to stand by ready to offer their help. For example, there was literature. All the famous novels of the world, with their well-known characters and their famous scenes, only asked, it seemed, to be put on the films. What could be easier and simpler? The cinema fell upon its prey with immense rapacity, and to the moment largely subsists upon the body of its unfortunate victim. But the results are disastrous to both. The alliance is unnatural. Eye and brain are torn asunder ruthlessly as they try vainly to work in couples. The eye says "Here is Anna Karenina." A voluptuous lady in black velvet wearing pearls comes before us. But the brain says, "That is no more Anna Karenina than it is Queen Victoria." For the brain knows Anna almost entirely by the inside of her mind—her charm, her passion, her despair. All the emphasis is laid by the cinema upon her teeth, her pearls, and her velvet. Then "Anna falls in love with Vronsky"—that is to say, the lady in black velvet falls into the arms of a gentleman in uniform and they kiss with enormous succulence, great deliberation, and infinite gesticulation, on a sofa in an extremely well-appointed library, while a gardener incidentally mows the lawn. So we lurch and lumber through the most famous novels of the world. So we spell them out in words of one syllable, written, too, in the scrawl of an illiterate schoolboy. A kiss is love. A broken cup is jealousy. A grin is happiness. Death is a hearse. None of these things has the least connexion with the novel that Tolstoy wrote, and it is only when we give up trying to connect the pictures with the book that we guess from some accidental scene—like the gardener mowing the lawn—what the cinema might do if left to its own devices.

But what, then, are its devices? If it ceased to be a parasite, how would it walk erect? At present it is only from hints that one can frame any conjecture. For instance, at a performance of Dr. Caligari the other day a shadow shaped like a tadpole suddenly appeared at one corner of the screen. It swelled to an immense size, quivered, bulged, and sank back again into nonentity. For a moment it seemed to embody some monstrous diseased imagination of the lunatic's brain. For a moment it seemed as if thought could be conveyed by shape more effectively than by words. The monstrous quivering tadpole seemed to be fear itself, and not the statement "I am afraid." In fact, the shadow was accidental and the effect unintentional. But if a shadow at a certain moment can suggest so much more than the actual gestures and words of men and women in a state of fear, it seems plain that the cinema has within its grasp innumerable symbols for emotions that have so far failed to find expression. Terror has besides its ordinary forms the shape of a tadpole; it burgeons, bulges, quivers, disappears. Anger is not merely rant and rhetoric, red faces and clenched fists. It is perhaps a black line wriggling upon a white sheet. Anna and Vronsky need no longer scowl and grimace. They have at their command—but what? Is there, we ask, some secret language which we feel and see, but never speak, and, if so, could this be made visible to the eye? Is there any characteristic which thought possesses that can be rendered visible without the help of words? It has speed and slowness; dartlike directness and vaporous circumlocution. But it has, also, especially in moments of emotion, the picture-making power, the need to lift its burden to another bearer; to let an image run side by side along with it. The likeness of the thought is for some reason more beautiful, more comprehensible, more available, than the thought itself. As everybody knows, in Shakespeare the most complex ideas form chains of images through which we mount, changing and turning, until we reach the light of day. But obviously the images of a poet are not to be cast in bronze or traced by pencil. They are compact of a thousand suggestions of which the visual is only the most obvious or the uppermost. Even the simplest image "My luve's like a red, red, rose, that's newly-sprung in June" presents us with impressions of moisture and warmth and the glow of crimson and the softness of petals inextricably mixed and strung upon the lift of a rhythm which is itself the voice of the passion and hesitation of the lover. All this, which is accessible to words and to words alone, the cinema must avoid.

Yet if so much of our thinking and feeling is connected with seeing, some residue of visual emotion which is of no use either to painter or to poet may still await the cinema. That such symbols will be quite unlike the real objects which we see before us seems highly probable. Something

abstract, something which moves with controlled and conscious art, something which calls for the very slightest
help from words or music to make itself intelligible, yet
justly uses them subserviently—of such movements and
abstractions the films may in time to come be composed.
Then indeed when some new symbol for expressing
thought is found, the film-maker has enormous riches at
his command. The exactitude of reality and its surprising
power of suggestion are to be had for the asking. Annas
and Vronskys—there they are in the flesh. If into this
reality he could breathe emotion, could animate the perfect form with thought, then his booty could be hauled in
hand over hand. Then, as smoke pours from Vesuvius, we
should be able to see thought in its wildness, in its beauty,
in its oddity, pouring from men with their elbows on a
table; from women with their little handbags slipping to
the floor. We should see these emotions mingling together
and affecting each other.

We should see violent changes of emotion produced
by their collision. The most fantastic contrasts could be
flashed before us with a speed which the writer can only
toil after in vain; the dream architecture of arches and
battlements, of cascades falling and fountains rising, which
sometimes visits us in sleep or shapes itself in half-darkened
rooms, could be realized before our waking eyes. No fan-
tasy could be too far-fetched or insubstantial. The past
could be unrolled, distances annihilated, and the gulfs
which dislocate novels (when, for instance, Tolstoy has
to pass from Levin to Anna and in doing so jars his story
and wrenches and arrests our sympathies) could by the
sameness of the background, by the repetition of some
scene, be smoothed away.

How all this is to be attempted, much less achieved, no one at the moment can tell us. We get intimations only in the chaos of the streets, perhaps, when some momentary assembly of colour, sound, movement, suggests that here is a scene waiting a new art to be transfixed. And sometimes at the cinema in the midst of its immense dexterity and enormous technical proficiency, the curtain parts and we behold, far off, some unknown and unexpected beauty. But it is for a moment only. For a strange thing has happened—while all the other arts were born naked, this, the youngest, has been born fully-clothed. It can say everything before it has anything to say. It is as if the savage tribe, instead of finding two bars of iron to play with, had found scattering the seashore fiddles, flutes, saxophones, trumpets, grand pianos by Erard and Bechstein, and had begun with incredible energy, but without knowing a note of music, to hammer and thump upon them all at the same time.

Walter Sickert

THOUGH talk is a common habit and much enjoyed, those who try to record it are aware that it runs hither and thither, seldom sticks to the point, abounds in exaggeration and inaccuracy, and has frequent stretches of extreme dullness. Thus when seven or eight people dined together the other night the first ten minutes went in saying how very difficult it is to get about London nowadays; was it quicker to walk or to drive; did the new system of coloured lights help or hinder? Just as dinner was announced, somebody asked: "But when were picture galleries invented?," a question naturally arising, for the discussing about the value of coloured lights had led somebody to say that in the eyes of a motorist red is not a colour but simply a danger signal. We shall very soon lose our sense of colour, another added, exaggerating, of course. Colours are used so much as signals now that they will very soon suggest action merely—that is the worst of living in a highly organized community. Other instances of the change wrought upon our senses by modern conditions were then cited; how buildings are changing their character because no one can stand still to look at them; how statues and mosaics removed from their old stations and confined to the insides of churches and private houses lose the qualities proper to them in the open air. This naturally led to the question when picture galleries were first opened, and as no precise answer was forthcoming the speaker went on to sketch a fancy picture of an inventive youth having to wait his turn to cross Ludgate Circus in the reign of Queen Anne. "Look," he said to himself, "how the coaches cut across the corner! That poor old boy," he said, "positively had to put his hand to his pigtail. Nobody any longer stops to look at St. Paul's. Soon all these swinging signboards will be dismantled. Let me take time by the forelock," he said, and, going to his bank, which was near at hand, drew out what remained of his patrimony, and invested it in a neat set of rooms in Bond Street, where he hung the first show of pictures ever to be displayed to the public. Perhaps that is the origin of the House of Agnews; perhaps their gallery stands on the site of the house that was leased, so foreseeingly, by the young man over two hundred years ago. Perhaps, said the others; but nobody troubled to verify the statement, for it was a bitter cold night in December and the soup stood upon the table.

In course of time the talk turned, as talk has a way of turning, back on itself—to colour; how different people see colour differently; how painters are affected by their place of birth, whether in the blue South or the grey North; how colour blazes, unrelated to any object, in the eyes of children; how politicians and business men are blind, days spent in an office leading to atrophy of the eye; and so, by contrast, to those insects, said still to be found in the primeval forests of South America, in whom the eye is so developed that they are all eye, the body a tuft of leather, serving merely to connect the two great chambers of vision. Somebody had met a man whose business it was to explore the wilder parts of the world in search of cactuses, and from him had heard of these insects who are born with the flowers and die when the flowers fade. A hard-headed man, used to roughing it in all parts of the world, yet there was something moving to him in the sight of these little creatures drinking crimson until they became crimson; then flitting on to violet; then to a vivid green, and becoming for the moment the thing they saw—red, green, blue, whatever the colour of the flower might be. At the first breath of winter, he said, when the flowers died, the life went out of them, and you might mistake them as they lay on the grass for shrivelled air-balls. Were we once insects like that, too, one of the diners asked; all eye? Do we still preserve the capacity for drinking, eating, indeed becoming colour furled up in us, waiting proper conditions to develop? For as the rocks hide fossils, so we hide tigers, baboons, and perhaps insects, under our coats and hats. On first entering a picture gallery, whose still-ness, warmth and seclusion from the perils of the street reproduce the conditions of the primeval forest, it often seems as if we reverted to the insect stage of our long life.

"On first entering a picture gallery"—there was silence for a moment. Many pictures were being shown in London at that time. There was the famous Holbein; there were pictures by Picasso and Matisse; young English painters were holding an exhibition in Burlington Gardens, and there was a show of Sickert's pictures at Agnew's. When I first went into Sickert's show, said one of the diners, I became completely and solely an insect—all eye. I flew from colour to colour, from red to blue, from yellow to green. Colours went spirally through my body lighting a flare as if a rocket fell through the night and lit up greens and browns, grass and trees, and there in the grass a white bird. Colour warmed, thrilled, chafed, burnt,

soothed, fed and finally exhausted me. For though the life
of colour is a glorious life it is a short one. Soon the eye
can hold no more; it shuts itself in sleep, and if the man
who looks for cactuses had come by he would only have
seen a shrivelled air-ball on a red plush chair.

That is an exaggeration, a dramatization, the others said.
Nobody who can walk down Bond Street in the year
1933 without exciting suspicion in the heart of the police-
man, can simplify sufficiently to see colour only. One
must be a fly in order to die in aromatic pain. And it is
many ages now since we lost "the microscopic eye." Ages
ago we left the forest and went into the world, and the
eye shrivelled and the heart grew, and the liver and the
intestines and the tongue and the hands and the feet.
Sickert's show proves the truth of that soon enough. Look
at his portraits: Charles Bradlaugh at the Bar of the House
of Commons; the Right Honourable Winston Churchill,
M.P.; Rear-Admiral Lumsden, C.I.E., C.V.O.; and Dr.
Cobbledick. These gentlemen are by no means simple
flowers. In front of Sickert's portraits of them we are reminded of all that we have done with all our organs since
we left the jungle. The face of a civilized human being is
a summing-up, an epitome of a million acts, thoughts,
statements and concealments. Yes, Sickert is a great biographer, said one of them; when he paints a portrait I read
a life. Think of his picture of the disillusioned lady in full
evening-dress sitting on a balcony in Venice. She has seen
every sort of sunrise and sunset whether dressed in diamonds or white night-gown; now all is ruin and ship-
wreck; and yet the tattered ship in the background still
floats. For though Sickert is a realist he is by no means
a pessimist . . . Laughter drowned the last words. The

portrait of the lady on the balcony had suggested nothing
of the kind to most of the others. Had she lovers or not—
it did not matter; did the ship sail or did it sink—they did
not care. And they fetched a book of photographs from
Sickert's paintings and began cutting off a hand or a head,
and made them connect or separate, not as a hand or a
head but as if they had some quite different relationship.

Now they are going into the silent land; soon they will
be out of reach of the human voice, two of the diners said,
watching them. They are seeing things that we cannot
see, just as a dog bristles and whines in a dark lane when
nothing is visible to human eyes. They are making passes
with their hands, to express what they cannot say; what
excites them in those photographs is something so deeply
sunk that they cannot put words to it. But we, like most
English people, have been trained not to see but to talk.
Yet it may be, they went on, that there is a zone of silence
in the middle of every art. The artists themselves live in
it. Coleridge could not explain *Kubla Khan*—that he left
to the critics. And those who are almost on a par with the
artists, like our friends who are looking at the pictures,
cannot impart what they feel when they go beyond the
outskirts. They can only open and shut their fingers. We
must resign ourselves to the fact that we are outsiders,
condemned for ever to haunt the borders and margins of
this great art. Nevertheless that is a region of very strong
sensations. First, on entering a picture gallery, the violent
rapture of colour; then, when we have soused our eyes
sufficiently in that, there is the complexity and intrigue of
character. I repeat, said one of them, that Sickert is among
the best of biographers. When he sits a man or woman
down in front of him he sees the whole of the life that has

been lived to make that face. There it is—stated. None of our biographers make such complete and flawless statements. They are tripped up by those miserable impediments called facts; was he born on such a day; was his mother's name Jane or Mary; then the affair with the barmaid has to be suppressed out of deference to family feeling; and there is always, brooding over him with its dark wings and hooked beak, the Law of Libel. Hence the three or four hundred pages of compromise, evasion, understatement, overstatement, irrelevance and downright falsehood which we call biography. But Sickert takes his brush, squeezes his tube, looks at the face; and then, cloaked in the divine gift of silence, he paints—lies, paltriness, splendour, depravity, endurance, beauty—it is all there and nobody can say, "But his mother's name was Jane not Mary." Not in our time will anyone write a life as Sickert paints it. Words are an impure medium; better far to have been born into the silent kingdom of paint.

But to me Sickert always seems more of a novelist than a biographer, said the other. He likes to set his characters in motion, to watch them in action. As I remember it, his show was full of pictures that might be stories, as indeed their names suggest—*Rose et Marie; Christine buys a house; A difficult moment*. The figures are motionless, of course, but each has been seized in a moment of crisis; it is difficult to look at them and not to invent a plot, to hear what they are saying. You remember the picture of the old publican, with his glass on the table before him and a cigar gone cold at his lips, looking out of his shrewd little pig's eyes at the intolerable wastes of desolation in front of him? A fat woman lounges, her arm on a cheap yellow chest of drawers, behind him. It is all over with them, one feels. The accumulated weariness of innumerable days has discharged its burden on them. They are buried under an avalanche of rubbish. In the street beneath, the trams are squeaking, children are shrieking. Even now somebody is tapping his glass impatiently on the bar counter. She will have to bestir herself; to pull her heavy, indolent body together and go and serve him. The grimness of that situation lies in the fact that there is no crisis; dull minutes are mounting, old matches are accumulating and dirty glasses and dead cigars; still on they must go, up they must get.

And yet it is beautiful, said the other; satisfactory; complete in some way. Perhaps it is the flash of the stuffed birds in the glass case, or the relation of the chest of drawers to the woman's body; anyhow, there is a quality in that picture which makes me feel that though the publican is done for, and his disillusion complete, still in the other world, of which he is mysteriously a part without knowing it, beauty and order prevail; all is right there—or does that convey nothing to you? Perhaps that is one of the things that is better said with a flick of the fingers, said the other. But let us go on living in the world of words a little longer. Do you remember the picture of the girl sitting on the edge of her bed half naked? Perhaps it is called *Nuit d'Amour*. Anyhow, the night is over. The bed, a cheap iron bed, is tousled and tumbled; she has to face the day, to get her breakfast, to see about the rent. As she sits there with her night-gown slipping from her shoulders, just for a moment the truth of her life comes over her; she sees in a flash the little garden in Wales and the dripping tunnel in the Adelphi where she began, where she will end, her days. So be it, she says, and yawns and shrugs and stretches a hand for her stockings and chemise. Fate has willed it so. Now a novelist who told that story would plunge—how obviously—into the depths of sentimentality. How is he to convey in words the mixture of innocence and sordidity, pity and squalor? Sickert merely takes his brush and paints a tender green light on the faded wallpaper. Light is beautiful falling through green leaves. He has no need of explanation; green is enough. Then again there is the story of Marie and Rose—a grim, a complex, a moving and at the same time a heartening and rousing story. Marie on the chair has been sobbing out some piteous plaint of vows betrayed and hearts broken to the woman in the crimson petticoat. "Don't be a damned fool, my dear," says Rose, standing before her with her arms akimbo. "I know all about it," she says, standing there in the intimacy of undress experienced, seasoned, a woman of the world. And Marie looks up at her with all her illusions tearfully exposed and receives the full impact of the other's knowledge, which, however, perhaps because of the glow of the crimson petticoat, does not altogether wither her. There is too much salt and savour in it. She takes heart again. Down she trips past the one-eyed char with a pail, out into the street, a wiser woman than she went in. "So that's what life is," she says, brushing the tear from her eye and hailing the omnibus. There are any number of stories and three-volume novels in Sickert's exhibition.

But to what school of novelists does he belong? He is a realist, of course, nearer to Dickens than to Meredith. He has something in common with Balzac, Gissing and the earlier Arnold Bennett. The life of the lower middle class interests him most—of innkeepers, shopkeepers, music-hall actors and actresses. He seems to care little for the life of the aristocracy whether of birth or of intellect. The reason may be that people who inherit beautiful things sit much more loosely to their possessions than those who have bought them off barrows in the street with money earned by their own hands. There is a gusto in the spending of the poor; they are very close to what they possess. Hence the intimacy that seems to exist in Sickert's pictures between his people and their rooms. The bed, the chest of drawers, the one picture and the vase on the mantelpiece are all expressive of the owner. Merely by process of use and fitness the cheap furniture has rubbed its varnish off; the grain shows through; it has the expressive quality that expensive furniture always lacks; one must call it beautiful, though outside the room in which it plays its part it would be hideous in the extreme. Diamonds and Sheraton tables never submit to use like that. But whatever Sickert paints has to submit; it has to lose its separateness; it has to compose part of his scene. He chooses, therefore, the casual clothes of daily life that have taken the shape of the body; the felt hat with one feather that a girl has bought with sixpence off a barrow in Berwick Market. He likes bodies that work, hands that work, faces that have been lined and suppled and seamed by work, because, in working, people take unconscious gestures, and their faces have the expressiveness of unconsciousness—a look that the very rich, the very beautiful and the very sophisticated seldom possess. And of course Sickert composes his picture down to the very castors on the chairs and the fire-irons in the grate just as carefully as Turgenev, of whom he sometimes reminds me, composes his scene.

There are many points one could argue in that statement, said the other. But certainly it would seem to be true that Sickert is the novelist of the middle class. At the same time, though he prefers to paint people who use their hands rather than the leisured, he never sinks below a certain level in the social scale. Like most painters, he has a profound love of the good things of life; well-cooked food, good wine, fine cigars. His world abounds in richness and succulence and humour. He could not draw breath in a starved, a stunted or a puritanical universe. His people are always well fed in body and mind; they excel in mother wit and shrewd knowledge of the world. Some of their sayings are really a little broad; I have always wondered that the censor has let them pass. There is always good company in his pictures. Nothing could be more enjoyable than to sit behind the shop with the French innkeeper—that formidable man in the frock-coat whose name I forget. He would offer us a very fine cigar; uncork a bottle kept for his private use; and Madame would join us from the glass-house where she keeps accounts, and we should sit and talk and sing songs and crack jokes.

Yes, and in the middle of our songs we should look up and see red-gold light dripping down into the green waters of the canal. We should suddenly become aware of a grey church looming over us and one pink cloud riding down the bosom of the west. We should see it suddenly over the shoulders of the innkeeper; and then we should go on talking. That is how Sickert makes us aware of beauty—over the shoulders of the innkeeper; for he is a true poet, of course, one in the long line of English poets, and not the least. Think of his Venice, of his landscapes; or of those pictures of music-halls, of circuses, of street markets, where the acute drama of human character is cut off; and we no longer make up stories but behold—is it too much to say a vision? But it would be absurd to class Sickert among the visionaries; he is not a rhapsodist; he does not gaze into the sunset; he does not lead us down glorious vistas to blue horizons and remote ecstasies. He is not a Shelley or a Blake. We see his Venice from a little table on the Piazza, just as we are lifting a glass to our lips. Then we go on talking. His paint has a tangible quality; it is made not of air and star-dust but of oil and earth. We long to lay hands on his clouds and his pinnacles; to feel his columns round and his pillars hard beneath our touch. One can almost hear his gold and red dripping with a little splash into the waters of the canal. Moreover, human nature is never exiled from his canvas—there is always a woman with a parasol in the foreground, or a man selling cabbages in the shadow of the arch. Even when he paints a formal eighteenth-century town like Bath, he puts a great cart-wheel in the middle of the road. And those long French streets of pale pink and yellow stucco are all patched and peeled; a child's pink frock hangs out to dry; there are marble-topped tables at the corner. He never goes far from the sound of the human voice, from the mobility and idiosyncrasy of the human figure. As a poet, then, we must liken him to the poets who haunt taverns and sea beaches where the fishermen are tumbling their silver catch into wicker baskets. Crabbe, Wordsworth, Cowper are the names that come to mind, the poets who have kept close to the earth, to the house, to the sound of the natural human voice.

But here the speakers fell silent. Perhaps they were thinking that there is a vast distance between any poem and any picture; and that to compare them stretches words too far. At last, said one of them, we have reached the edge where painting breaks off and takes her way into the silent land. We shall have to set foot there soon, and all our words will fold their wings and sit huddled like rooks on the tops of the trees in winter. But since we love words let us dally for a little on the verge, said the other. Let us hold painting by the hand a moment longer, for though they must part in the end, painting and writing have much to tell each other: they have much in common. The novelist after all wants to make us see. Gardens, rivers, skies, clouds changing, the colour of a woman's dress, landscapes that bask beneath lovers, twisted woods that people walk in when they quarrel—novels are full of pictures like these. The novelist is always saying to himself, How can I bring the sun on to my page? How can I show the night and the moon rising? And he must often think that to describe a scene is the worst way to show it. It must be done with one word, or with one word in skilful contrast with another. For example, there is Shakespeare's "Dear as the ruddy drops that visit this sad heart." Does not "ruddy" shine out partly because "sad" comes after it; does not "sad" convey to us a double sense of the gloom of the mind and the dullness of colour? They both speak at once, striking two notes to make one chord, stimulating the eye of the mind and of the body. Then again there is Herrick's

> "More white than are the whitest creams,
>   Or moonlight tinselling the streams"

where the word "tinselling" adds to the simplicity of "white" the glittering, sequined, fluid look of moonlit water. It is a very complex business, the mixing and marrying of words that goes on, probably unconsciously, in the poet's mind to feed the reader's eye. All great writers are great colourists, just as they are musicians into the bargain; they always contrive to make their scenes glow and darken and change to the eye. Each of Shakespeare's plays has its dominant colour. And each writer differs of course as a colourist. Pope has no great range of colours; he is more draughtsman than colourist; clear washes of indigo, discreet blacks and violets best suit his exquisite sharp outlines—save that in the *Elegy to an Unfortunate Lady* there is a mass of funeral black; and the great image of the Eastern King glows, fantastically, if you like, dark crimson. Keats uses colour lavishly, lusciously, like a Venetian. In the *Eve of St. Agnes* he paints four lines at a time, dipping his pen in mounds of pure reds and blues. Tennyson on the other hand is never luscious; he uses the hard brush and the pure bright tints of a miniature painter. *The Princess* is illuminated like a monk's manuscript; there are whole landscapes in the curves of the capital letters. You almost need a magnifying glass to see the minuteness of the detail.

Undoubtedly, they agreed, the arts are closely united. What poet sets pen to paper without first hearing a tune in his head? And the prose-writer, though he makes believe to walk soberly, in obedience to the voice of reason, excites us by perpetual changes of rhythm following the emotions with which he deals. The best critics, Dryden, Lamb, Hazlitt, were acutely aware of the mixture of elements, and wrote of literature with music and painting in their minds. Nowadays we are all so specialized that critics keep their brain fixed to the print, which accounts for the starved condition of criticism in our time, and the attenuated and partial manner in which it deals with its subject.

But we have gossiped long enough, they said; it is time to make an end. The silent land lies before us. We have come within sight of it many times while we were talking; when, for example, we said that Rose's red petticoat satisfied us; when we said that the chest of drawers and the arm convinced us that all was well with the world as a whole. Why did the red petticoat, the yellow chest of drawers, make us feel something that had nothing to do with the story? We could not say; we could not express in words the effect of those combinations of line and colour. And, thinking back over the show, we have to admit that there is a great stretch of silent territory in Sickert's pictures. Consider once more the picture of the music-hall. At first it suggests the husky voice of Marie Lloyd singing a song about the ruins that Cromwell knocked about a bit; then the song dies away, and we see a scooped-out space filled curiously with the curves of fiddles, bowler hats, and shirt fronts converging into a pattern with a lemon-coloured splash in the centre. It is extraordinarily satisfying. Yet the description is so formal, so superficial, that we can hardly force our lips to frame it; while the emotion is distinct, powerful and satisfactory.

Yes, said the other, it is not a description at all; it leaves out the meaning. But what sort of meaning is that which cannot be expressed in words? What is a picture when it has rid itself of the companionship of language and of music. Let us ask the critics.

But the critics were still talking with their fingers. They were still bristling and shivering like dogs in dark lanes when something passes that we cannot see.

They have gone much farther into the forest than we shall ever go, said one of the talkers, sadly. We only catch a glimpse now and then of what lives there; we try to describe it and we cannot; and then it vanishes, and having seen it and lost it, exhaustion and depression overcome us; we recognize the limitations which Nature has put upon us, and so turn back to the sunny margin where the arts flirt and joke and pay each other compliments.

But do not let us fall into despair, said the other. I once read a letter from Walter Sickert in which he said, "I have always been a literary painter, thank goodness, like all the decent painters." Perhaps then he would not altogether despise us. When we talk of his biographies, his novels, and his poems we may not be so foolish as it seems. Among the many kinds of artists, it may be that there are some who are hybrid. Some, that is to say, bore deeper and deeper into the stuff of their own art; others are always making raids into the lands of others. Sickert it may be is among the hybrids, the raiders. His name itself suggests that he is of mixed birth. I have read that he is part German, part English, part Scandinavian perhaps; he was born in Munich, was educated at Reading, and lived in France. What more likely than that his mind is also cosmopolitan; that he sings a good song, writes a fine style, and reads enormously in four or five different languages? All this filters down into his brush. That is why he draws so many different people to look at his pictures. From his photograph you might take him for a highly distinguished lawyer with a nautical bent; the sort of man who settles a complicated case at the Law Courts, then changes into an old serge suit, pulls a yachting-cap with a green peak over his eyes and buffets about the North Sea with a volume of Æschylus in his pocket. In the intervals of hauling up and down the mainsail he wipes the salt from his eyes, whips out a canvas and paints a divinely lovely picture of Dieppe, Harwich, or the cliffs of Dover. That is the sort of man I take Walter Sickert to be. You should call him Richard Sickert, said the other—Richard Sickert, R.A. But since he is probably the best painter now living in England, whether he is called Richard or Walter, whether he has all the letters in the alphabet after his name or none, scarcely matters. Upon that they were all agreed.

Flying over London

FIFTY or sixty aeroplanes were collected in the shed like a flock of grasshoppers. The grasshopper has the same enormous thighs, the same little boatshaped body resting between its thighs, and if touched with a blade of grass, he too springs high into the air.

The mechanics ran the aeroplane out on to the turf; and Flight-Lieutenant Hopgood, at whose invitation we had come to make our first flight, stooped down and made the engine roar. A thousand pens have described the sensation of leaving earth; "The earth drops from you," they say; one sits still and the world has fallen. It is true that the earth fell, but what was stranger was the downfall of the sky. One was not prepared within a moment of taking off to be immersed in it, alone with it, to be in the thick of it. Habit has fixed the earth immovably in the centre of the imagination like a hard ball; everything is made to the scale of houses and streets. And as one rises up into the sky, as the sky pours down over one, this little hard granular knob, with its carvings and frettings, dissolves, crumbles, loses its domes, its pinnacles, its firesides, its habits, and one becomes conscious of being a little mammal, hot-blooded, hard boned, with a clot of red blood in one's body, trespassing up here in a fine air; repugnant to it, unclean, anti-pathetic. Vertebrae, ribs, entrails, and red blood belong to the earth; to the world of brussels sprouts and sheep going awkwardly on four pointed legs. Here

203

are winds tapering, vanishing, and the untimed manœuvre
of clouds, and nothing permanent, but vanishing and melting at the touch of each other without concussion, and the
fields that with us are meted into yards and grow punctually wheat and barley are here made and remade perpetually with flourishes of rain and flights of hail and
spaces tranquil as the deep sea, and then all is chop and
change, breeze and motion. Yet, though we flew through
territories with never a hedge or stick to divide them,
nameless, unowned, so inveterately anthropocentric is the
mind that instinctively the aeroplane becomes a boat and
we are sailing towards a harbour and there we shall be
received by hands that lift themselves from swaying garments; welcoming, accepting. Wraiths (our aspirations and
imaginations) have their home here; and in spite of our
vertebrae, ribs, and entrails, we are also vapour and air,
and shall be united.

Here Flight-Commander Hopgood, by a touch on the
lever, turned the nose of the Moth downwards. Nothing
more fantastic could be imagined. Houses, streets, banks,
public buildings, and habits and mutton and brussels
sprouts had been swept into long spirals and curves of
pink and purple like that a wet brush makes when it
sweeps mounds of paint together. One could see through
the Bank of England; all the business houses were transparent; the River Thames was as the Romans saw it, as
paleolithic man saw it, at dawn from a hill shaggy with
wood, with the rhinoceros digging his horn into the roots
of rhododendrons. So immortally fresh and virginal London looked and England was earth merely, merely the
world. Flight-Lieutenant Hopgood kept his finger still on
the lever which turns the plane downwards. A spark

glinted on a greenhouse. There rose a dome, a spire, a factory chimney, a gasometer. Civilization in short emerged; hands and minds worked again; and the centuries vanished and the wild rhinoceros was chased out of sight for ever. Still we descended. Here was a garden; here a football field. But no human being was yet visible; England looked like a ship that sails unmanned. Perhaps the race was dead, and we should board the world like that ship's company who found the ship sailing with all her sails set, and the kettle on the fire, but not a soul on board. Yet a spot down there, something squat and minute, might be a horse—or a man. . . . But Hopgood touched another lever and we rose again like a spirit shaking contamination from its wings, shaking gasometers and factories and football fields from its feet.

It was a moment of renunciation. We prefer the other, we seemed to say. Wraiths and sand dunes and mist; imagination; this we prefer to the mutton and the entrails. It was the idea of death that now suggested itself; not being received and welcomed; not immortality but extinction. For the clouds above were black. Across them there passed in single file a flight of gulls, livid white against the leaden background, holding on their way with the authority of owners, having rights, and means of communication unknown to us, an alien, a privileged race. But where there are gulls only, life is not. Life ends; life is dowsed in that cloud as lamps are dowsed with a wet sponge. That extinction has become now desirable. For it was odd in this voyage to note how blindly the tide of the soul and its desires rolled this way and that, carrying consciousness like a feather on the top, marking the direction, not controlling it. And so we swept on now up to death.

Hopgood's head cased in leather with a furry rim to it had the semblance of a winged pilot, of Charon's head, remorselessly conducting his passenger to the wet sponge which annihilates. For the mind (one can but repeat these things without claiming sense or truth for them—merely that they were such) is convinced in its own fastness, in its solitude, of extinction, and what is more, proud of it, as if it deserved extinction, extinction profited it more and were more desirable than prolongation on other terms by other wills. Charon, the mind prayed to the back of Flight-Lieutenant Hopgood, carry me on; thrust me deep, deep; till every glimmer of light in me, of heat of knowledge, even the tingling I feel in my toes is dulled; after all this living, all this scratching and tingling of sensation, that too-darkness, dullness, the black wet—will be also a sensation. And such is the incurable vanity of the human mind that the cloud, the wet sponge that was to extinguish, became, now that one thought of a contact with one's own mind, a furnace in which we roared up, and our death was a fire; brandished at the summit of life, many tongued, blood red, visible over land and sea. Extinction! The word is consummation.

Now we were in the skirts of the cloud and the wings of the aeroplane were spattered with hail; hail shot past silver and straight like the flash of steel railway lines. Innumerable arrows shot at us, down the august avenue of our approach.

Then Charon turned his head with its fringe of fur and laughed at us. It was an ugly face, with high cheek bones, and little deep sunk eyes, and all down one cheek was a crease where he had been cut and stitched together. Perhaps he weighed fifteen stone; he was oak limbed and angular. But for all this nothing now remained of Flight-Lieutenant Hopgood but a flame such as one sees blown thin and furtive at a street corner; a flame that for all its agility can hardly escape death. Such was the Flight-Lieutenant become; and ourselves too, so that the clinging hands, the embraces, the companionship of those about to die together was vanished; there was no flesh. However, just as one comes to the end of an avenue of trees and finds a pond with ducks on it, and nothing but lead-coloured water, so we came through the avenue of hail and out into a pool so still, so quiet, with haze above and cloud below it, so that we seemed to float as a duck floats on a pond. But the haze above us was compact of whiteness. As colour runs to the end of a paint brush, so the blue of the sky had run into one blob beneath it. It was white above us. And now the ribs and the entrails of the sprout-eating mammal began to be frozen, pulverized, frozen to lightness and whiteness of this spectral universe, and nothingness. For no clouds voyaged and lumbered up there; with light fondling them and masses breaking off their slopes or again towering and swelling. Here was no feather, no crease to break the steep wall ascending for ever up, for ever and ever.

And those yellowish lights, Hopgood and oneself, were put out effectively as the sun blanches the flame on a coal. No sponge effaced us, with its damp snout. Nothingness was poured down upon us like a mound of white sand. Then as if some part of us kept its ponderosity, down we fell into fleeciness, substance, and colour; all the colours of pounded plums and dolphins and blankets and seas and rain clouds crushed together, staining—purple, black, steel, all this soft ripeness seethed about us, and the eye felt as a fish feels when it slips from the rock into the depths of the sea.

For a time we were muffled in the clouds. Then the fairy earth appeared, lying far far below, a mere slice or knife blade of colour floating. It rose towards us with extreme speed, broadening and lengthening; forests appeared on it and seas; and then again an uneasy dark blot which soon began to be pricked with spires and blown into bubbles and domes. Nearer and nearer we came together and had again the whole of civilization spread beneath us, silent, empty, like a demonstration made for our instruction; the river with the steamers that bring coal and iron; the churches, the factories, the railways. Nothing moved; nobody worked the machine, until in some field on the outskirts of London one saw a dot actually and certainly move. Though the dot was the size of a blue bottle and its movement minute, reason insisted that it was a horse and it was galloping, but all speed and size were so reduced that the speed of the horse seemed very very slow, and its size minute. Now, however, there were often movements in the streets, as of sliding and stopping; and then gradually the vast creases of the stuff beneath began moving, and one saw in the creases millions of insects moving. In another second they became men, men of business, in the heart of the white city buildings.

Through a pair of Zeiss glasses one could indeed now see the tops of the heads of separate men and could distinguish a bowler from a cap, and could thus be certain of social grades—which was an employer, which was a working man. And one had to change perpetually air values into land values. There were blocks in the city of traffic sometimes almost a foot long; these had to be translated into eleven or twelve Rolls Royces in a row with city magnates waiting furious; and one had to add up the fury of the magnates; and say—even though it was all silent and the block was only a few inches in length, how scandalous the control of the traffic is in the City of London.

But with a turn of his wrist Flight-Lieutenant Hopgood flew over the poor quarters, and there through the Zeiss glasses one could see people looking up at the noise of the aeroplane, and could judge the expression on their faces. It was not one that one sees ordinarily. It was complex. "And I have to scrub the steps," it seemed to say grudgingly. All the same, they saluted, they sent us greeting; they were capable of flight. And after all, here the head was turned down again and the scrubbing brush was grasped tightly, to fall on the pavement wouldn't be nice. And they shook their heads; but they looked up at us again. But further on, over Oxford Street perhaps it was, nobody noticed us at all, but went on jostling each other with some furious desire absorbing them, for a sight of something (there was a yellowish flash as we passed overhead) in a shop window. Further, by Bayswater perhaps, where the press was thinner, a face, a figure, something odd in hat or person suddenly caught one's eye. And then it was odd how one became resentful of all the flags and surfaces and of the innumerable windows symmetrical as avenues, symmetrical as forest groves, and wished for some opening, and to push indoors and be rid of surfaces. Up in Bayswater a door did open, and instantly, of course, there appeared a room, incredibly small, of course, and ridiculous in its attempt to be separate and itself, and then—it was a woman's face, young, perhaps, at any rate with a black cloak and a red hat that made the furniture—

here a bowl, there a sideboard with apples on it, cease to be interesting because the power that buys a mat, or sets two colours together, became perceptible, as one may say that the haze over an electric fire becomes perceptible. Everything had changed its values seen from the air. Personality was outside the body, abstract. And one wished to be able to animate the heart, the legs, the arms with it, to do which it would be necessary to be there, so as to collect; so as to give up this arduous game, as one flies through the air, of assembling things that lie on the surface.

And then the field curved round us, and we were caught in an eddy of green cloth and white racing palings that flew round us like tape, and touched earth and went at an enormous speed, pitching, bumping upon a rocky surface, hard curves, after the plumes of air. We had landed, and it was over.

As a matter of fact, the flight had not begun; for when Flight-Lieutenant Hopgood stooped and made the engine roar, he had found a defect of some sort in the machine, and raising his head, he had said very sheepishly, " 'Fraid it's no go today."

So we had not flown after all.

The Sun and the Fish[1]

IT is an amusing game, especially for a dark winter's morning. One says to the eye Athens; Segesta; Queen Victoria; and one waits, as submissively as possible, to see what will happen next. And perhaps nothing happens, and perhaps a great many things happen, but not the things one might expect. The old lady in horn spectacles—the late Queen—is vivid enough; but somehow she has allied herself with a soldier in Piccadilly who is stooping to pick up a coin; with a yellow camel who is swaying through an archway in Kensington Gardens; with a kitchen chair and a distinguished old gentleman waving his hat. Dropped years ago into the mind, she has become stuck about with all sorts of alien matter. When one says Queen Victoria, one draws up the most heterogeneous collection of objects, which it will take a week at least to sort. On the other hand, one may say to oneself Mont Blanc at dawn, the Taj Mahal in the moonlight; and the mind remains a blank. For a sight will only survive in the queer pool in which we deposit our memories if it has the good luck to ally itself with some other emotion by which it is preserved. Sights marry, incongruously, morganatically (like the Queen and the Camel), and so keep each other alive. Mont Blanc, the Taj Mahal, sights which we travelled and toiled to see, fade and perish and disappear because they failed to find the right mate. On our deathbeds we shall see nothing

[1] Written in 1928.

211

more majestic than a cat on a wall or an old woman in a
sun-bonnet.

So, on this dark winter's morning, when the real world
has faded, let us see what the eye can do for us. Show me
the eclipse, we say to the eye; let us see that strange spec-
tacle again. And we see at once—but the mind's eye is
only by courtesy an eye; it is a nerve which hears and
smells, which transmits heat and cold, which is attached to
the brain and rouses the mind to discriminate and speculate—it is only for brevity's sake that we say that we "see"
at once a railway station at night. A crowd is gathered at
a barrier; but how curious a crowd! Mackintoshes are
slung over their arms; in their hands they carry little cases.
They have a provisional, extemporized look. They have
that moving and disturbing unity which comes from the
consciousness that they (but here it would be more proper
to say "we") have a purpose in common. Never was there
a stranger purpose than that which brought us together
that June night in Euston Railway Station. We were come
to see the dawn. Trains like ours were starting all over
England at that very moment to see the dawn. All noses
were pointing north. When for a moment we halted in the
depths of the country, there were the pale yellow lights
of motor cars also pointing north. There was no sleep, no
fixity in England that night. All were on the roads; all
were travelling north. All were thinking of the dawn. As
the night wore on, the sky, which was the object of so
many million thoughts, assumed greater substance and
prominence than usual. The consciousness of the whitish
soft canopy above us increased in weight as the hours
passed. When in chill early morning we were turned out
on a Yorkshire roadside, our senses had orientated them-

selves differently from usual. We were no longer in the same relation to people, houses, and trees; we were related to the whole world. We had come, not to lodge in the bedroom of an inn; we were come for a few hours of disembodied intercourse with the sky.

Everything was very pale. The river was pale and the fields, brimming with grasses and tasselled flowers which should have been red, had no colour in them, but lay there whispering and waving round colorless farmhouses. Now the farmhouse door would open, and out would step to join the procession the farmer and his family in their Sunday clothes, neat, dark and silent as if they were going up hill to church; or sometimes women merely leant on the window sills of the upper rooms watching the procession pass with amused contempt, it appeared—they have come such hundreds of miles, and for what? they seemed to say—in complete silence. We had an odd sense of keeping an appointment with an actor of such vast proportions that he would come silently and be everywhere.

By the time we were at the meeting place, on a high fell where the hills stretched their limbs out over the flowing brown moorland below, we had put on too—though we were cold and with our feet stood in red bog water were likely to be still colder, though some of us were squatted on mackintoshes among cups and plates, eating, and others were fantastically accoutered and none were at their best— still we had put on a certain dignity. Rather, perhaps, we had put off the little badges and signs of individuality. We were strung out against the sky in outline and had the look of statues standing prominent on the ridge of the world. We were very, very old; we were men and women of the primeval world come to salute the dawn. So the worship-

pers at Stonehenge must have looked among tussocks of
grass and boulders of rock. Suddenly, from the motor car
of some Yorkshire squire, there bounded four large, lean,
red dogs, hounds of the ancient world, hunting dogs, they
seemed, leaping with their noses close to the ground on
the track of boar or deer. Meanwhile, the sun was rising.
A cloud glowed as a white shade glows when the light is
slowly turned up behind it. Golden wedge-shaped stream-
ers fell from it and marked the trees in the valley green
and the villages blue-brown. In the sky behind us there
swam white islands in pale blue lakes. The sky was open
and free there, but in front of us a soft snowbank had
massed itself. Yet, as we looked, we saw it proving worn
and thin in patches. The gold momentarily increased,
melting the whiteness to a fiery gauze, and this grew
frailer and frailer till, for one instant, we saw the sun in
full splendour. Then there was a pause, a moment of sus-
pense, like that which precedes a race. The starter held his
watch in his hand, counting the seconds. Now they were
off.

The sun had to race through the clouds and to reach the
goal, which was a thin transparency to the right, before
the sacred seconds were up. He started. The clouds flung
every obstacle in his way. They clung, they impeded. He
dashed through them. He could be felt, flashing and flying
when he was invisible. His speed was tremendous. Here
he was out and bright; now he was under and lost. But
always one felt him flying and thrusting through the murk
to his goal. For one second he emerged and showed himself to us through our glasses, a hollowed sun, a crescent
sun. Finally, he went under for his last effort. Now he was
completely blotted out. The moments passed. Watches

were held in hand after hand. The sacred twenty-four
seconds were begun. Unless he could win through before
the last one was over, he was lost. Still one felt him tear-
ing and racing behind the clouds to win free; but the
clouds held him. They spread; they thickened; they slack-
ened; they muffled his speed. Of the twenty-four seconds
only five remained, and still he was obscured. And, as the
fatal seconds passed, and we realized that the sun was
being defeated, had now, indeed, lost the race, all the
colour began to go from the moor. The blue turned to
purple; the white became livid as at the approach of a
violent but windless storm. Pink faces went green, and it
became colder than ever. This was the defeat of the sun,
then, and this was all, so we thought, turning in disappointment from the dull cloud blanket in front of us to
the moors behind. They were livid, they were purple; but
suddenly one became aware that something more was
about to happen; something unexpected, awful, unavoid-
able. The shadow growing darker and darker over the
moor was like the heeling over of a boat, which, instead
of righting itself at the critical moment, turns a little further and then a little further on its side; and suddenly cap-
sizes. So the light turned and heeled over and went out.
This was the end. The flesh and blood of the world was
dead; only the skeleton was left. It hung beneath us, a frail
shell; brown; dead; withered. Then, with some trifling
movement, this profound obeisance of the light, this
stooping down and abasement of all splendour was over.
Lightly, on the other side of the world, up it rose; it
sprang up as if the one movement, after a second's tremendous pause, completed the other, and the light which
had died here rose again elsewhere. Never was there such

a sense of rejuvenescence and recovery. All the convalescences and respites of life seemed rolled into one. Yet, at first, so light and frail and strange the colour was, sprinkled rainbow-like in a hoop of colour, that it seemed as if the earth could never live decked out in such frail tints. It hung beneath us, like a cage, like a hoop, like a globe of glass. It might be blown out; it might be stove in. But steadily and surely our relief broadened and our confidence established itself as the great paint-brush washed in woods dark on the valley, and massed hills blue above them. The world became more and more solid; it became populous; it became a place where an infinite number of farmhouses, of villages, of railway lines have lodgement; until the whole fabric of civilization was modelled and moulded. But still the memory endured that the earth we stand on is made of colour; colour can be blown out; and then we stand on a dead leaf; and we who tread the earth securely now have seen it dead.

But the eye has not done with us yet. In pursuit of some logic of its own, which we cannot follow immediately, it now presents us with a picture, or generalized impression rather, of London on a hot summer day, when, to judge by the sense of concussion and confusion, the London season is at its height. It takes us a moment to realize, first, the fact that we are in some public gardens, next, from the asphalt and paper bags thrown about, that they must be the Zoological Gardens, and then without further preparation we are presented with a complete and perfect effigy of two lizards. After destruction, calm; after ruin, steadfastness—that, perhaps, is the logic of the eye at any rate. One lizard is mounted immobile on the back of another, with only the twinkle of a gold eyelid or the suction of a green flank to show that they are the living flesh, and not made of bronze. All human passion seems furtive and feverish beside this still rapture. Time seems to have stopped and we are in the presence of immortality. The tumult of the world has fallen from us like a crumbling cloud. Tanks cut in the level blackness enclose squares of immortality, worlds of settled sunshine, where there is neither rain nor cloud. There the inhabitants perform forever evolutions whose intricacy, because it has no reason, seems the more sublime. Blue and silver armies, keeping a perfect distance for all their arrowlike quickness, shoot first this way, then that. The discipline is perfect, the control absolute; reason there is none. The most majestic of human evolutions seems feeble and fluctuating compared with theirs. Each of these worlds too, which measures perhaps four feet by five, is as perfect in its order as in its method. For forests, they have half a dozen bamboo canes; for mountains, sandhills; in the curves and crinkles of a sea-shell lie for them all adventure, all romance. The rise of a bubble, negligible elsewhere, is here an event of the highest importance. The silver bead bores its way up a spiral staircase through the water to burst against the sheet of glass, which seems laid flat across the top. Nothing exists needlessly. The fish themselves seem to have been shaped deliberately and slipped into the world only to be themselves. They neither work nor weep. In their shape is their reason. For what other purpose except the sufficient one of perfect existence can they have been thus made, some so round, some so thin, some with radiating fins upon their backs, others lined with red electric light, others undulating like white pancakes on a frying pan, some armoured in blue mail, some given prodigious claws, some outrageously fringed with huge whiskers? More care has been spent upon half a dozen fish than upon all the races of men. Under our tweed and silk is nothing but a monotony of pink nakedness. Poets are not transparent to the backbone as these fish are. Bankers have no claws. Kings and Queens themselves have neither ruffs nor frills. In short, if we were to be turned naked into an aquarium—but enough. The eye shuts now. It has shown us a dead world and an immortal fish.

Gas[1]

IT is not necessary, perhaps, to dwell upon the circumstances. There can be few people who have not at one time or another had a tooth out under gas. The dentist stands very clean and impersonal in his long white overcoat. He tells one not to cross one's legs and arranges a bit under one's chin. Then the anæsthetist comes in with his bag as clean and impersonal as the dentist and only as black as the other is white. Both seem to wear uniform and to belong to some separate order of humanity, some third sex. The ordinary conventions lapse, for in ordinary life one does not after shaking hands with an unknown man at once open one's mouth and show him a broken tooth. The new relation with the third sex is stony, statuesque, colourless, but nevertheless humane. These are the people who manage the embarcations and disembarcations of the human spirit; these are they who stand on the border line between life and death forwarding the spirit from one to the other with clean impersonal antiseptic hands. Very well, I resign myself to your charge, one says, uncrossing one's legs; and at your command I cease to breathe through the mouth and breathe through the nose; breathe deep, breathe quietly, and your assurance that one is doing it very nicely is a parting salute, a farewell from the officer who presides over the ritual of disembarcation. Soon one is beyond his care.

[1] Written in 1929.

With each breath one draws in confusion; one draws in darkness, falling, scattering, like a cloud of falling soot flakes. And also one puts out to sea; with every breath one leaves the shore, one cleaves the hot waves of some new sulphurous dark existence in which one flounders without support, attended only by strange relics of old memories, elongated, stretched out, so that they seem to parody the world from which one brought them, with which one tries to keep still in touch by their means; as the curved glass at a fair makes the body seem tapering and then bloated. And as we plunge deeper and deeper away from shore, we seem to be drawn on in the wake of some fast flying always disappearing black object, drawn rapidly ahead of us. We become aware of something that we could never see in the other world; something that we have been sent in search of. All the old certainties become smudged and dispersed, because in comparison with this they are unimportant, like old garments crumpled up and dropped in a heap, because one needs to be naked, for this chase, this pursuit; all our most cherished beliefs and certainties and loves become like that. Scudding under a low dark sky we fly on the trail of this truth which, if we could grasp it, we should be for ever illuminated. And we rush faster and faster and the whole world becomes spiral and like wheels and circles about us, pressing closer and closer until it seems by its pressure to force us through a central hole, very narrow through which it hurts us, squeezing us with its pressure on the head, to pass. Indeed we seem to be crushed between the upper world and the lower world and then suddenly the pressure is lessened; the whole aperture widens up; we pass through a gorge, emerge into daylight, and behold a glass dish and hear a voice saying, "Rinse the mouth. Rinse the mouth," while a trickle of warm blood runs from between the lips. So we are received back by the officials. The truth that was being drawn so fast ahead of us vanishes.

Such is a very common experience. Everybody goes through it. But it seems to explain something that one observes very often in a third-class railway carriage for example. For it is impossible not to ask some questions as one looks down the long narrow compartment where so many different people sit facing each other. If they begin originally like that, one muses, looking at a child of three, what is the process that turns them into that? And here one looks at a heavy old man with a despatch box; or at an overdressed red-faced woman. What has made that extraordinary change? What sights, what experiences? For except in some very rare cases it seems as if the passing of sixty or seventy years had inflicted a most terrible punishment on the smooth pink face, had imparted some very strange piece of information, so that, however the features differ, the eyes of old people always have the same expression.

And what is that piece of information? one asks. Is it probably that all these people have been several times under gas? Gradually they have been made to think that what passes before them has very little substance. They know that they can be rid of it for a small sum. They can then see another thing, more important, perhaps drawn through the water. But what hardly any of them knows is whether he or she wishes to be rid of it. There they sit, the plumber with his leaden coil, the man with his despatch box, the middle-class woman with her parcel from Selfridges, revolving often unconsciously the question whether there is any meaning in this world compared with the other, and what the truth is that dashed ahead through the water. They woke before they had seized it. And the other world vanished. And perhaps to forget it, to cover it over, they went to the public house, they went to Oxford Street and bought a hat. As one looks down the third-class carriage, one sees that all the men and women over twenty have often been under gas; it is this that has done more than anything to change the expression of the face. An unchanged face would look almost idiotic. But, of course, there are a few faces which look as if they had caught the thing that dashes through the water.

Thunder at Wembley [1]

IT is nature that is the ruin of Wembley; yet it is difficult
to see what steps Lord Stevenson, Lieutenant-General Sir
Travers Clarke, and the Duke of Devonshire could have
taken to keep her out. They might have eradicated the
grass and felled the chestnut trees; even so the thrushes
would have got in, and there would always have been the
sky. At Earls Courts and the White City, so far as memory
serves, there was little trouble from this source. The area
was too small; the light was too brilliant. If a single real
moth strayed in to dally with the arc lamps, he was at once
transformed into a dizzy reveller; if a laburnum tree shook
her tassels, spangles of limelight floated in the violet and
crimson air. Everything was intoxicated and transformed.
But at Wembley nothing is changed and nobody is drunk.
They say, indeed, that there is a restaurant where each
diner is forced to spend a guinea upon his dinner. What
vistas of cold ham that statement calls forth! What pyramids of rolls! What gallons of tea and coffee! For it is un-
thinkable that there should be champagne, plovers' eggs,
or peaches at Wembley. And for six and eightpence two
people can buy as much ham and bread as they need. Six
and eightpence is not a large sum; but neither is it a small
sum. It is a moderate sum, a mediocre sum. It is the prevailing sum at Wembley. You look through an open door
at a regiment of motor cars aligned in avenues. They are

[1] Written in 1924.

not opulent and powerful; they are not flimsy and cheap. Six and eightpence seems to be the price of each of them. It is the same with the machines for crushing gravel. One can imagine better; one can imagine worse. The machine before us is a serviceable type and costs, inevitably, six and eightpence. Dress fabrics, rope, table linen, old masters, sugar, wheat, filigree silver, pepper, birds' nests (edible and exported to Hong Kong), camphor, bees-wax, rattans, and the rest—why trouble to ask the price? One knows beforehand—six and eightpence. As for the buildings themselves, those vast smooth grey palaces, no vulgar riot of ideas tumbled expensively in their architect's head; equally, cheapness was abhorrent to him, and vulgarity anathema. Per perch, rod, or square foot, however ferroconcrete palaces are sold, they too work out at six and eightpence.

But then, just as one is beginning a little wearily to fumble with those two fine words—democracy, mediocrity—Nature asserts herself where one would least look to find her—in clergymen, school children, girls, young men, invalids in bath-chairs. They pass quietly, silently, in coveys, in groups, sometimes alone. They mount the enormous staircases; they stand in queues to have their spectacles rectified gratis; to have their fountain-pens filled gratis; they gaze respectfully into sacks of grain; glance reverently at mowing machines from Canada; now and again stoop to remove some paper bag or banana skin and place it in the receptacle provided for that purpose at frequent intervals along the avenues. But what has happened to our contemporaries? Each is beautiful; each is stately. Can it be that one is seeing human beings for the first time? In streets they hurry; in houses they talk; they are bankers in banks, sell shoes in shops. Here against the enormous background of ferro-concrete Britain, of rosy Burma, at large, unoccupied, they reveal themselves simply as human beings, creatures of leisure, civilization, and dignity; a little languid, perhaps, a little attenuated, but a product to be proud of. Indeed they are the ruin of the Exhibition. The Duke of Devonshire and his colleagues should have kept them out. As you watch them trailing and flowing, dreaming and speculating, admiring this coffee-grinder, that milk and cream separator, the rest of the show becomes insignificant. And what, one asks, is the spell it lays upon them? How, with all this dignity of their own, can they bring themselves to believe in that?

But this cynical reflection, at once so chill and so superior, was made, of course, by the thrush. Down in the Amusement Compound, by some grave oversight on the part of the Committee, several trees and rhododendron bushes have been allowed to remain; and these, as anybody could have foretold, attract the birds. As you wait your turn to be hoisted into mid-air, it is impossible not to hear the thrush singing. You look up and discover a whole chestnut tree with its blossoms standing; you look down and see ordinary grass scattered with petals, harbouring insects, sprinkled with stray wild flowers. The gramophone does its best; they light a horse-shoe of fairy-lamps above the Jack and Jill; a man bangs a bladder and implores you to come and tickle monkeys; boatloads of serious men are poised on the heights of the scenic railway; but all is vain. The cry of ecstasy that should have split the sky as the boat dropped to its doom patters from leaf to leaf, dies, falls flat, while the thrush proceeds with his statement. And then some woman in the row of red-brick villas outside the grounds comes out and wrings a dish-cloth in the backyard. All this the Duke of Devonshire should have prevented.

The problem of the sky, however, remains. Is it, one wonders, lying back limp but acquiescent in a green deck-chair, part of the Exhibition? Is it lending itself with exquisite tact to show off to the best advantage snowy Palestine, ruddy Burma, sand-coloured Canada, and the minarets and pagodas of our possessions in the East? So quietly it suffers all these domes and palaces to melt into its breast; receives them with such sombre and tender discretion; so exquisitely allows the rare lamp of Jack and Jill and the Monkey-Teasers to bear themselves like stars. But even as we watch and admire what we would fain credit to the forethought of Lieutenant-General Sir Travers Clarke, a rushing sound is heard. Is it the wind, or is it the British Empire Exhibition? It is both. The wind is rising and shuffling along the avenues; the Massed Bands of Empire are assembling and marching to the Stadium. Men like pin-cushions, men like pouter pigeons, men like pillar-boxes, pass in procession. Dust swirls after them. Admirably impassive, the bands of Empire march on. Soon they will have entered the fortress; soon the gates will have clanged. But let them hasten! For either the sky has misread her directions, or some appalling catastrophe is impending. The sky is livid, lurid, sulphurine. It is in violent commotion. It is whirling water-spouts of cloud into the air; of dust in the Exhibition. Dust swirls down the avenues, hisses and hurries like erected cobras round the corners. Pagodas are dissolving in dust. Ferro-concrete is fallible. Colonies are perishing and dispersing in spray of inconceivable beauty and terror which some malignant power illuminates. Ash and violet are the colours of its decay. From every quarter human beings come flying—clergymen, school children, invalids in bath-chairs. They fly with outstretched arms, and a vast sound of wailing rolls before them, but there is neither confusion nor dismay. Humanity is rushing to destruction, but humanity is accepting its doom. Canada opens a frail tent of shelter. Clergymen and school children gain its portals. Out in the open under a cloud of electric silver the bands of Empire strike up. The bagpipes neigh. Clergy, school children, and invalids group themselves round the Prince of Wales in butter. Cracks like the white roots of trees spread themselves across the firmament. The Empire is perishing; the bands are playing; the Exhibition is in ruins. For that is what comes of letting in the sky.

Memories of a Working Women's Guild [1]

WHEN you asked me to write a preface to a book which you had collected of papers by working women I replied that I would rather be drowned than write a preface to any book whatever. Books should stand on their own feet, my argument was (and I think it is a sound one). If they need shoring up by a preface here, an introduction there, they have no more right to exist than a table that needs a wad of paper under one leg in order to stand steady. But you left me the papers, and, turning them over, I saw that on this occasion the argument did not apply; this book is not a book. Turning the pages, I began to ask myself what is this book then, if it is not a book? What quality has it? What ideas does it suggest? What old arguments and memories does it rouse in me? and as all this had nothing to do with an introduction or a preface, but brought you to mind and certain pictures from the past, I stretched my hand for a sheet of note-paper and wrote you the following letter.

You have forgotten (I wrote) a hot June morning in Manchester in the year 1913, or at least you will not remember what I remember, because you were otherwise

[1] These pages, written in 1930, relating to the Women's Co-operative Guild, are addressed to a former officer of this organization who had placed in Mrs. Woolf's hands a collection of letters written by its members. Copyright 1930 by Yale University Press (*The Yale Review*).

engaged. Your attention was entirely absorbed by a green table, several sheets of paper, and a bell. Moreover, you were frequently interrupted. There was a woman wearing something like a Lord Mayor's chain round her shoulders; she took her seat perhaps at your right; there were other women without ornament save fountain pens and despatch boxes—they sat perhaps on your left. Soon a row had been formed up there on the platform, with tables and inkstands and tumblers of water; while we, many hundreds of us, scraped and shuffled and filled the entire body of some vast municipal building beneath. Perhaps an organ played. The proceedings somehow opened. The talking and laughing and shuffling suddenly subsided. A bell struck; a figure rose; she took her way from among us; she mounted a platform; she spoke for precisely five minutes; she descended. Directly she sat down another rose; mounted the platform; spoke for precisely five minutes and descended; then a third rose; then a fourth—and so it went on, speaker following speaker, one from the right, one from the left, one from the middle, one from the background—each took her way to the stand, said what she had to say, and gave place to her successor. There was something military in the regularity of the proceeding. They were like marksmen, I thought, standing up in turn with rifle raised to aim at a target. Sometimes they missed, and there was a roar of laughter; sometimes they hit, and there was a roar of applause. But whether the particular shot hit or missed there was no doubt about the carefulness of the aim. There was no beating about the bush; there were no phrases of easy eloquence. The speaker made her way to the stand primed with her subject. Determination and resolution were stamped on her face. There was so much to be said between the strokes of the bell that she could not waste a second. The moment had come for which she had been waiting perhaps for many months. The moment had come for which she had stored hat, shoes, and dress—there was an air of discreet novelty about her clothing. But, above all, the moment had come when she was going to speak her mind, the mind of her constituency, the mind of the women who had sent her from Cornwall perhaps or Sussex, or some black mining village in Yorkshire, to speak their mind for them in Manchester.

It soon became obvious that the mind which lay spread over so wide a stretch of England was a vigorous mind working with great activity. It was thinking of June, 1913, of the reform of the divorce laws; of the taxation of land values; of the minimum wage. It was concerned with the care of maternity; with the Trades Board Act; with the education of children over fourteen; it was unanimously of opinion that adult suffrage should become a government measure—it was thinking, in short, about every sort of public question, and it was thinking constructively and pugnaciously. Accrington did not see eye to eye with Halifax, nor Middlesborough with Plymouth. There was argument and opposition; resolutions were lost and amendments won.

Meanwhile—let me try after seventeen years to sum up the thoughts that passed through the minds of your guests, middle-class people who had come from London and elsewhere not to take part, but to listen—meanwhile, what was it all about? What was the meaning of it? These women were demanding divorce, education, the vote—all good things. They were demanding higher wages and shorter hours—what could be more reasonable? And yet though it was all so reasonable, much of it so forcible, some of it so humorous, a weight of discomfort was settling and shifting itself uneasily from side to side in your visitors' minds. All those questions, I found myself thinking—and perhaps this was at the bottom of it—which matter so intensely to the people here, questions of sanitation and education and wages, this demand for an extra shilling, or another year at school, for eight hours instead of nine behind a counter or in a mill, leave me, in my own blood and bones, untouched. If every reform they demand was granted this very instant it would not matter to me a single jot. Hence my interest is merely altruistic. It is thin spread and mooncoloured. There is no life blood or urgency about it. However hard I clap my hands or stamp my feet, there is a hollowness in the sound which betrays me. I am a benevolent spectator. I am irretrievably cut off from the actors. I sit here hypocritically, clapping and stamping, an outcast from the flock.

On top of this too, my reason (it was in 1913, remember) could not help assuring me that even if the resolution, whatever it was, were carried unanimously, the stamping and the clapping was an empty noise. It would pass out of the open windows and become part of the clamour of the lorries and the striving of the hooves on the Manchester cobbles beneath—an inarticulate uproar. The mind might be active; the mind might be aggressive; but the mind was without a body; it had no legs and arms with which to enforce its will. In all that audience, among all those women who worked, women who had children, women who scrubbed and cooked and bargained and knew to a penny what they had to spend, there was not a single woman with a vote. Let them fire off their rifles if they liked, but they would hit no target; there were only blank cartridges inside. The thought was irritating and depressing.

The clock had now struck half past eleven; there were still then many hours to come. And if one had reached this stage of irritation and depression by half past eleven in the morning, into what depths of boredom would one not be plunged by half past five in the evening? How could one sit out another day of speechifying? How, above all, could one face you, our hostess, with the information that your Congress had proved so insupportably depressing that one was going back to London by the very first train? The only chance lay in some happy conjuring trick, some change of attitude by which the mist and blankness of the speeches could be turned to blood and bone. Otherwise they remained intolerable.

But suppose one played a childish game; suppose one said, as a child says, "Let's pretend . . ."? "Let's pretend," one said to oneself, looking at the speaker, "that I am Mrs. Giles of Durham City." A woman of that name had just turned to address us. "I am the wife of a miner. He comes back thick with coal grime. First he must have his bath. Then he must have his dinner. But there is only a wash tub. My range is filled with saucepans. There is no getting on with the work. All my crocks are covered with dust again. . . . Why in the Lord's name have I not hot water laid on and electric light when middle-class women . . ." So up I jump and demand passionately "labour-saving appliances and housing reform." Up I jump in the person of Mrs. Giles of Durham; in the person of Mrs. Phillips of Bacup; in the person of Mrs. Edwards of Wolverton. But, after all, the imagination is largely the child of the flesh. One could not be Mrs. Giles because one's body had never stood at the wash tub; one's hands had never wrung and scrubbed and chopped up whatever the meat may be that makes a miner's dinner. The picture was always letting in irrelevancies. One sat in an armchair or read a book. One saw landscapes or seascapes, in Greece or perhaps in Italy, where Mrs. Giles or Mrs. Edwards must have seen slag heaps and row upon row of slate roofs in a mining village. Something at any rate was always creeping in from a world that was not their world and making the picture false and the game too much of a game to be worth playing.

It was true that one could always correct these fancy portraits by taking a look at the actual person—at Mrs. Thomas, or Mrs. Langrish, or Miss Bolt of Hebden Bridge. Certainly, there were no armchairs, electric light, or hot water laid on in their homes, no Greek hills or Mediterranean bays in their lives. They did not sign a cheque to pay the weekly bills, or order, over the telephone, a cheap but quite adequate seat at the Opera. If they travelled it was on excursion day, with paper bags and hot babies in their arms. They did not stroll through the house and say, that cover must go to the wash, or those sheets need changing. They plunged their arms in hot water and scrubbed the clothes themselves. In consequence they had thickset muscular bodies. They had large hands; they had the slow emphatic gestures of people who are often stiff and fall tired in a heap on hard-backed chairs. They touched nothing lightly. They gripped papers and pencils as if they were brooms. Their faces were firm, with heavy folds and deep lines. It seemed as if their muscles were always taut and on the stretch. Their eyes looked as if they were always set on something actual—on saucepans that were boiling over, on children who were getting into mischief. Their faces never expressed the lighter and more detached emotions that come into play when the mind is perfectly at ease about the present. They were not in the least detached and cosmopolitan. They were indigenous and rooted to one spot. Their very names were like the stones of the fields, common, grey, obscure, docked of all the splendours of association and romance. Of course they wanted baths and ovens and education and seventeen shillings instead of sixteen and freedom and air and . . . "And," said Mrs. Winthrop of Spenny Moor, breaking into these thoughts with words that sounded like a refrain, "we can wait." "Yes," she repeated, at the conclusion of her speech—what demand she had been making I do not know—"we can wait." And she got down rather stiffly from her perch and made her way back to her seat, an elderly woman dressed in her best clothes.

Then Mrs. Potter spoke. Then Mrs. Elphick. Then Mrs. Holmes of Edgbaston. So it went on, and at last after innumerable speeches, after many communal meals at long tables and many arguments—after seeing jams bottled and biscuits made, after some song singing and ceremonies with banners—the new President received the chain of office with a kiss from the old President; the Congress dispersed; and the separate members who had stood up and spoken out so boldly while the clock ticked its five minutes went back to Yorkshire and Wales and Sussex and Cornwall and hung their clothes in the wardrobe and plunged their hands in the wash tub again.

Later that summer the thoughts, here so inadequately described, were again discussed, but not in a public hall

hung with banners and loud with voices. The head office
of the Guild, the centre from which speakers, papers, inkstands, and tumblers, as I suppose, were issued, was then
in Hampstead. There, if I may remind you again of what
you may well have forgotten, you invited us to come; you
asked us to tell you how the Congress had impressed us.
But I must pause on the threshold of that very dignified
old house with its eighteenth-century carvings and panel-
ling, as we paused then in truth, for one could not enter
and go upstairs without encountering Miss Wick. Miss
Wick sat at her typewriter in the outer office. Miss Wick,
one felt, was set as a kind of watch-dog to ward off the
meddlesome middle-class wasters of time who come pry-
ing into other people's business. Whether it was for this
reason that she was dressed in a peculiar shade of deep
purple I do not know. The colour seemed somehow sym-
bolic. She was very short, but owing to the weight which
sat on her brow and the gloom which seemed to issue from
her dress she was also very weighty. An extra share of the
world's grievances seemed to press upon her shoulders.
When she clicked her typewriter, one felt that she was
making that instrument transmit messages of foreboding
and ill omen to an unheeding universe. But she relented
and, like all relentings after gloom, hers came with a
sudden charm. We went upstairs and upstairs was a very
different figure—there was Miss Janet Erskine, indeed, and
Miss Erskine may have been smoking a pipe—there was
one on the table. She may have been reading a detective
story—there was a book of that kind on the table—at any
rate, she seemed the image of detachment and equanimity.
Had one not known that Miss Erskine was to the Congress what the heart is to the remoter veins—that the great

engine at Manchester would not thump and throb without her—that she had collected and sorted and summoned and arranged that very intricate but orderly assembly of women—she would never have enlightened one. She had nothing whatever to do—she came to the office because an office is a good place in which to read detective stories— she licked a few stamps and addressed a few envelopes—it was a fad of hers—that was what her manner conveyed. It was Miss Erskine who moved the papers off the chairs and got the teacups out of the cupboard. It was she who answered questions about figures and put her hand on the right file of letters.

Again let me telescope into a few sentences and into one scene many random discussions at various places. We said then—for you now emerged from an inner room and if Miss Wick was purple and Miss Erskine was coffee-coloured, you, speaking pictorially (and I dare not speak more explicitly), were kingfisher blue and as arrowy and decisive as that quick bird—we said then that the Congress had roused thoughts and ideas of the most diverse nature. It had been a revelation and a disillusionment. We had been humiliated and enraged. To begin with, all their talk, we said, or the greater part of it, was of matters of fact. They want baths and money. When people get together communally they always talk about baths and money: they always show the least desirable of their characteristics—their lust for conquest and their desire for possessions. To expect us, whose minds, such as they are, fly free at the end of a short length of capital, to tie ourselves down again upon that narrow plot of acquisitiveness and desire is impossible. We have baths and money. Society has supplied us with all we need in that direction. Therefore however much we sympathized, our sympathy was largely fictitious. It was æsthetic sympathy, the sympathy of the eye and of the imagination, not of the heart and of the nerves; and such sympathy is always physically uncomfortable. Let us explain what we mean, we said.

The women are magnificent to look at. Ladies in evening dress are lovelier far, but they lack the sculpturesque quality that these working women have. Their arms are undeveloped. Fat has softened the lines of their muscles. And though the range of expression is narrower in working women, their expressions have a force and emphasis, of tragedy or humour, which the faces of ladies lack. But at the same time, it is much better to be a lady; ladies desire Mozart and Cézanne and Shakespeare; and not merely money and hot water laid on. Therefore to deride ladies and to imitate, as some of the speakers did, their mincing speech and little knowledge of what it pleases them to call "reality" is not merely bad manners, but it gives away the whole purpose of the Congress, for, if it is better to be a working woman, by all means let them remain so and not claim their right to undergo the contamination of wealth and comfort.

In spite of this, we went on, apart from prejudice and bandying compliments, undoubtedly the women at the Congress possess something which ladies have lost, something desirable, stimulating, and at the same time very difficult to define. One does not want to slip easily into fine phrases about "contact with life," about "facing facts," "the teaching of experience," for they invariably alienate the hearer, and moreover no working man or woman works harder with his hands or is in closer touch with reality than a painter with his brush or a writer with his pen. But the quality that they have—judging from a phrase caught here and there, a laugh, or a gesture seen in passing—is a quality that Shakespeare would have liked. One can fancy him slipping away from the brilliant salons of educated people to crack a joke in Mrs. Robson's back kitchen. Indeed, we said, one of our most curious impressions at your Congress was that "the poor," "the working classes," or by whatever name you choose to call them are not down-trodden, envious, and exhausted; they are humorous and vigorous and thoroughly independent. Thus, if it were possible to meet them not as sympathizers, as masters or mistresses with counters between us or kitchen tables, but casually and congenially as fellow beings with the same ends and wishes even if the dress and body are different, a great liberation would follow. How many words, for example, must lurk in those women's vocabularies that have faded from ours! How many scenes must lie dormant in their eyes unseen by us! What images and saws and proverbial sayings must still be current with them that have never reached the surface of print; and very likely they still keep the power which we have lost of making new ones. There were many shrewd sayings in the speeches at the Congress which even the weight of a public meeting could not flatten out entirely.

But, we said, and here perhaps fiddled with a paper knife or poked the fire impatiently by way of expressing our discontent, what is the use of it all? Our sympathy is fictitious, not real. Because we pay our bills with cheques and our clothes are washed for us and we do not know the liver from the lights, we are condemned to remain forever shut up in the confines of the middle classes wearing tail coats and silk stockings and called Sir or Madam as the case may be, when we are all, in truth, simply Johns and Susans. And they remain equally deprived. For we have as much to give them as they us—wit and detachment, learning and poetry and all those good gifts which those who have never answered bells or touched their foreheads with their forefingers enjoy by right. But the barrier is impassable. And nothing perhaps exasperated us more at the Congress (you must have noticed at times a certain irritability) than the thought that this force of theirs, this smouldering heat which broke the crust now and then and licked the surface with a hot and fearless flame, is about to break through and melt us together so that life will be richer and books more complex, and society will pool its possessions instead of segregating them—all this is bound to happen inevitably thanks to you, very largely, and to Miss Erskine and to Miss Wick—but only when we are dead.

It was thus that we tried in the Guild office that afternoon to explain the nature of fictitious sympathy and how it differs from real sympathy and how defective it is because it is not based upon sharing the same important emotions unconsciously. It was thus that we tried to describe the contradictory and complex feelings which beset the middle-class visitor forced to sit out a congress of working women in silence.

Perhaps it was at this point that you unlocked a drawer and took out a packet of papers. You did not at once untie the string that fastened them. Sometimes, you said, you got a letter which you could not bring yourself to burn; once or twice a Guildswoman at your suggestion had written a few pages about her life. It might be that we should find these papers interesting; it might be that if we read them the women would cease to be symbols and become instead individuals. But they were very fragmentary and ungrammatical; they had been jotted down in the intervals of housework. Indeed, you could not at once bring yourself to give them up, as if to expose their simplicity were a breach of confidence. It might be that their illiteracy would only perplex, you said; that the writing of people who do not know how to write—but at this point we burst in. In the first place, every English woman knows how to write, in the second, even if she does not she has only to take her own life for subject and write the truth and not fiction or poetry for our interest to be so keenly roused that—in short, we cannot wait but must read the packet at once.

Thus pressed you did by degrees and with many delays—there was the war for example, and Miss Wick died, and you and Janet Erskine retired from the Guild, and a testimonial was given you in a casket, and many thousand working women tried to say how you had changed their lives—tried to say what they will feel for you to their dying day—after all these interruptions, you did at last gather the papers together and finally put them in my hands. There they were, typed and docketed with a few snapshots and rather faded photographs stuck between the pages. And when, at last, I began to read, there started up in my mind's eye the figures that I had seen all those years ago at Manchester with such bewilderment and curiosity. But they were no longer addressing a large meeting in Manchester from a platform, dressed in their best clothes. The hot June day with its banners had vanished, and instead one looked back into the past of the women who had stood there; into the four-roomed houses of miners, into the homes of small shopkeepers and agricultural labourers, into the fields and factories of fifty or sixty years ago. Mrs. Barrows for example had worked in the Lincolnshire fens when she was eight with forty or fifty other children, and an old man had followed the gang with a long whip in his hand "which he did not forget to use." That was a strange reflection. Most of the women had started work at seven or eight, earning a penny on Saturday for washing a doorstep, or two pence a week for carrying suppers to the men at the iron foundry. They had gone into factories when they were fourteen.

They had worked from seven in the morning till eight or nine at night and had made thirteen or fifteen shillings a week. Out of this money they had saved some pence with which to buy their mother gin—she was often very tired in the evening and had borne perhaps thirteen children in as many youthful years; or they fetched opium to assuage some miserable old woman's ague in the fens. Betty Potter killed herself when she could get no more. They had seen half-starved women standing in rows to be paid for their match boxes while they snuffed the roast meat of their employers' dinner cooking within. The smallpox had raged in Bethnal Green, and they had known that the boxes went on being made in the sick room and sold to the public with the infection thick on them. They had been so cold working in the wintry fields that they could not run when the ganger gave them leave. They had waded through floods when the Wash overflowed its banks. Kind old ladies had given them parcels of food which turned out to contain only crusts and rancid bacon rind.

All this they had done and seen and known when other children were still dabbling in seaside pools and spelling out fairy tales by the nursery fire. Naturally their faces

had a different look on them. But they were also, one remembered, firm faces, faces with something indomitable in
their expression. And the reason can only be that human
nature is so tough that it will take such wounds, even at
the tenderest age, and survive them. Keep a child mewed
up in Bethnal Green and she will somehow snuff the country air from seeing the yellow dust on her brother's boots,
and nothing will serve her but she must go there, and see
the "clean ground" as she calls it for herself. It was true
that at first the "bees were very frightening," but all the
same she got to the country and the blue smoke and the
cows came up to her expectations. Put girls after a childhood of minding smaller brothers and sisters and washing
doorsteps into a factory when they are fourteen and their
eyes will turn to the window and they will be happy because, as the work room is six stories up, the sun can be
seen breaking over the hills "and that was always such a
comfort and a help."

Still stranger, if one needs additional proof of the
strength of the human instinct to escape from bondage
and attach itself to a country road or a sun rising over distant hills, is the fact that the highest ideals of duty flourish
in an obscure hat factory as surely as on a battlefield.
There were women in Christie's hat factory, for example,
who worked for "honour." They gave their lives to the
cause of putting straight stitches into the bindings of men's
hat brims. Felt is hard and thick; it is difficult to push the
needle through; there are no rewards or glory to be won;
but such is the incorrigible idealism of the human mind
that there were "trimmers" in those obscure places who
would never put a crooked stitch in their work and ruthlessly tore out the crooked stitches of others. And as they

drove in their straight stitches they reverenced Queen Victoria and thanked God, drawing up to the fire, that they were all married to good Conservative working men.

Certainly that story explained something of the force, of the obstinacy which one had seen in the faces of the speakers at the Congress in Manchester. And then if one went on reading these papers, one came upon other signs of the extraordinary vitality of the human spirit. The dauntless energy which no amount of childbirth and washing up can quench entirely had reached out, it seemed, and seized upon old copies of magazines; had attached itself to Dickens; had propped the poems of Burns against a dish-cover to read while cooking. They read at meals; they read before going to the mill. They read Dickens and Scott and Henry George and Bulwer-Lytton and Ella Wheeler Wilcox and Alice Meynell and would like "to get hold of any good history of the French Revolution, not Carlyle's, please," and B. Russell on China, and William Morris and Shelley and Florence Barclay and Samuel Butler's Note Books—they read with the indiscriminate greed of a hungry appetite that crams itself with toffee and beef and tarts and vinegar and champagne all in one gulp.

Naturally, such reading led to argument. The younger generation had the audacity to say that Queen Victoria was no better than an honest charwoman who had brought up her children respectably. They had the temerity to doubt whether to sew straight stitches into men's hat brims should be the sole aim and end of a woman's life. They started arguments and even held rudimentary debating societies on the floor of the factory. In time the old trimmers even were shaken in their beliefs and came to think that there might be other ideals in the world besides straight stitches and Queen Victoria. Ideas, indeed, were seething in their brains. A girl, for instance, would reason, as she walked along the streets of a factory town, that she had no right to bring a child into the world if that child must earn its living in a mill. A chance saying in a book would fire her imagination and make her dream of future cities where there were to be baths and kitchens and wash houses and art galleries and museums and parks.

The minds of working women were humming and their imaginations were awake. But how were they to realize their ideals? How were they to express their needs? Of middle-class organizations there were many. Women were beginning to found colleges, and even here and there to enter the professions. But these were middle-class women with some amount of money and some degree of education behind them. How could women whose hands were full of work, whose kitchens were thick with steam, who had neither education nor encouragement nor leisure remodel the world according to the ideas of working women? It was then, I suppose, some time early in the eighties, that the Women's Guild crept modestly and tentatively into existence, occupying for a time a certain space in the "Co-operative News" which was called the "Woman's Corner." It was there that Mrs. Acland asked, "Why should we not hold our Co-operative Mothers' Meetings, when we may bring our work and sit together, one of us reading some co-operative work aloud, which may afterwards be discussed?" And on April 18th, 1883, she announced that there were seven members who had achieved this object.

This was the tiny magnet that drew to itself all that restless wishing and dreaming. This was the central meeting place where was formed and solidified what was else so scattered and incoherent. The Guild must have given the older women, with their husbands and children, what "clean ground" had given the little girl in Bethnal Green, or the view of day breaking over the hills had given to the girls in the hat factory. It gave them in the first place a room where they could sit down and think remote from boiling saucepans and crying children; and then that room became a place where one could make, and share with others in making, the model of what a working woman's house should be. Then as the membership grew and twenty or thirty women made a practice of meeting weekly, that one house became a street of houses; and if you have a street of houses you must have stores and drains and post boxes; and at last the street becomes a town, and a town brings in questions of education and finance and the relation of one town to another town. And then the town becomes a country; it becomes England; it becomes Germany and America; and so from debating questions of butter and bacon, working women at their weekly meetings have to consider the relations of one great nation to another.

So it was that in the year 1913 Mrs. Robson and Mrs. Potter and Mrs. Wright were getting up and asking not only for baths and wages and electric light, but also for co-operative industry and adult suffrage and the taxation of land values and divorce law reform. It was thus that they were to ask, as the years went by, for peace and disarmament and the sisterhood of nations. And the force that lay behind their speeches was compact of many things—of men with whips, and sick rooms where match boxes are made, of hunger and cold, and many and difficult childbirths, of much scrubbing and washing up, of reading

Shelley and William Morris and Samuel Butler, of meetings of the Women's Guild, and committees and congresses at Manchester and elsewhere. All this lay behind the speeches of Mrs. Robson and Mrs. Potter and Mrs. Wright. The papers which you sent me certainly threw some light upon those old curiosities and bewilderments.

But it cannot be denied that, as I began by saying, they do not make a book, as literature they have many limitations. The writing lacks detachment and imaginative breadth, even as the women themselves lacked variety and play of feature. Here are no reflections; no view of life as a whole; no attempt to enter into the lives of other people. It is not from the ranks of working class women that the next great poet or novelist will be drawn. Indeed, we are reminded of those obscure writers before Shakespeare who had never been beyond the borders of their own parishes and found expression difficult and words few and awkward to fit together.

And yet since writing is an impure art much infected by life, the letters you gave me seem to possess some qualities even as literature that the literate and instructed might envy. Listen, for instance, to Mrs. Scott the midwife, "I have been over the hilltops when the snowdrifts were over three feet high, and six feet in some places. I was in a blizzard in Hayfield and thought I should never get round the corners. But it was life on the moors; I seemed to know every blade of grass and where the flowers grew and all the little streams were my companions." Could she have said that better if Oxford had made her a doctor of letters? Or take Mrs. Layton's description of a match box factory in Bethnal Green, and how she "looked through the fence and saw three ladies sitting in the shade doing some kind of fancy work." It has something of the accuracy and clarity of a description by Defoe. And when Mrs. Burrows brings to mind that very bitter day when the children were about to eat their cold dinner and drink their cold tea under the hedge and the ugly woman asked them in to her parlour saying, "Bring these children into my house and let them eat their dinner there," one must admit that she gets her effect, and brings the scene before us—the frozen children eating hot boiled potatoes in a ring on the floor—by whatever means she manages it. And then there is a fragment of a letter from Miss Wick, the sombre purple figure who typed as if the weight of the world rested on her shoulders. "When I was a girl of seventeen," she writes, "my then employer, a gentleman of good position and high standing in the town, sent me to his home one night ostensibly to take a parcel of books, but really with a very different object. When I arrived at the house all the family were away, and before he would allow me to leave he forced me to yield to him. At eighteen I was a mother." The stiff words, which conceal all emotion conventionally enough, are yet illuminating. Such then was the burden that rested upon that squat and sombre figure—such were the memories that she stored as she sat typing your letters, guarding your door with such tremendous fidelity in her purple dress.

But I will quote no more. These letters are only fragments. These voices are beginning only now to emerge from silence into half articulate speech. These lives are still half-hidden in profound obscurity. To write even what is written has been a task of labour and difficulty. The writing has been done in kitchens, at odds and ends of time, in the midst of distractions and obstacles—but really there is no need for me, in a letter addressed to you, to lay stress upon the hardships of working women's lives. Have not you and Janet Erskine given your best years—but hush! you will not let me finish that sentence and therefore, with the old messages of friendship and admiration, I will make an end.